ACKNOWLEDGEMENTS

God(dess) – thank you for this life, this path and this message. May the words you gave me to write be interpreted exactly as you intended.

Billy, the world's best husband - you rarely had a problem telling the self-defeatist in me to shut the hell up. Even when you where placed on the backburner, you urged me to continue. To simply thank you for your undying support is an injustice to the level of gratitude I have for you and your love. This book would not be what it is without you.

Mom - I so appreciate the incredible amounts of help you provided me. You edited, you suggested, but most importantly, you told me it was great – even after I asked you to read it over and over…and over. The time you spent on this is precious to me, as are you.

Robin, my sister and best friend - your laughter let me know I was on the right track and so did your endless faith in my work. I draw courage from you.

My amazing editor, Jennifer Ciotta – you're a machine, sister. There are no words to describe how grateful I am that I had the opportunity to work with you. You inspire me with your tirelessness and I look forward to future projects with you.

Monica Rodriguez – your eye baffles me. How can you tell when a *period* is italicized? Unbelievable.

Christina Sell, my yoga teacher - your lessons taught me what kind of car I am and, I'm delighted to say, 230 mph feels pretty damn good.

To all of my supportive friends who cheered from the sidelines, your love warms my heart and I thank the heavens for your presence in my life.

And lastly, I'd like to acknowledge New York City. You changed everything. Thanks for the tenacity.

Namaste, y'all...

Michelle

STYLISH BUT SHALLOW:

"The upside is you have great taste. The downside is you're completely shallow."

Now who doesn't love a little self-introspection? I'm a normal, self-absorbed woman in America, and I, too, enjoy the enlightenment of a daily horoscope or a three-page-long quiz in a fashion magazine. Like most of my peers, when the results of said horoscope or quiz are positive, I feel pleased by their accuracy and happily apply their wisdom to whichever area of my life is in need of such illumination. However, when the results aren't so positive, like being told I'm shallow, for example, I write them off as total bullshit. Little did I know one of these seemingly innocuous quizzes had the power to propel a major turning point in my life.

2009 had come to an end and I was looking forward to the promise of a new year. I didn't have any resolutions or particular goals in mind; frankly, I gave up on those a long time ago. Instead, I had a feeling 2010 was going to be a good year. My husband, Shawn, had just been promoted from selling computer anti-virus software to managing his own sales team—a much more lucrative position. We'd finally moved into our new house in the 'burbs. And even though my three children of two, five, and twelve fought incessantly and drove me nuts, God love 'em, they were all growing, developing and in good health. I didn't have anything to bitch about is my point. I'm not saying I never complained, but I had a hard time finding anyone who would listen.

So, there I was one January night, rinsing the dinner plates and stacking them in the dishwasher. My flannel pajama pants paired nicely with the oversized bear claw slippers my kids had gotten me for Christmas. I was looking drop dead sexy with my hair pulled back in my Mickey Mouse scrunchie. Yes, my getup screamed, "I'm depressed and so is my fashion sense!" But my spirits were actually high. It was after 9:00 p.m., and with the children in bed and my husband away on business (the only downside to managing an outside sales team), I was delighted to have the house all to myself. My Petit Syrah of excellent vintage had been breathing for two hours. At least 99.9% of the germs on my countertops were dying a quick and painless death thanks to my EPA-approved all-purpose cleaner. And as if quiet time, good wine and a lemon-scented kitchen weren't enough, I had a brand new issue of *Cosmopolitan* magazine waiting to be perused on the table. I scrubbed quickly, impatient to flip through *Cosmo*'s glossy pages, knowing it was chock full of fashion advice, intimidating sexual positions and a lengthy personality quiz to ring in the New Year. I poured my wine, taking in the spicy aroma of oak and plum, and dove right into the January issue. I had been looking forward to this moment all day. With my hot pink bejeweled pen poised and ready, I sat down at my kitchen table and flipped to the survey. As usual, I read through each question, enthusiastically circling whatever answers I assumed would provide me with the most favorable results.

When gift shopping for a friend, you:

A. *Have a hard time choosing just one. I love my friends and I'm such a giver!*

B. *Choose something personal. I like my loved ones to know I put thought into it.*

C. *End up buying more items for me than anyone else. There's just so much good stuff out there!*

Of course my honest answer was C, but A sounded so much better. Did it occur to me that lying on my own personality quiz might be the first indication that something was amiss?

Nah.

I finished answering all thirty-two questions and tallied up my points with fervor, totally expecting to be validated as the kind, deep and genuine woman I thought I was.

Stylish but Shallow.

What the hell?

It wasn't exactly the profile I had anticipated. I was hoping for "Warm and Grounded" or maybe "Slow and Steady." I even went back and retook the test with honest answers to see if I could get different results. No dice. "Stylish but Shallow" slapped the self-righteous expression right off my face. I poured myself another glass of wine, doing my best to blow it off as I held back tears. I flipped open the lid to the recycling bin and threw in the $8 magazine. Try as I might to ignore my growing suspicion that the quiz makers at *Cosmo* might be on to something, it was too late. The seed had been planted. For the next several days, through the hustle and bustle of being a wife and mother of three, the words of that stupid quiz haunted me. *Stylish…but shallow.* I didn't want to be shallow. I wanted to be

AWESOME. Revered as graceful and loving, a humanitarian who was compassionate to mankind, a friggin SAINT! Even though I might not be particularly deserving of such a title...

"Haunted" turned into "obsessed." In between shuttling kids back and forth from place to place, avoiding household chores and trying to convince my husband that *Cosmo* was a credible psychological resource, I found myself scavenging the Self-Help section at my local bookstore on a regular basis, searching for something to fill my newly discovered void. This went on for over four months, and by the end of spring, I had purchased no less than a dozen books aimed toward personal healing. I found myself growing more and more jaded with all the promises that left me wanting more.

"Uncover Who You're REALLY Mad At!"

"Free Yourself of Low Self-Esteem!"

"Quit Eating Your Hate!"

"Find Your Inner Child!"

"Restrain Your Inner Child!"

"Become Your Inner Child and then BREAK that Child's Spirit!"

I bought them all, even when the message didn't apply to me in the least. I even got a book on how to quit smoking in hopes it might contain some nugget of wisdom that could help me with whatever I *thought* I needed help with. Since I don't smoke, it goes without saying I got nothing out of "Quit Smoking in 37 Seconds!" Another $21.95 well spent.

I felt like I had read the first three chapters of every book written on the subject of "Healing My Inner [Whatever]." So when I spotted a workbook journal titled *Discover Your Inner Goddess*, I felt a tinge of excitement. Mainly because it was the only thing on the shelf I had yet to defeat, and I love a good challenge.

Oh, you think you can heal me? Bring it on, bitch.

At the same time, I was intrigued. There was something about the word "goddess" that resonated with me, even though on the surface I felt the need to belittle it.

Inner Goddess? It's probably some bra-burning, hippie-dippie, feminist crap.

I bought it immediately, of course. I was skeptical, but deep down I hoped that maybe this would be "the one"—the key to unlocking the answers as to why I felt so empty when I was "perfectly happy" before.

But was I really?

I didn't know it at the time, but in retrospect, I was wasting my days with boredom by watching TV, daydreaming about greener pastures, regretting unmet goals... Five o'clock was something to be celebrated on a daily basis as I poured myself a tall glass of *whatever*, in hopes it would help me deal with the stress of fighting kids and a messy house. This was the norm. Does that sound like a happy and motivated woman who's living each day like it's her last? No way. It sounds more like a woman who woke up each day, already looking forward to going back to bed. I was in a stagnant place in my life. But since I had little faith in myself and an extreme aversion to failure, I chose to live vicariously though the achievements of my loved ones while I remained safe within my comfort zone.

"No pain, no gain...and that's just fine, because I hate pain, so screw the gain."

This was my credo. It worked quite well. The downside was, eventually this route led me to the point where I felt nothing, and "nothing" was mistaken for "happy." Then all of a sudden, there I was at my kitchen table, sobbing in my Petit Syrah because a superficial personality quiz told me I was shallow. This was when I realized that even the most positive of circumstances, like a supportive husband, joyful children and financial security, could only make up for one half of a whole. On the inside I was suffering, and all of the sunshine on the outside wasn't changing it. It was like wearing a cheap, itchy suit that was three sizes too small, and I wanted to rip it off, seam by seam. It was undeniable: my transformation had to come from within.

I bought this workbook in May of 2010, frustrated with my life, not knowing the first thing about who I was or what it meant to love myself. As with all of the other self-help books I had purchased before it, I fully expected to roll my eyes and toss it to the side by the time I reached the third chapter. However, I'm glad to say, this is not what happened. Unbeknownst to me, committing to the lessons in this book would inspire a year of self-discovery, extreme discomfort, some new beginnings, a few humiliating moments, but ultimately, it would bestow upon me the most beautiful suit of all...the one I'm wearing now.

Discover Your Inner Goddess!

*A Beginner's Guide to
Getting In Touch with Your True Self*

By

Devi Phoenix

TABLE OF CONTENTS

THE BEGINNING   1

INTRODUCTION: *You & Your Goddess*   3

PART 1 *Looking Within*   9

LESSON 1: *Why Are You Here?*   11

LESSON 2: *Daydreaming*   27

LESSON 3: *Fear*   43

LESSON 4: *Your Anti-Goddesses*   57

LESSON 5: *Negative Habits*   83

LESSON 6: *Instilling Positive Habits*   93

PART 2: *Breaking Down Barriers*   113

LESSON 7: *Cleanse*   115

LESSON 8: *Union*   143

LESSON 9: *Meditation & Affirmation*   165

LESSON 10: *Goddess Essence, Part I:*
            The Body Temple   183

LESSON 10: *Goddess Essence, Part II:*
            Your Goddess Center   195

PART 3: *Personal Growth*   211

LESSON 11: *A Day for Ritual*   213

LESSON 12: *Learn Something New*   229

LESSON 13: *Get to Know the World*   *249*

LESSON 14: *Be One with Nature*   *261*

LESSON 15: *Giving Back, Part I*   *285*

LESSON 15: *Giving Back, Part II*   *295*

LESSON 16: *Reflection*   *301*

THE BEGINNING

What is an Inner Goddess, you might be wondering? I am honored to tell you, my dear sister, your Inner Goddess is your True Self. She is the spirit of pure love, joy and energy that lives inside of you. She is your connection, your oneness with Source. She is your greatest good, and your highest potential. Your Inner Goddess is the guide to your soul's purpose on this earth.

Welcome to the beginning of a new path, my sister! I want to commend you for having the courage and Goddess Power to embark on such a beautiful adventure—and an adventure it will be! Going to the depths of yourself is not an easy task and in the months ahead you might come face to face with some pretty uncomfortable truths. Throughout this process, remain compassionate and loving towards yourself. Change is never easy. I want you to take a moment to acknowledge your strength and commit to yourself that you will persevere, even in moments when everything inside of you is telling you to RUN.

The workbook is comprised of three parts: "Looking Within" asks you to take a look at the mental and emotional scenery of your current path. The lessons in this section consist of some basic exercises to get you familiar with the areas of your life in need of attention. "Breaking Down Barriers" focuses on chipping away at the blockages that have developed over the years due to stagnancy or lack of growth. "Personal Growth" is all about rebuilding what you deconstructed in "Breaking Down Barriers."

This course is writing-intensive; every lesson involves daily journaling. You will need to commit time for this, so budget according to your schedule. This is also a great way to help you develop the habit of journaling on a regular basis, which is an indispensible tool of self-discovery. The only criteria are that you be completely honest and pace yourself. Everyone is different and some chapters might be easier for you than others. It's perfectly normal for progress to fluctuate from lesson to lesson. Clock time has no place in a process as important as releasing your Inner Goddess, dear one—be mindful of that.

Before you begin, I want you to introduce yourself. What are you about? What do you do? Who are you...or better yet, who do you *think* you are? Once you feel satisfied with your "profile," write about your Inner Goddess. Have you ever met her? If so, what is she like? Is she graceful or thunderous? Beautiful or faceless? Does she *do* or does she *teach*? I also want you to consider what you hope to gain from this workbook and journal about any aspirations you may have. When you write, remember there are no restrictions! Be creative, have fun and get excited, because, my sister, you are on your way to meeting your TRUE self! Blessings to you on your journey!

INTRODUCTION

You & Your Goddess

Name: Holly
Date: 5/01/10

Who am I? Doesn't this kind of question seem like it should always have some deep, existential answer?

"I am but a woman. A delicate and unique snowflake, floating on the subtle and ever-churning breeze of humanity..."

So poetic. However, since existentialism has never been my thing, I'll stick with the basics.

Hi, my name is Holly. I'm thirty-four years old and from Pasadena, California. I'm a Libra, a housewife, and I buy classic literature for my bookshelves in order to feel well-read, even though I prefer dime-store erotica. If I could find a way to cover a cheesy romance novel in a Hemingway jacket, I would totally do it. But since all of mine are paperback, I'm stuck reading my guilty pleasures behind closed doors and away from judgment.

I like to do arts and crafts. However, I'm too lazy to see a project through to completion, and the thought of cleaning up a glittery mess is never appealing. So in actuality, I love coveting the finished product of someone else's art or craft, only to wonder why I never do arts and crafts myself.

I don't watch useless TV shows because I feel guilty if I spend the day catching up on soaps or other such nonsense. Reality TV and crime shows, on the other hand, are a completely different story. I feel watching the Food Network is a lot like going to school, and *CSI*, set in any city, gives me the sense that I'm staying on top of cutting-edge forensic science. On top of that, being a real housewife myself, how could I NOT keep up with what my peers are doing in Orange County?

I honestly think flowers are a waste of money and a bit cliché when given as a gift. Still, that doesn't keep me from getting irritated when my husband, Shawn, fails to deliver on our anniversary or any other occasion of the like. "No long stem roses???" W-T-F!

Shawn and I have three kids, Tyler, Ryan and Zoe; two enormous dogs, Leo and Lucy; and we share a brand new, 2,800-square-foot farm-style house in a small town outside of Houston, Texas. I like to refer to it as "NOT Pasadena, California;" however, the locals call it Richmond. There's a porch swing, a riding lawn mower and a community pond we can't fish in because the goddamn ducks eat all the perch.

Shawn is cute, funny and annoyingly chipper at all the wrong times. My oldest son, Tyler, is close to becoming a teenager and he's really, REALLY good at it. Ryan, my five-year-old, has an ongoing obsession with Batman, or maybe he thinks he is Batman? Zoe is my two-year-old princess and can eat her weight in pancakes.

I'm the middle sister of three. The youngest, Katy, is studying abroad in Spain, so, needless to say, I rarely talk to her and am extremely jealous that she's living the life of adventure I never had the balls to lead. Libby, my older sister, lives in Santa Monica, not too far from where we grew up in Pasadena. We talk on the phone at least eight times a day to compensate for the distance between us. Though, ironically, I hate talking on the phone. Why? It's pointless. My children have the patience of crackhead monkeys and can never wait until I'm done with my conversation before they bombard me with tattle tales and complaints.

"MOM! Ryan took my doll!"

"MOM! Zoe trashed my room!"

"MOM! Tyler mashed his gum in my hair!"

Does it matter that they wanted nothing to do with me *before* I got on the phone? No. With that being said, the next logical thing to add would be that I dislike when my kids bombard me while I'm on the phone. Bless their precious hearts.

I love fashion. A lot. Most of my community wouldn't know Barney's from Beall's, nor would they care. But I do… Oh yes, I do.

I love good music. Genre doesn't matter. If it sounds good and raises some sort of feeling or movement, I love it. I love good food. I don't care about cuisine. If it causes a warm and fuzzy sensation, I love it. I love good alcohol and I don't care about type. If it makes me an easy-breezy mom… You get the idea.

I have medium-brown hair that styles well, but I'll typically throw in a comment about how it's too stringy when someone compliments its fullness. I have hazel eyes that are moderately sized and don't see well past ten feet. Unfortunately, I'm too vain to get glasses and contacts make my eyes itchy, so I just walk around with a headache most of the time. I'm fair skinned and freckled and when taking my short temper into account, I actually would make more sense as a redhead (although I don't know if that stereotype is well-founded). I have soft features when I'd love to be a little more angular, but I like my button nose even though I complain about it. I'm five feet two inches of pure torso. I long for the days of my youth when I could eat a full sleeve of butter crackers without worrying about the calories but, as it stands now, I weigh in at 140 pounds of nothing but atrophied muscle mass, and I'm pretty sure my arms are longer than my legs. As ideal for runway modeling as I might sound, making shitloads of money to be beautiful has never appealed to me. I'd rather look like a fireplug at no extra cost to the taxpayers. You're welcome, America.

I'm incredibly flexible but relatively out of shape. I have a giant tattoo of a butterfly on my lower back that I got during my stoner days in college, and even though I talk about how much I hate it, I secretly love it and want more. If I had the balls, I'd pierce my nose because I think a tiny little diamond stud would add a sexy edge to my otherwise mundane appearance. But since I live in a small town, I'm afraid of what people would say about me.

This is about all I can come up with on that front. While I'd love to be mint chocolate chip or cookies 'n' cream, I'm pretty vanilla, I think.

Who is my Inner Goddess? Let's see… I would like her to be a gorgeous, talented, vivacious, organized clean freak. Then again, I'm not really sure what an Inner Goddess is supposed to be like. I really wish I was that person who could ooze effortless perfection at all times. Is that what an Inner Goddess does? I was raised to talk to the big man in the sky, so the idea of having a divine female inside of me is a new concept to say the least. How about I channel the vibes from my Baptist youth group days and get down with the prayer requests?

throat clear

Dear Goddess of the deep, my house is a sucking vortex of positive energy and I've got the organizational skills of a hoarder. I beckon you to emerge with grace and make sense of my storage space. Awaken, oh perfect one, and clean my house until it shines as you shine.

I also invite you, Goddess, to express through me your undying passion for exercise, combined with an inherent preference for lean protein and vegetables. Wrap this child in your muscular yet feminine embrace and allow the body of your host to be free of stretch marks and cellulite, as you are free of them, I'm sure. And if you have breasts larger than an A cup, that would be fantastic.

Goddess, I invoke thee, rise to the surface and bring with you your insatiable sexual appetite, as my libido is nowhere to be found. Through me, set free the ravenous sex kitten you so crave to unleash. With hungry eyes, look upon my husband as if he were a very large filet, smothered in some sort of peppery butter sauce. With a side of garlic mashed potatoes and a healthy serving of creamed spinach. Devour him, holy one, as I would a gigantic friggin brownie. I'm here to do your bidding, Goddess. Release the hounds...seriously, dude, release the hounds.

Goddess, Divine Mother, She who resides somewhere inside this woman, raise my children for me. Nurture them as you do the animals of the forest, since their behavior can be so closely related to that of wild animals. Love compassionately through me. Understand, unconditionally, through me. Mess be damned, be serene through me while they eat their meals, dropping more food on the floor than they put in their mouths. Settle their disputes with patience THROUGH ME, so I can experience a day when I don't want to strangle at least one of them, oh Goddess…

Emerge, your Highness. Experience yourself as the woman I have NO clue how to be…Amen?

I don't know if I did that right, but I think I've pretty much summed it up. If my Inner Goddess could be a smokin' hot, well-dressed, organized sex maven who poops rice crispy treats and is an annual contender for "Mother of the Year," that would work out swimmingly for me.

The end.

PART 1

Looking Within

When seeking your True North, you must know where you currently stand before taking a step forward. Many people begin new paths only to travel in circles because they were unclear from where they began. Going within to examine your habitual thoughts and behavior patterns can shed light on certain tendencies of which you may, or may not, be aware. By searching within yourself you can identify the good and improve upon it, as well as recognize the "less than good" to pinpoint the areas of your life you desire to change.

LESSON 1

Why Are You Here?

You made the decision to purchase this workbook, but have you stopped to ask yourself *why*? Is it because you've been soul searching and you thought the exercises in this book would help you to find clarity? Have you been feeling alone, helpless, separate from a power you sense should be a part of you? Did you feel drawn to the title and the possibilities it suggests? Or was it simply for fun? Whatever the reason, in this lesson and the week to come, you should explore where you are on your current path, and maybe learn a little bit about why you chose to begin a new one. You will do this by going within each day and journaling about the state of your thoughts and emotions. This can help you get a clear picture of where you are in your life and discover where there is lack and/or separation. It may seem like a slow start to what you're anticipating will be an AMAZING journey, but this is important. Before you can take a step forward, you need to know where you stand right now. Take your time and be thoughtful. No one day is the same and what you write is affected by your moods. If you are having difficulty with this, begin the lesson with a brief centering exercise. Find a quiet place, sit still with your eyes closed and take a few deep breaths. Go within and really *feel* what's going on inside of you. You might come across days when journaling is the last thing you want to do. Remember the commitment you made to yourself and do it anyway. If you don't feel like writing, then write about why you don't feel like writing. Before you know it, you will have a clear picture of your emotional state, my friend. At the end of the week, read it as if you were reading a stranger's diary. Be objective. No judgments. What do the entries tell you about this woman? Conclude the lesson with a summary of what you read and then answer the question, "Why are you here?"

Go within and find your strength, dear sister. *BLESSED BE!*

5/03/10

Where am I today? I think it's safe to say that I'm currently setting up shop in "I'm On My Period and I Hate Everyone Land." All I want to do is eat peanut butter and complain about how fat I am while I retain 75% of the water covering the earth's surface.

God help me, my kids have been home from school less than an hour and are already driving me bananas (a great accompaniment to peanut butter). Shawn can do nothing right. He doesn't answer my calls and I'm pissed because he doesn't want to talk to me. He calls me back and I'm irritated because he won't leave me alone. My house is a disaster. What a shock. But why bother cleaning it? As soon as the last plastic truck is tossed into the toy box, my kids will be pulling out the giant tub of Legos. After two hours of effort, my house will be returned to ruins in a matter of minutes. Destroyed...just like they've destroyed any silence the Universe has to offer, along with what USED to be my abs.

And you know what else I find annoying? Being told to "go within" when I don't even know what that means, much less how to effing do it. I feel like I'm back in grade school with that teacher who told me to "look it up" every time I asked her how to spell a word. How in the hell can I look it up when I don't know how to effing spell it?!

What I want to know is this: If my Inner Goddess were to emerge, would I still suffer from this menstrual-induced insanity? Does an Inner Goddess even deal with PMS? Does she experience fits of rage combined with uncontrollable crying? Does she ever hate every inch of her cramp-ridden, bloated body? Does she ever want to run away to a deserted island because she knows that's the only place on the planet where she won't be exposed to societal pressure to choose between Team Jacob and Team Edward? Does she ever resent the fact that she can't have thirty-eight seconds of quiet time? THIRTY-EIGHT GODDAMN SECONDS! IS THAT TOO MUCH TO ASK?!

Does my Inner Goddess share the weight of this burden? If not, I'd like to go within, punch her in the face and then help myself to more peanut butter.

5/04/10

So, maybe I was a little dramatic yesterday. At first I was thinking it was a mistake to begin this workbook during such an emotionally tumultuous period of time. In fact, I almost threw this book in the burn pile with the rest of the self-helpers who ended in failure. But I decided to push through it, and I'm glad I did. I'm feeling recharged and spry this morning, ready to give it a fresh start. I'm hoping my Inner Goddess won't judge my bipolarity too harshly.

Due to a string of hormonally charged fits yesterday, I was exhausted by eight-thirty, making it easy to go to bed at a decent hour. Yes, the Shiraz helped, but let's not get lost in the details. I slept well and didn't dream about chocolate or swimming for my life against a powerful current. This tells me the end of my cycle is on the horizon (a celebration worthy of cracking open another bottle).

My chemicals have managed to balance themselves out, so today can be handled with optimism and patience. Of course, my kids are still asleep so my sunny disposition is subject to change, but I won't start worrying about that just yet. I'm enjoying my morning coffee and my positive attitude. It's a Saturday. The kids will be in a good mood, too. Good vibes for everyone. I will it to be so!

I'm looking forward to a great family day. Shawn has to travel tomorrow for work, and we won't be able to celebrate Mother's Day together, so we're doing it today. Burgers, homemade ice cream, fishing at the pond and S'mores. Does it get more Norman Rockwell than that? No. It's going to be a goddamn Country Time Lemonade commercial come to life.

Weather changes, fighting kids, bread dough that won't double in size due to inactive yeast; all of this could possibly take place today. Should any of the abovementioned occur, I will NOT flip my shit. I will remain calm and accepting without seeking the comfort of overly processed baked goods. Step off Little Debbie!

MAY THE 4TH BE WITH YOU!

• • •

The day has come to an end and it took a slightly different turn than anticipated. Our water pump broke right before lunch. Shawn worked all day getting water back into the house. It rained on and off and we weren't able to go fishing. We couldn't make ice cream because we're out of rock salt and the nearest store was completely sold out.

Upside? The beer was cold and bubbly, the buttery homemade hamburger buns were soft and fluffy, and it stopped raining long enough to make gooey S'mores outside in the fire pit. The day did not turn out as expected, but I refuse to be upset. I will, however, help myself to another S'more...or possibly two.

Yes, I promised myself I wouldn't rely on food for comfort... but I break promises to myself all the time, so I'm really not all that disappointed.

5/05/10

I'm blah. I ate three S'mores at ten o'clock last night and I feel disgusting. I should workout but I don't feel like it. My five-year-old, Ryan, came to me completely naked complaining he has no clean underwear. I should do laundry but I don't feel like it. I have a bruise the size of a quarter on the bottom of my foot because I stomped on a Lego while running to answer the phone. Tidying my house would be a good idea but I don't feel like it. My children are bored and restless and need to expel some energy. I should take them out to do something fun but I don't feel like it. I, myself, am bored and restless but I only have enough motivation to bitch about it. Saddle up, kids. I smell a vicious cycle developing. Looks like Shawn's getting out just in time.

Happy Mother's Day—this one should be a hoot.

5/06/10

Yesterday ended up being a great day, despite my earlier crappy attitude. Shawn surprised me with rescheduling his business trip to Baton Rouge for today and the flowers I was upset about not receiving arrived just in time. He and the kids cooked me a spaghetti dinner and cleaned up the dishes while I hung out at the table, drinking wine and flipping through this month's issue of *InStyle*. And what made it even better was the homemade sculpture Ryan made for me out of orange construction paper and aluminum foil. I don't exactly know what it's supposed to be, but who am I to deny the Picasso of a new generation?

I wish I could be as enthusiastic about today but since I have no idea "where I am" it's hard to write about it. I almost blew it off, but then it occurred to me how stupid it is to buy a self-help workbook and not do the exercises. That's like hiring a therapist only to ditch the appointments. As brilliant a strategy as that may seem on the surface, I can't expect a great deal of personal growth to spring forth from the decision to quit on the third day. Mind you, I'm choosing to overlook the mass of half-read self-help books in my office right now.

So anyway, here I am, dedicating myself to the process, sitting in front of my blank workbook, looking around my country kitchen, trying to decide "where am I today." It's kind of annoying. I'm just here. That's it. I'm not sad, happy, angry, joyful. I feel nothing. I mean, I still have a pulse and the ability to appreciate the everyday pleasures in life, like eating super-awesome guacamole and watching syndicated *Law & Order* reruns. Other than going to lunch with Shawn before he left and shopping for summer clothes while the boys were in school, the day's been business as usual. I put off my chores and my workout. I scolded Zoe for grinding Play-Doh into the carpet. I heated up a frozen meal for dinner because the *Law & Order* marathon I previously mentioned caused me to lose track of time and it was too late to actually cook something. That pretty much brings us up to speed.

On a side note, is it pathetic that the guacamole seems to have been the highlight of my day? My instincts could be off, but something tells me that's pretty effing sad. Nonetheless, I'm sure my goddess would totally approve. Each ingredient in my guacamole was 100% organic and fair trade, so I've got that going for me.

Wherever my Inner Goddess lives, she's probably rubbing her temples in frustration...

5/07/10

The kids are asleep and I'm guzzling my second bowl of Shiraz after a carb-free dinner. I feel fantastic!

We're in the middle of a tropical depression and the third storm in six weeks is expected to blow in tomorrow. But who likes predictable, weather-related catastrophes? Not me, my friend, no, no—I like my hurricanes nice and early.

Living less than seventy miles from Galveston Bay, hurricane season can be pretty intimidating and we typically get out of town if the storm is forecasted to be a big one. This one, however, hits right in the middle. Not powerful enough to blow the house away, but at the same time, we may end up finding the patio furniture tossed 100 yards from the porch if it isn't properly secured. Granted, the storm would only be liable for a fraction of that mess. Our dogs would be responsible for dragging the furniture, piece by piece, farther out into the brush. "Sweet! New chew toys!" Those two troublemakers are more destructive than the hurricane itself.

Let me fill you in on my day up to this point. The school was closed due to the storm, which means I've been trapped inside a house with kids that were annoying each other to no end. My twelve-year-old, Tyler, wanted to play Xbox alone, while Ryan was ready to fight crime in his Batman gear. He was puzzled as to why his older brother didn't want to play the role of Robin. They argued back and forth for what felt like hours over the difference between an awesome game and a stupid one. It sounded something like this:

"That's stupid."

"No it's not, it's awesome."

"No, dude, it's stupid."

"YOU'RE stupid, this game is awesome."

Compelling, yes?

While they impressed Mensa with their mad debate skills, I played tea party with Zoe until I heard a loud thud and the sound of shattering plastic.

Ah, good…that would be Ryan throwing Tyler's Xbox remote against the wall.

After I broke up the wrestling match between my two sons, I escorted Ryan to his room for a time out and told him he would be pulling weeds for the next month to work off his debt for the cost of the broken remote. Then I told Tyler he could break something of Ryan's. In retrospect, it was a bad idea. But hell, it's what *I* would've done.

Anyone who says being a stay-at-home mom is easy can come say that to my face and then prepare to have a size six shoved right up their ass.

A quiet work place with nothing but adults? No cookie crumbs to clean out of my freshly made bed? No fights to settle over who can watch what? No thank you, I'd much rather be reduced to the fetal position by three children who refuse to get along. It's even better in a house with hardwood floors. The acoustic affects are mind-boggling!

deep sigh

If only they would use their powers for good.

What's better? This weather is expected to last until Friday. It's only Tuesday, help me, God—Tuesday!!! And Shawn's not due back from his trip until Thursday, lucky him. So after the day I've had, where am I this evening, oh goddess? Well, let's see...

–The thought of going for a long run in the middle of a Category Three hurricane is beginning to sound appealing.

–I've never wanted to be deaf so badly in my life.

–My two-gallon bucket of cookie dough is empty, and I don't have the ingredients to make my own.

–Earlier, I locked myself in the bathroom and told the kids I was practicing tornado safety drills.

It seems pretty bleak. The silver lining? I stocked up on wine and ibuprofen at the grocery store the other day, and I honestly believe I was guided by the Universe to do so.

There I was, picking out wine in aisle six, when suddenly there was a voice of wisdom, speaking to me from the heavens.

"My child," It said. "Think reasonably. You save ten percent when you buy six bottles... Why go with three? Buy twelve instead..." The angels sang. I heard it. I swear.

As if that wasn't enough, after removing some of the produce from the basket in order to squeeze in the case of wine, my sunglasses fell from the top of my head and when I bent down to pick them up, what did I find on the floor but a coupon for ibuprofen. Coincidence? I think not. It was the Universe, yet again, communicating with me to stock up on essentials. I give thanks to you, my Inner Goddess. Your ability to plan ahead is unparalleled.

I have been submerged in chaos, yet I remain unfazed. My kids are sleeping peacefully, and I have a Bordeaux stem filled to the brim, a bendy-straw and a complete disregard for wine etiquette. I need nothing else but the air in my lungs!

I will say I'm feeling a smidge guilty for the superfluous 1300 calories I'm taking in from alcohol alone, so I'm thinking I may hop on the treadmill later to burn some of this shit off. Or I might just pass out, slumped over my journal... I haven't decided yet. Cheers, bitches!

5/08/10

God in Heaven, what was I thinking? My entire body is throbbing, from my brain down to the tips of my puffy toes. The pounding inside my head is like my very own Broadway showing of *Stomp*, less the Tony Award.

I have road rash on my knees and a genuine sense of memory loss. Did I *seriously* go run on the treadmill? Oh my freaking God! I know I spoke to Shawn on the phone at some point; did he not talk me out it? Seriously, how exactly did that conversation go?

"Yeah honey, running on the treadmill while you're drunk is actually scientifically proven to reverse the effects of alcohol. I say go for it!"

If the situation were reversed, I can't say I wouldn't have done the same. But I'm still disappointed in him. With all his self-control, he always claims to be the mature one in this relationship, but now I'm starting to think he's full of shit. I talked to my sister Libby for the third time today and she's still laughing. I'm not calling her anymore until she can grow up and act more supportive.

Anyway, the only difference between today and yesterday is that I'm hung over. The weather conditions suck, school is still closed, so I'm stuck inside with my energetic kids who seem louder today than ever before.

My only saving grace is the stack of leftover pancakes from yesterday's breakfast. Why is this my saving grace? Because I already know there will not be a point in the day when I'll feel like making myself something to eat. A heaping load of simple carbohydrates is the effortless kind of snack I'm looking for. If only I could fashion some sort of "bucket necklace" to put them in, I could spare myself the repeated trips to the kitchen. And if those kids think they're getting a crumb of those pancakes, they've got another thing coming. I can see it now…

"Mommy, can I have one of your—"

"NO—this is MY pancake bucket!!! Where's my chocolate milk?"

Luckily Tyler knows how to heat up frozen pizza pockets, so he'll be the one making lunch today. I wonder if my children know how blessed they are to have such a responsible and giving mother. *eye roll*

I was supposed to meet up with friends in the city for lunch today. We get together once a week. Casey, Marissa and Sandy all live in Houston, and Blair, the one I'm closest with, lives in Sugarland. She's about fifteen minutes away. Our husbands work together, which is how we all met. Cool chicks. I'm obviously not meeting them today since the weather's bad and I feel like I'm dying, so I plan to submerge myself in movies that intensify my sense of self-loathing instead. I'll start out with *The Dukes of Hazzard* and then move right into *Cat Woman*, followed up with the knock out, one-two punch of *Charlie's Angels* and *Charlie's Angels: Full Throttle*. There's nothing like a good 'ole montage of Hollywood hot-bods to make you feel like shit when you're already feeling like shit. I call it "shit²" since "shit sandwich" has already been coined.

Dude, even my aura is hung over. *barf*

5/9/10

Now that the hangover has healed, I've sworn off drinking and I'm feeling rather motivated today. Yes, the torrential downpour outside has yet to cease and school is still closed, but since I no longer feel like throwing up with every breath I take, I don't mind it so much. And since it looks super cold outside, I'm going to take advantage of the illusion and do what I always do during the winter months. Bake!

So, what should it be? Chocolate chip cookies? Pecan pie squares? Peanut butter brownies? Fudge cake.

Oh, the possibilities! There's so much to choose from. Of course, I don't have to decide right now, it's only nine a.m. I just ate breakfast, after all. Perhaps I'll drop some hints to the kids and coerce one of them into asking me to bake something. That way I'm absolved of any glutton-related guilt. You know how it goes. If the treat is for the children and not me, then I don't need to invest any creative energy in coming up with a justifiable excuse for making fudge cake at nine o'clock in the morning. On top of that, Shawn comes home from his business trip today, and I can say I baked it for him. I could even get the kids involved! Spending time together in the kitchen will be a precious memory for us…even though I know deep down I won't let the kids help me bake. They're too messy, and more cake batter will end up on the walls than in the cake pan. Just the thought of that mess stresses me out. But if I let them lick the bowl, I still come out looking like a cool mom. CAKE!!!

5/10/10

I'm glad to say yesterday was a great day. I did make fudge cake, and the kids ended up helping out after all. It was actually pretty fun. Tyler did all the measuring. I let Ryan crack the eggs and, aside from the few pieces of eggshell I had to fish out, he did a great job. Zoe stirred the whisk a few times but then I had to take over because she kept sticking it in her mouth. She's just like her mother. We worked well as a team, but the best part of the experience was the clean up. Tyler got the spatula; I gave Zoe her whisk back; and Ryan and I split the bowl. Every single face in that kitchen was covered in cake batter. After the frosting set, Tyler wrote "Welcome Home Dad" in M&Ms for Shawn. Of course, the cake was half gone by the time he got home so the message only read "welcome ho," but he was touched, nonetheless.

"Aw, honey," he said. "You baked me your favorite cake!"

Doh! He saw right through me.

So here we are today. The weather has lightened and the boys are back at school. Zoe's coloring in the kitchen and the house is quiet for the first time all week. *sigh*

I'm now at the end of the first lesson and my next step is to go back and read all my entries since day one, pretending it's someone else's journal. Minus judgments and editing. I'm supposed to go over it and summarize what these entries tell me about the "woman who wrote them."

Typically I'd be thrilled to go back and read what I've written since no one thinks I'm funnier or more insightful than I do. But assessing from someone else's perspective? That may not be quite as much fun. And it will be hard doing it objectively and without judgment. So, I'll do what I always do…put it off. I have a busy morning anyway. What with laundry, last night's dinner mess and a closet that needs reorganizing, well, gosh, I'm just swamped.

What gets me motivated to complete the list of chores I've been avoiding? Something I want to avoid even more. I'll do it later. I promise.

· · ·

Okay, so it's now the end of the day, and I can't put this off any longer. It's really hard to write a serious summary, I'll admit it. My instinctive reaction to what I read was sarcasm, and the one thing twenty-eight self-help books taught me over the course of five months is that I make jokes out of serious situations in order to effectively shirk having to confront them. It's what I do. However, my gut's telling me that I won't get much out of this workbook if I'm making fun of the process throughout the whole thing. I guess I should take it seriously this time. Maturity. *ugh*

Here we go:

I'd like to say the woman who wrote these journal entries is a bitch and a drunk, but since I'm not supposed to judge, I'll say she seems to be struggling with her life situation. She clearly has trouble prioritizing, and comes across as mentally unsound. She doesn't appear to be completely miserable, but she isn't exactly radiating joy. Emotionally detached, she tries to escape, finding fulfillment in alcohol and fudge cake. It's also clear that she's easily stressed by her domestic responsibilities and the pressures of motherhood. She's sarcastic and critical, and, at times, seems a little bitter. She probably feels guilty for it, too.

Is this assessment correct? Of course it is. These are things I've known about myself for some time...and things I've hated. Here's the big question: Why am I here?

I have a great life. I'm married to a good guy who provides very well for me and the kids. Yes, he's gone a lot, but that's something I have to get used to, I guess. I have three children whom I love (even when I'm losing my cool). I have a great family and friends. I have my health, financial security and a nice car. I am living a dream life. So why isn't this enough? Why do I want more? Why do I feel the need to search for anything when I seem to have it all?

Because I don't know who I am. That's why I'm here, and that's what I want to find out.

LESSON 2

Daydreaming

Do you ever daydream? Of course you do, we all do! Some of us do it to find inspiration, to plan or to create. Some of us daydream about achieving a special goal or starting a new hobby or career. On the other hand, some of us use daydreaming as a means of escape, to fantasize about the proverbial greener grass. It's important to understand the difference between the two because our desires are trying to communicate with us. If we can examine those desires and fantasies, we might be able to better understand the areas in need of attention, the parts of us that are seeking growth, or more importantly, our desires could guide us to a greater purpose.

What do you find yourself daydreaming about? From traveling the world to telling off your boss, do you have a favorite scenario you think about more than others? Maybe you have more than one. If so, is there a common theme among them, or do they relate to different areas of your life? Now think about this: Do you ever experience jealousy with the happiness or success of others? Is it common to find yourself thinking, "I'd be so much happier if I had..." or "Why don't I ever get what I want?" Do your daydreams ever make you regret decisions you've made, or leave you feeling unhappy with your life? If you regularly entertain thoughts of regret—*If I had just done this instead of that, I'd have the life I want*—this will be an important lesson for you, sister.

I want you to spend time with your thoughts, observe them. What mental "movies" do you notice pop up more than others, and what emotions do they evoke? Do they promote motivation to grow or feelings of lack and resentment? Write about what you discover daily, then at the end of each week (or however often you choose, depending on the amount of time you dedicate to this), reread what you've written and see if there's a theme developing. The goal of this exercise is to write and reflect so you can begin to get a better idea of where to go from here.

Release any judgment you may have of your dreams and be honest with yourself. If we examine our life-long desires, we can, perhaps, detect patterns and similarities that can very well point us in the direction Destiny wants to take us. I also believe it's important to shine light on the negative thought patterns that are no longer serving you. This can be a fun assignment as well as an emotional one. Just remain open to the experience. The Universe has guided you here, so do not resist the process. *BLESSED BE!*

5/12/10

Well, when I was six I wanted a flying horse. Does that mean anything? Sadly, I'm being serious. I prayed for her every night, waiting [im]patiently for God to deliver.

I still remember her; she was so cool. Her color would change according to my moods. Sometimes she was luminously white, other times, black as pitch. Every now and then she was pink and purple, but it really depended on how flashy I was feeling that day. Her name was Princess and she was loyal only to me, doing my bidding on command. I imagined when I was bored or in trouble she would swoop down from the heavens and whisk me away to some magical, faraway place where I ruled with a forceful, yet accommodating hand. In my head, I was so immersed within the fantasy that I almost believed it was real at times. A lot like the subculture of gamers who have confused real life with *World of Warcraft*, only I wasn't twenty-five and living in my parents' basement.

Come to think of it, I'm pretty sure I used to tell other kids in my neighborhood she was real. Some of them actually believed me. All those who didn't got threatened or punched in the arm. I was a real charmer; a lying, bullying, imaginative charmer. But enough about my childhood character flaws, let's talk about the basis for this lesson. U2 sang about it, strip clubs are full of it and there was a streetcar named after it. That's right folks, I'm talkin' about DEE-ZY-UH.

This could take a small eternity since I have a boatload of desires and daydreams all the time. I have to go get the boys from school, so I'll put some thought into this and come back later.

05/15/10

I intended to take a few days and pay attention to my daydreams. I thought if I did this, I could write some things out, giving me a better understanding of what's on my mind more than anything. Sounds great, right? I know, I thought so too.

Well, I didn't do that.

I guess I was so caught up in whatever I was thinking about, I forgot to write it down. So I decided to sit down and make a list of what I fantasize about on a regular basis, which is pretty much the same thing the author of this workbook told me to do. What can I say? I have a knack for following directions. Here we go, in order from most often to least:

–Having the perfect body

–Owning an immaculate wardrobe

–Being famous (because I'm still nine, evidently)

–Traveling the world

–Being by myself (sad, I know)

–Party scenarios (mainly when I listen to music, I'll explain later)

That's what came to mind without having to think about it very hard. Of course, I left the sexual stuff off. I'd hate to freak Shawn out in case he gets curious and picks this up for some light reading. Although, on second thought, I probably should've written that out, too. Those daydreams might've added some cool points to my otherwise sad list. Seriously? Being famous?

I guess I'm supposed to dissect each item and figure out what's behind it, but I'd rather pop open a bottle of bubbly and watch the kids play on the jungle gym in the backyard while I wait for Shawn to bring home burgers for dinner. And oh yeah, the whole "I've sworn off drinking" thing fell through about two days after I declared myself to be a nondrinker. Heads up. This happens a lot.

I'll come back tomorrow.

5/16/10

At first I was feeling stupid about the thoughts that occupy my time, but I suppose I shouldn't feel too diminished by yesterday's entry. I've always daydreamed about cheesy stuff. I didn't limit the fantasizing to flying horses when I was little, you know. Along with conquering the unknown realm of equestrian flight, I wanted to be queen of the world, master of kung fu, grand ballerina, Michelle Pfeiffer, lead singer of a rock band and a twirler. I was ambitious. Being the imaginative child that I was, I guess it's not completely unnatural to be a creative adult? That feels good. Let's go with it.

On to the biology lesson. Today I'll be dissecting my daydreams. Pinning them down, slicing them open and doing my best to ignore the creepy smell of formaldehyde as they stare up at me blankly. I know this process is supposed to help me figure out if my desires are "ego based" or "goddess based," but let's be frank. I don't need to channel Freud for help on this one. It's not my "connection with the Universe" telling me I need a better body, or that being famous would kick ass. I'm still going to do the lesson, of course. I'm just stating the obvious for "I told you so" purposes when I'm done.

DAYDREAM #1: HAVING THE PERFECT BODY

Allow me to touch base with a bit of history before I begin.

My first "fat fear" memory dates back to the ripe age of six. We lived on a cul-de-sac in a Pasadena neighborhood and my best friend lived directly across the circle from me. We practically lived together, bouncing back and forth between her house and mine.

Her mom was always on a "diet," which, in retrospect, is hilarious. That family lived on hotdogs, white bread and frozen pizza (this being the reason her mom's ass was the size of a barn). I remember sitting in their kitchen, watching this woman measure portions and weighing chicken on her food scale, only to then polish off the pizza us kids didn't eat. Big, HUGE ass.

One day she said to me, "That'll make you fat," as I sat with her daughter eating corndogs she had prepared for us. I'll never forget it. Being only six, I didn't understand the full extent of her comment, but I did understand the negativity of her tone. I was terrified right then and there.

I remember imagining this gigantic woman, towering over the houses in our neighborhood. She wore a pink, floral-printed moo-moo with roses on it the size of trampolines. Atop of her gargantuan, egg-shaped body was her tiny head. I don't know why it was so disproportionate to the rest of her body, but I recall being unnerved by it.

I don't want to be huge with a tiny head!

I didn't want to become that monster, and I've been afraid of it ever since.

Thanks a lot, Mrs. Taylor. Moo-moo wearing bitch.

Side note: I'm not trying to go off on some autobiographical rant here. I know I'm not writing my life's story. But I feel that since this is what's on my mind more than anything, I should do a little digging into the history of it. Moving on...

I went on my first diet when I was twelve. Junior high was really the time of my life where I began shaping my idea of the perfect body. In the sixth grade I weighed 116 lbs. and I had pretty much topped out at five feet two inches. Fat? Absolutely not. However, in comparison to the other four foot eight inch, eighty-pound girls in my class, I felt like a giant. At least my head was the right size.

By the time I got into high school, the daydream was fully developed and on its way to becoming an obsession. The ideal body for me was a C cup, flat abs, a bubble butt and thighs with equal circumference to the calves; the typical cheerleader standard held by most teenage girls in America. However, since I was too busy skipping school and smoking pot to do much more than fantasize, it goes without saying that I did not live up to this standard.

"God! Why can't I be thin??? Dude, don't Boggart the Funions…" Yeah, I was seriously baffled as to why my goal weight continued to elude me. *duh* I'm glad brain cells have the power to regenerate themselves… Uh…they do, right?

Anyway, after high school, I got a bit closer to achieving my goal of "perfection" due to diet pills and starvation. It's probably the closest I've ever been to being happy with my body. Of course, I said close. At five feet two inches, 110 lbs. wasn't quite thin enough. "Just five more pounds," I'd tell myself.

I got married and things got worse before they got better. There are certain people who have to completely crash before they can heal and, according to my former therapist, I'm one of them. I remember the night I hit rock bottom. We had moved to Richmond and Shawn had begun traveling a lot more with his new position as sales manager. With such a huge amount of change happening so quickly, I felt really out of control in my life and started to take it out on my body more than usual. The desperate act of binging and purging was occurring on a more regular basis. Not quite daily, but getting there. So one night I was sitting in the kitchen alone. Shawn was at a team dinner in Houston and Tyler was asleep. I was bored and my sweet tooth was flaring up, so I decided to bake a dessert: butter cake with fudge frosting, yum. I salivated as I mixed the dry ingredients with the wet. The sound of the whisk scraping against the metal mixing bowl was like music to my ears. I sat on my kitchen floor and watched the cake rise and bake through the window of the oven door, taking in the sweet smell of the comforting confection. Sadly, I already knew what I planning to do. As soon as the cake was out of the oven and frosted to perfection, I cut myself a piece…and didn't stop until the cake was gone. I immediately ran to my bathroom to purge myself of my sins, crying the whole time. Imagine how mortified I was when Shawn asked me the next day, "Did you get sick last night? I got home and there was a mess in the toilet." I was usually good about cleaning up after myself, but that night I didn't care. Maybe I wanted to get caught? Before I knew it, I was crying again and telling my husband what I had done. It felt like a goddamn AA meeting.

"Hi, I'm Holly, and I ate an entire cake and then threw it up. It's nice to be here."

Shawn listened with wide eyes, surprised to have never noticed this behavior from his wife of eight years.

"How could this have gotten past me?" he asked. "We've been together for almost a decade. How could I have not known?"

I was embarrassed to talk to him about it. He's so freaking perfect all the time. Shawn told me he wished I loved myself more than that. To this day I don't know how I feel about that response.

Anyway, I'm getting off track. That day, I researched therapists who specialize in eating disorders and the rest is history. I saw Dr. Appolito once a week until I was able to at least heal the physical side of the disease, the binging and purging. However, I can admit to myself that I should've stuck with the therapy longer. The emotional side of the disease, the critical eye, the counting, the obsessing, it never really went away.

So yes, at the age of thirty-four, I habitually daydream of emulating the image of that seventeen-year-old cheer captain I coveted in high school. Healthy? You Bet'cha! *eye roll*

Shawn tells me all the time that I'm "Beautiful. Sexy. Perfect." I typically scoff and say, "Yeah right," or "You have to say that because you're my husband." I wish his finding me attractive was enough for me…but it's not.

Zoe's up from her nap. I'm done for today.

5/17/10

Today was a lunch with the girls in Houston, so I took Zoe to Mother's Day Out. It's this childcare program at the Baptist church where you can drop your kids off for a few hours at a time throughout the week. It's kind of like daycare, but calling it "Mother's Day Out" absolves me of the guilt I associate with being a stay-at-home mom and still taking my daughter to daycare, but I digress.

After dropping her off, I met up with my girls at Casa Garcia, which is where we typically meet to gorge on tortilla chips and the best damn margaritas in town. I'm trying to enjoy it while I can. Once the boys are out of school, our get-togethers will become more difficult. I managed to hold off drinking too much so I could do my lesson today. Only two weeks into this workbook and I'm already becoming more responsible. Success is mine!

DAYDREAM #2: AN IMMACULATE WARDROBE

Ah, clothes, my second favorite thing to daydream about, and definitely the most fun. It makes sense, doesn't it? The perfect body might as well be dressed in the perfect outfit. Haute couture, salon shoes, super-fine handbags, drool, drool, wipe.

Growing up in Pasadena, my friends and I used to spend our Saturdays in LA, shopping, star gazing and trying to pretend that we were rich enough to step foot on Rodeo Drive. So with that being said, I have a bit of an affinity for fashion and dressing up. I'm not saying that Texas doesn't have its own sense of style or its own material world. It does, especially Houston. But I don't live in Houston. I live in Richmond. So over the years, I've gotten used to lounge pants and T-shirts because there's no place in my life for Dior anymore. But I'd be lying if I said I didn't miss "getting dressed" or savoring every catalogue, fantasizing about "where I would wear that."

I've always, always loved clothes. I played dress up in my mom's cocktail gowns when I was five; I never missed an opportunity to walk around in whatever high heels fit me at the department store; and by the age of eleven, I had a notebook of outfits I had designed and sketched out. There were even a few garments I sewed haphazardly together by hand from scraps of old material.

So yes, I think about the perfect outfit for any occasion that comes to mind. Lunch with friends in town, followed by a pedicure and a grocery trip; I'd go with nautical stripes and dolman sleeves, bellbottom jeans and a cute wedge heel. Date night to the movies... trapeze top with a shrunken blazer, skinny jeans and ballet flats. An outing to the petting zoo…I'd say a maxi dress with a structured denim jacket and cowboy boots, but since I don't go to the petting zoo, it's obsolete. The spontaneous trip to New York that never happens…what says 'effortless but runway-ready'? The story takes off from there. If I don't already have the ensemble in my closet, I obsessively search for it online until I find it.

I get it. I'm materialistic. I'm sure I'm the only woman who does this. *psh*

It's time to get the boys from school. Peace out.

5/20/10

I finished conversation #4 with Libby and it's only ten-thirty in the morning. Shawn says we have an unusual relationship but I don't see it. I told her about this workbook: what it's about, what's involved in it. I'm supposed to keep her in the loop of any changes I see or discoveries I make so she can make the decision whether or not to buy a copy for herself. This is the norm for us, by the way. Libby's only a year older than I am, so we're a lot like twins, following each other's trends. However, when it comes to trying something new, I always end up being the Guinea pig. She'll sell me on an idea; hair extensions, microdermabrasion, P90X.

"Dude, they say you'll have a completely different body in less than twelve weeks!"

"Seriously? I think I'm going to try it!"

"Totally! Get it and let me know if it works."

I usually find myself irritated when she says, "Oh, you didn't like it? Hmm, well then, I'm not going to do it." I understand her logic, but I always end up feeling used.

Moving on.

DAYDREAM #3: BEING FAMOUS

This is embarrassing so I don't want to spend too much time on this, but yes, I daydream about what it would be like to be famous, okay?

I wanted to be an actor when I was little and it's one of the fantasies I've held onto ever since. I actually wrote a play when I was in first grade. Yes, it only had one act and I spent more time on wardrobe than storyline, but it could've been big if I had actors to fill the cast.

All throughout junior high and high school acting was genuinely what I wanted to do. I never pursued it, of course, because I had shit for confidence, but I thought about it every day.

As an adult, the prospect of acting is gone. Now I think it would be cool to have access to celebrity trainers, stylists and surgeons. I will say I don't envy the lack of privacy at all. I'm sure taking out the trash without having to put on heels and makeup is a luxury I take for granted.

I'm over this one. Let's move forward, k?

5/25/10

This one's going to be brief today. It's the last day of school and the boys will be home right after lunch. I'm going to take them to Houston and meet up with Shawn for dinner at their favorite pizza place to celebrate the end of the school year. It was totally my idea. Aren't I awesome?

DAYDREAM #4: TRAVELING THE WORLD

Yeah, totally. Seeing the world would be so amazing. That's why I love getting updates from my sister, Katy. She studies in Spain but goes all over the place. It's nothing for her to hop on a train to Paris for the weekend, or go clubbing in Germany. Last week she updated her Facebook picture and I could see the hills of Tuscany in the background. Man, what I wouldn't give. That's exactly what I would've done in my early twenties if I could have. Fly to Europe, jump from country to country...sleep with every hot guy I met. Well, that's a little extreme, I can't say EVERY guy, but it sure is fun to think about having so much freedom. I never really got to experience the irresponsibility of that age. Hell, I didn't even get to party on my twenty-first birthday because I was three months pregnant. Tyler was a bit of a surprise, see. While most people my age were running wild, I was learning how to breastfeed and heal a diaper rash with homeopathic remedies. I know, I know—sob, sob, sob, right? Don't get me wrong, I'm not throwing myself a pity party. I wouldn't trade my family for anything. Still, it doesn't stop me from wanting to live vicariously through Katy's adventures. So yeah, I daydream about traveling the world. I'd start with Italy and eat a shit ton of pasta. Then I'd go to Greece for some hummus, France for champagne, enjoy the tapas in Spain, buy a kilt and drink cold beer in Ireland, then I'd go look for Nessy in Scotland. And everyone I know would get some world-class postcards along the way. I'm thoughtful like that.

DAYDREAM #5: BEING BY MYSELF

I'm ashamed to admit it, but sometimes I wonder what life would be like if I were single without children. Not because I want to go out and party like a "free woman." That doesn't really appeal to me as much as it used to. I just think it would be nice to have alone time. Without the TV constantly chattering. Quiet time. I could buy groceries for one. Make dinner for one. Do laundry for one. Deep down, I have moments when that sounds really appealing. And then I feel really guilty about it. A lot like I do right now. So I'm going to take my kids out to do something fun in order to absolve myself of said guilt.

5/29/10

DAYDREAM #6: PARTY SCENARIOS

Okay, Zoe's taking a nap, the boys are watching a movie and I have a lunch date in fifteen minutes. Let's make this quick!

So I mentioned earlier that I love music. LOVE music. The only thing I love more than music? Dancing to music. I can be in the worst mood, but you put on "Boom, Boom, Pow" and this bitch is shakin' it. It's only natural then, while listening to my jams, to start thinking about a great scenario that matches the song. Classic rock: I want a patio and margaritas. Club music is self-explanatory with a vodka soda. Alternative rock: I want dark beer and a get-together with friends. Country: give me a pool hall and cold beer.

Of course each scenario has the right outfit, which should go without saying after I explained daydream #2. Classic rock on the patio: I see a tunic top with bellbottom jeans and sandals. Club music: I want a tastefully slutty cocktail dress and sky-high stilettos. Alternative rock: I'm thinking worn-in cords with a vintage Cyndi Lauper T-shirt and Converse chucks. It should also go without saying that these clothes are being worn on the perfect body, and in each scenario I'm doing something really cool that's impressive to everyone within eyeshot.

God, I'm such a loser.

I'm headed to Casa Garcia to meet up with my girls. I went ahead and did my lesson first so that way I can drink all I want! What's better, Blair, one of my best friends, is bringing her fourteen-year-old daughter over to hang with my kids while we're gone. Last but not least, it's her turn to drive so I don't have to worry about pacing myself. A margarita binge is totally in my cards today! *FIST PUMP*

6/1/10

My day started out pretty good until I went back and read through what I've written for this lesson. I have to say, I'm a bit disappointed. Examining all of my ridiculous daydreams was not fun; if anything, it was embarrassing and shameful.

Should I go ahead and insert the "I told you so" that was predicted when I began this chapter? All of my daydreams are ego based! Clearly I use fantasizing as a tool for escape. Beauty, fame, wanderlust, mythical creatures; yeah, I would say there's a common theme. I spend a great portion of my life wanting to be somebody else in a land far, far away. Jesus, I *am* shallow! Six months later, that damn *Cosmo* quiz is STILL effing haunting me!

I'm hoping Lesson Three will be more uplifting. If not, I'm throwing this workbook in the "bullshit" pile. And I'll probably tell Libby to buy it.

LESSON 3

Fear

Now that we've discussed desire, let's talk about what holds us back. Fear. It is the root of all negative emotions and thoughts. It takes on many forms and doesn't always present itself as blatantly as the sensation of fright. It can disguise itself as anger, greed, sadness, sarcasm, cynicism, stress and even as lethargy or apathy. Fear keeps us trapped in restrictive comfort zones and is responsible for bad habits. It's what causes us to hold on to negative emotional "baggage," turning such baggage into a sense of "who I am." It is an extremely poisonous delusion and it must be eliminated. But its power cannot be denied and its roots are deeply ingrained in the way we think, feel and act. How do we go about ridding ourselves of something so incredibly influential? We start by examining our discomforts or discontentment. We ponder our unmet goals and desires and question WHY they remain dreams and not reality.

Again, be thoughtful throughout this lesson. Take as much time as you need, it is crucial. Write about it each day because, again, each day is different. On Monday you may be aloof and totally at ease, whereas Tuesday you might be rigid and irritable. Pay attention to your actions. See if you notice fear in the way you behave or in the decisions you make. Journal about what you come up with, as well as how you handle day-to-day occurrences, work, family or your spiritual journey, for instance. When you find yourself in the position to react, observe what's going on inside of you before you do. If you sense a negative feeling, try not to get lost in it. Instead, take the opportunity to monitor the emotion. Notice if shifting your awareness changes how you might normally handle an off-putting situation. Bringing awareness to what you do brings quality to what you do, leaving very little space for negativity. Fear is an illusion and your Goddess Essence, your True Self, knows nothing of it. Know this, and you will be free. *BLESSED BE!*

6/4/10

If this were a text message, I would've started out this entry with "LOL!" Seriously, if fear is the root of all negativity then I'm absolutely stunned I can function at all as a normal human being.

By all rights and purposes, my negativity means I'm afraid of everything. My sarcasm alone suggests I'm a quip away from the effing nuthouse. Uh-oh, I'm being snide. This must mean I'm terrified right now. *eye roll*

Can't I become a better person and still get to complain and make fun of other people? Why must these things be mutually exclusive?

I don't feel like doing this shit today, so I'll end my entry on this note: The ONLY thing I'm afraid of is someone telling me the foundation of my sense of humor needs to be *eliminated*. Well…that and obesity. But other than those two things, nothing scares me. Except burning alive. That sounds pretty terrifying. But it's not something I think about all the time, so it doesn't count.

6/6/10

Well, let's go within and see how afraid I am today. I have the overwhelming desire to call a certain author a hippie douche. Yep, I'd say I'm still experiencing too much fear to take this lesson seriously.

6/8/10

I guess I should consider changing my attitude if I ever plan on moving on with this workbook, huh? It probably didn't help that I was at the tail end of a hormonal overcharge when I began the lesson. I love being able to use that excuse.

6/9/10

So, even after adjusting my attitude, I'm still having a hard time figuring out my fears. I'm trying to pay attention to what I feel, as suggested in the lesson plan. Since my sister knows me better than anyone, I thought I would ask her if she knew of anything that maybe I couldn't see.

"Well, you're terrified of being fat and burning alive, that's all I know." She's the master of insight.

Here's what I've come up with on my own. If fear is related to discomfort, and that discomfort is being caused by annoyance, then I feel disheartened. I experience annoyance more than I experience most emotions. According to the author, this means I spend a lot of time being afraid. In fact, you could say this lesson is making me "afraid" right now.

I don't know. This chapter isn't coming easily to me. I want to skip it and move on to Lesson Four.

6/15/10

After several days of writer's block, I went back and read my previous entries. I'd like to say I was being proactive and searching for any clues to help me out with Lesson Three. However, in all honesty, I wanted to read what I had written because I'm strangely vain in that way. There have been times I've opened my "Sent Items" to reread some of my funny emails, so I could relive how impressed I was with my sense of humor. I'm really glad no one else is going to read this. That's kind of embarrassing.

Anyway, the whole point in bringing this up is that my rereading did, in fact, point me in the right direction for this lesson. Since

I'm a bit of a prideful gal, it's no surprise that admitting fear on my part makes me squeamish. I don't mind admitting my faults because there seems to be strength in one's ability to do so. But being presently afraid? I don't like it. Again, I find myself having to be reminded that this workbook will do me no good if I stonewall the process. Even *I* know, deep down, exploring and dissolving one's fear is probably not the best lesson to hit the "pass" button on. I'm not stupid. I'm hardheaded.

Getting back to what I read in the previous entries, I found that I was opening the clichéd can of worms I was trying to avoid in the first place. I don't need to be super observant to catch the undertones of laziness, escape, impatience, overindulgence, lack of self worth and separation. Even though I don't want to admit it, something tells me the author is right. These are all rooted in fear. This led me to ask: "Why? What am I afraid of?"

If I'm being lazy, where does fear fit in? Let's take unpacking a full suitcase, for example; I hate unpacking. I always put it off because I don't feel like dealing with it. No kidding, I've had a full suitcase sit in my closet for weeks on end, simply because I didn't feel like putting away the clothes. The positive thing about that is, when I finally do get motivated to unpack, it's like I'm getting new clothes. "Oh! I love this shirt! I was wondering where this went..."

I'm getting off track. FEAR. What's the fear underneath my laziness and procrastination? In this case, what am I experiencing when I think about having to unpack? Let's see. I guess I feel put out. I know it's going to take forever to put all those clothes away. And, with dresser drawers that are overfilled as it is, it's going to be a pain in the ass putting the clothes back in their places. I'd rather be doing something that didn't take all that effort.

So let's break that down even further. When I'm feeling lazy, is it pure disdain for work, or do I "fear" the discomfort of the impending pain in the ass? I know the task at hand is going to be unenjoyable, so I put it off because I want to avoid that experience…?

What about "escape"? What am I feeling when I want to procrastinate or run away? Overwhelmed by the task; fed up with the stress. Helpless. I don't think we're talking about unpacking anymore.

The kids are asking for a snack and I need a break. I'll come back tomorrow.

6/20/10

I thought about this lesson all day yesterday, and I woke up this morning with a better sense of what's going on, I think. When I step back and look, I can see how all my negative behavior comes from fear, and knowing I'm not alone had me feeling better for a while. Screaming kids that don't belong to me, screaming kids that do belong to me, inattentive bartenders, traffic jams, flight delays—these things are annoying to everyone. By the time I finished my morning coffee, I found myself on the phone with Libby, validating my reasoning for being an irritable person.

"The world's full of jaded people. We're like one big crabby family!"

"You know what really pisses me off?" she asked. "Those stupid traffic light cameras!"

It was off topic, but since she was in the mood to complain, I was totally in.

"Are you still having issues with determining green lights from red lights, Lib?"

"They don't give you a chance! As soon as that yellow light turns red, BAM! They snap a picture. It's bullshit!"

"How long before you get your license suspended, dude?"

"Like that will stop me from driving? Sorry, Po-Po, I got shit to do. It's not MY fault the timing of the traffic lights is off. They need to take care of that, seriously."

"But Libby, isn't there anything the Junior League can do about it?"

"No, I don't think so…wait, are you making fun of me?"

She's so funny. Big sis, queen of the Santa Monica Junior League. Ever since she quit working for the Chamber of Commerce she has submerged herself in every committee and advisory board available to her. Libby only has one daughter, McKenna. But I swear, I think she would have more children just so she could perpetuate her role as "Homeroom Mom." But what's even funnier is that she joins everything, only to complain about how much time she doesn't have.

"I've joined the parade committee at McKenna's school again this year! Why do I keep doing this?!"

"Because you're a former events planner and you can't help but show off your wicked party-planning skills to all the other moms that aren't as cool as you."

"Oh…yeah."

Libby loves to have a good time. It's her sole purpose in life. She came out of the womb planning parties. This being the reason it took her seven years to finish college…without a doctorate. But an affinity for fun does not keep this woman from hopping on the wagon to "Bitch-and-Moan-ville," which is why she's the one I call when I want to complain about something.

Once I got off the phone with my big sister, I felt completely validated in my right to be a complaining hag if I wanted to be. But all that confirmation began to dwindle as I sat on the porch swing, watching my happy kids play on the play set without a care in the world.

This isn't about everyone else, it occurred to me out of nowhere.

I didn't buy this workbook to become more cynical and I didn't buy it to help me justify why it's acceptable to be unhappy. If I start preserving my entitlement to be irritated then aren't I setting myself up for a lifetime of irritation? That doesn't sound like a screaming victory to me. If I want to do this lesson right, if I want to do this workbook right, I should start asking myself some questions in order to move forward. Questions like: What do I feel beneath the laziness? What's behind the sense of being overwhelmed? What's up with the self-criticizing? Why am I so bitter and annoyed all the time? I feel uncomfortable and out of control. The vulnerability in being out of control makes me feel anxious and separated, and at the base of it, I feel alone and afraid.

So do all of these emotions come from something as simple as rambunctious children or being cut off in traffic? When I feel like someone's taking away my control...yes.

I'm not trying to have a *Full House* moment when all of a sudden everything is cleared up and A-OK after one sit-down talk with Uncle Jessie. Nevertheless, I do have a better understanding of what the author means when she said all negativity is rooted in fear. I got it. It's unsettling how quickly I went from an oblivious, "I'm not afraid!" to a concerned, "Ooohhh...hmm..."

I can hear my Inner Goddess now. "I won't say I told you so, but I told you so."

At least it's what I'd be saying if I were her.

Getting back to it, I guess the fear that's most obvious to me at this point deals with control, or better yet, the fear of having none. And when taking all of my negative thought patterns into account, it would appear that control is a pretty big deal to me; although I wouldn't have thought it was before. I guess that's how unaware I was.

Here's what gets me. I understand no one can possibly have complete control over everything at all times. That's a ridiculous expectation. So what does that mean for me? It means I now have realized there's never a time when I'm completely comfortable, because there is never a time when I'm completely in control. In other words, I'm a nervous wreck the majority of the time and didn't know it until about fifteen minutes ago. Maybe it's just me, but I would consider this to be a pretty sobering realization. I'm interested to learn the areas of my life that are most affected. And since I can feel the tension rising because I hear Tyler and Ryan fighting in the other room, I'd be willing to wager motherhood is a big'un.

6/27/10

I haven't written in a few days. I wish I could say it's because I've been off with the family, adventure-hopping and being productive, but that isn't the case. Shawn's been home in between business trips, so I've been spending time with him, which sounds like a really good excuse for not writing, right? However, if I had a backbone, I'd admit that after my little discovery about being riddled with fear, I've been avoiding this workbook like the plague. Why? When I know I look like shit, I avoid looking in the mirror. I guess it's the same thing with inner reflection.

At the same time, I haven't been able to help but question all of my negative behavior over the last few days. When I'm annoyed, when I'm putting off productivity, when I'm craving a drink at 11:45 in the morning, the awareness pops up.

Crap! What am I afraid of right now?

It's annoying. So even though I had actually decided to blow this workbook off, now I feel like I can't. I guess it's a good thing.

I'm hosting a dinner club get-together tonight, so I'm off to go prep for that. I'll write tomorrow.

6/28/10

It's 1:12 in the morning and I've had quite a bit to drink. I should be passed out or doing something self-destructive like bingeing on cookies...because cookies sound really good...but I felt it was important to write about something I experienced this evening. I know if I were to put it off until I wake up, I wouldn't remember it; "strike while the iron's hot," and all that.

So like I said earlier, I hosted my dinner club tonight and it was a lot of fun; hence the whole "heavy buzz" thing. It's called a "dinner club," but it's really a good excuse for twelve to fifteen women to get together for fattening snacks, gossip and way too much sangria... way, WAY too much sangria. It should be called the "Good Excuse to Get Drunk Club," because dinner has nothing to do with it.

Now, I already know overindulgence is one of my weaknesses; I typically blow it off because... I don't know... I just do. Anyway, I went into this evening trying to be all "aware" since that's the point of all this goddess shit.

Not Fun.

The voice in my head that usually says, "OK, that's enough," was louder tonight, and was harder to ignore. Instead of the typical passive suggestion, it was more like, "You're overdoing it again, Holly, stop. This is what you're trying to grow out of. STOP!" This is a tad more assertive than, "You might want to consider slowing down." I tried arguing, "No. All my friends are here and everyone's having fun. I'm not going to miss out on a party at my own house, dude."

"This isn't what you want." Over and over again, "This isn't what you want." Calling to me from some untouchable place—my own little "Tell-Tale Heart."

This isn't what you want. This isn't what you want. This isn't what you want!

I ignored this voice with passionate resentment. Like a spoiled brat, I placed my hands over my ears and stomped my feet. It felt like rebellion, as if I needed to protect my right to destroy myself.

This is what I've done for as long as I can remember. I'm the fun party girl. It's what I do.

So here's my realization: I'm afraid if I follow the guidance of my "Goddess," then I'll lose my sense of identity. *Who am I without that which comforts me?*

I'm so afraid if I listen to her I'll miss out on the pleasure of indulgence. Without alcohol, I'm afraid of not being the life of the party because I'm nothing special when I don't drink. I'm not funny,

I'm not lively. In that same vein, I'm afraid if I abandon my cravings I, myself, will feel abandoned because feeding my cravings is how I show myself love.

Sangria hurts the next day. I'm going to be so mad at myself when I wake up.

6/28/10 (cont'd)

Well, I've felt worse. Surprisingly, I'm not that hung over. I bet my saving grace was ingesting a metric ton of chips and queso. Sweet mercy, there's something magically healing about fried tortillas and cheese dip made with heavy cream. It coats the stomach and does that of wonders, amen. It apparently also aids in revelation because what occurred to me so early this morning was a pretty big deal. It turns out my issue with overindulgence is precisely as bad as I've always suspected. Of course, my initial reaction when I read my early morning entry was denial.

You're such a queen! "Tell-Tale Heart," Holly? This is a bit theatrical, don't you think?

Yes, I do. But it doesn't make it any less true.

I may have been writing soap opera-worthy stuff at one o'clock in the morning, but at least it was without inhibition. Easily put, the predominant side of me that's in denial at all times passed out, and the honest part of me was finally free to tell the truth, the whole truth and nothing but the truth, so help me Goddess.

My fear of vulnerability, my fear of abandonment, my fear of exposure that I'm a complete fraud, my fear of being imperfect, my fear of being NOTHING, my fear of living my entire life and never knowing what it's like to feel my soul—everything comes down to this. Not only do I clearly have issues with who I think I am, I have no sense of security whatsoever. And since a part of me is rolling its eyes at the sound of all this, I evidently have a fear of sounding dramatic.

I am a living, breathing legion of fears. They are all so closely interwoven it's hard for me to tell which one is which. So I run away from them. And whatever I can't run away from, I try to numb because, on top of everything else, I'm afraid of feeling the fear. I'm afraid of being afraid. It's insane! Completely insane!

If it's possible that something so pervasive is "just an illusion," then a great deal of my life has been wasted.

Christ! There's another fear! *UGH* Lesson Four, please!

LESSON 4

Your Anti-Goddesses

In this lesson, you will use your imagination. Lesson Three was a bit heavy. Exploring one's fear is an emotional process and admitting weakness is never simple or painless. Kudos to you for coming this far, sister. However, we still have quite a journey ahead of us, and fear is a tricky character. It will not stop just because you acknowledged its presence, and you need to be able to identify it when it rears its ugly head. That's where Lesson Four comes in. Now you must take what you learned from Lesson Three, all those fears you expressed, and assign them identities, like a list of characters in a Playbill. Think of them as "anti-goddesses." Each has her own particular modus operandi. However, these entities serve only *one* purpose: to hinder your evolution.

They do this by creating and maintaining the illusion that you are separate from your Source. Lethargy keeps us from taking action, anger keeps us from letting go, mistrust keeps us from acceptance or loving completely, and so on. Get to know your anti-goddesses so when they show up, you have the power of awareness to say, "Ah ha! I see you and I know what you're trying to do!" It will help you to know that feelings of discontentment are not really YOU. You are NOT your fears! Your true essence is pure love and cannot co-exist with negativity. As we continue to shine light on each fear, they will weaken and eventually vanish. Get as creative as you want. Paint a clown face on them all! The more fun you have with this, the more likely you will be able to recognize the fear when it arrives, and more importantly, the less likely you'll be to take it seriously when it does. *BLESSED BE!*

7/3/10

I'm not questioning the process. I have no sarcastic remark. No, THIS I'm looking forward to. If I apply the screenwriting skills from my early elementary school days, this lesson is bound to be a freaking breeze! I was born to do character write-ups, are you kidding? *psh*

Hold onto your toga, goddess. Things are about to get awesome.

. . .

I've been sitting in front of my notebook for twenty minutes and I have no idea what to write. This lesson sucks.

Tomorrow I won't have the chance to work on this because we're meeting our Houston friends and some of Shawn's coworkers in Galveston. We're celebrating the Fourth together by going to some beach festival, then heading back to grill burgers and light fireworks at a beach house Blair and her husband Pete are renting for the holiday. While I'm really looking forward to seeing my friends, quite frankly I'm dreading the events of the day. I fully acknowledge the fact that I come from California and therefore, by all rights and purposes, should embrace the beach like I'm one with it. However, I can honestly say I'm the one person from California who does not fit that stereotype. I hate the beach—really, REALLY hate the beach. And I'm on my freaking period. Like I want to have fun in the sun right now? Come on.

Nevertheless, I'll keep the lesson in the back of my mind while I'm gone. Who knows? Maybe I'll light a sparkler and suddenly have a revelation about the meaning of life.

7/4/10

What's the meaning of life? Well, I lit four sparklers tonight and never figured it out.

I wasn't expecting to write until tomorrow, but since the beach house wasn't big enough to sleep all of us comfortably, we ended up driving home. It's late, I'm exhausted and this was a terrible day. But since it ended well, and I've gotten used to journaling so frequently, I thought I'd jot some stuff down while Shawn's getting the kids to bed.

Like I said, today flat out sucked for the most part. But in retrospect, it makes for a pretty funny story, and we all know how much I love impressing myself with my own witty anecdotes. I'll probably come back in a few weeks and read it again so I can laugh at my ability to spin a tale. Okay, okay. I'll get to the point.

So we went to the Fourth of July Sand Fest today, which is a sand sculpture contest and carnival of sorts. To lay it out there, I'm fair skinned and burst into flames when exposed to UV rays for longer than fifteen minutes. I couldn't get a golden brown tan if I tried, hence the reason I'm not a sun worshipper, and spending the day at the beach is unappealing to me. Libby's the exact opposite. While I got the Irish skin, she got the Italian. She goes out to get the mail and comes back looking like Miss Hawaiian Tropic. *eye roll*

Anyway, I'd never heard of this Sand Fest and was told by Blair that it was a rather small event, even though people from all over the country come to participate in the contest. I guess, in retrospect, I should blame myself for not questioning the inconsistency in that description.

"It's nationally recognized, but don't worry, hardly anyone shows."

Blair's no dummy. She put a different spin on it in order to get me to concede. In other words, she effing LIED. She knows I hate crowded places, I hate traffic, I hate the beach and I really don't like carnivals. But even after she played the whole thing down, I still had to take a few moments to weigh out the pros and cons of going. Aside from moderately cold beer and ridiculously yummy treats deep fried in animal fat, the most any carnival can offer is good quality people watching, second only to strip clubs. As appealing as Coors Light and fried Twinkies may sound, eating on the beach sucks. Every time the wind blows, you run the risk of losing your food, spilling your drink or getting sand in your mouth. With that in mind, I knew shamelessly making fun of people would be the only thing I had to look forward to.

Now, don't get me wrong. I won't dismiss the orgy of guilty pleasures offered by the "Human Behavior Variety Hour." The inspiring image of hickey-laden carnie folk on the beach had my inner critic salivating, and just the idea of the tattooed biker granny in a Brazilian bikini was like throwing a bucket of chum into a pool of ravenous sharks. Toss in a geriatric banana hammock (it's a Speedo, kids), a baby drinking soda through a bottle and that drunk dude with the third degree sunburn, and I should be a happy camper.

Unfortunately, the prospect of comedy gold wasn't enough to balance out the misery I was anticipating. Straight up, I didn't want to go. Nonetheless, I know my lack of motivation this summer has made me a bit of a stick in the mud. I'll be the first to admit, I never want to do anything fun and it has to suck for my kids. Sadly, even with this in mind, I still tried to play it down to the kids by making something really boring sound awesome.

"Hey, kids, I know all of you really want to go to the beach and see all the cool sand castles and eat cotton candy and swim. But mommy really hates the beach and the whole thing sounds like a giant pain in the ass. So let's just hang out at home and we'll pull out the inflatable pool! Who's with me?" I had no takers.

"I'm telling you, this is going to suck, Shawn," I said to him as we loaded up our Suburban with extra clothes, towels and beach toys.

"Well, yeah, with a bad attitude like that..."

I hate when he pulls that motivational salesman crap with me.

Don't tell me I have a bad attitude... YOU have a bad attitude. That's what I wanted to say.

Shawn loves the beach, so of course he didn't mind going. And he's one of those assholes that have muscles without working out, so of course he has no problem walking around in broad daylight with his shirt off.

"It'll be fun and I bet we'll get some good pictures," he said, even though we both know we won't. We're good about bringing the camera, but we always forget to use it. It happens every time. For instance, we went on a ski trip to New Mexico a few months before Zoe was born. We played in the snow, skied, saw cool forest animals, it was a hoot. You want to know how many pictures we came back with? Two.

I wasn't on board with Shawn's enthusiasm about the Sand Fest is what I'm saying.

"Pictures, yeah, right. Are you new here?" I sneered.

"I hope you're not going to be this irritated the whole day, Holly, because I can tell you, *I'm* going to make the most of it."

"Yes, I know, Jesus..."

"What'd you say?"

Back to my story, Blair ended up orchestrating a huge affair. Siblings, cousins, grandparents, in-laws, pets; if they were kin to our group of friends in any way, they were there. We all piled into a few SUVs, a minivan and a Ford Festiva, heading out from the rental house on what should have been a thirty-minute drive to the beach. I realized after an hour and a half of sitting in line less than a mile away from the fairgrounds that this "little" Sand Fest might possibly be a smidge more crowded than what was explained to me. An hour and a half after that, while waiting in line for beach parking, it occurred to me that every sibling, cousin, grandparent, in-law and dog in the entire South Texas region had decided to show up today.

"This is my nightmare!" I complained to Shawn. "This is why I hate doing crap like this! It's effing ridiculous!" I picked up my phone and decided to text everyone I could think of about what a giant mistake we made by going.

Yeah—we're STILL in line waiting for parking—we've been at this for 3 G-D hours—OMFG!!! I clicked away in my mass message.

My friend Casey was in the car ahead of us and I texted her to see if she was as put out as I was. *I'm going 2 get drunk*, she replied.

Not exactly the fuel I was looking for, but at least we agreed on that much. This day was going even worse than expected, and complaining incessantly was the only thing I could do to make myself feel better. Tyler kept sighing to convey his annoyance. Ryan kept reminding us, "This is taking FOREVER!" Zoe kept attempting to get out of her car seat while whining and pointing longingly to the "big pool" beyond the sand dunes. I couldn't do much for her but I told Ryan, since we were traveling at the speed of spilled peanut butter, he could roll the window down and stick his head out. This worked for a few minutes, but he kept yelling at people who were passing us on foot.

"HEY!!! WHOO-HOOO!!! YEAH!!!"

I don't know what he was trying to accomplish, but honestly, it was the most entertainment I had experienced all day.

"Ryan, sit down, dude," Shawn said to him. "You're making people feel uncomfortable."

He slumped back down in his seat and rolled the window up.

We finally found a parking spot about a mile past the festival. Normally I would've been put out that we had to park so far away, but I was so friggin happy to get out of the car. THREE HOURS, for the love of GOD! It took us three hours to get from the ferry line to the beach! We got out, stretched our legs, and almost immediately I was reminded of the second reason I am not a beach person. Sand. Floating along with the slightest breeze. Sand. Instantly it was in my shoes, hair, ears, eyelashes, inside every pore that covers my body.

"I already have sand in my goddamned underwear, Shawn! How is that possible?!"

He shook his head, trying to hold back laughing at me. I could've killed him.

Oh, I was furious. I hate sand. Evidently Zoe shared my resentment because as soon as her tiny feet hit the ground, a huge gust of wind blew a handful of it right into her face. She immediately began to scream while rubbing her eyes with her fists, making it worse no doubt.

"Awesome. I'll take this disaster of an outing with a steaming side of screaming toddler, thank you. Stop laughing, Shawn!"

I was so aggravated, my insides quivered, my head throbbed, and all I wanted to do was pack everyone up and go home, despite the effort it took to get there. I could tell that everyone in our caravan was well aware that I was not only epically unimpressed, my deep breathing wasn't helping, and I was about to FLIP MY SHIT.

Blair approached us by my car and asked if I was okay. "You seem tense, girlfriend. You doin' alright?"

"You conned me and you're a bitch. You know how much I hate this shit, Blair."

"Oh, you'll be fine. Just grab a beer. Casey's got a cooler in her trunk." She slapped me on the butt and walked away, like a coach sending one of his players onto the field.

Why am I the only one who's irritated here? I wondered. No one else seemed nearly as uncomfortable as me. My misery wanted some company and it had no takers.

The rest of the family went for vendor food and to look at the sand castles while I stayed behind with Zoe, who was uninterested in walking around. She amused herself by burying her legs then kicking the sand off so it could blow all over me. She had clearly hopped off my "I freaking hate freaking sand" bandwagon. Traitor.

It wasn't very long before the group had come full circle, buzzing about which sand sculpture they liked most. Some of the kids wanted to go feel the water but, for the most part, everyone but Zoe was ready to go...forty-five minutes after arriving. When all was said and done, the whole gaggle piled back into the cars to face the same traffic on the way out that we had battled on our way in. I literally felt as though I could throw up at any moment. My headache had turned into a migraine. My body was exhausted from carrying a thrashing toddler while power walking a mile through what felt like quicksand. Compounded with hunger from avoiding the carnie food, I felt sick. It was like a bad hangover, only more stressful.

After we got settled with seatbelts on, Shawn looked over at me with a smirk on his face.

"How much fun was *that*, huh, babe? You really gave it the ole college try."

"Please don't condescend me, Shawn."

"I'm not trying to condescend you, Holly. But, Jesus, all you did was make things worse for yourself. It's like once you decide that something's going to suck, you won't allow yourself to see any other possible outcome. Today was a lot of fun for everyone else and I hate that you weren't a part of it, that's all."

"Whatever. If the kids had fun, that's all that matters. It's the only reason I agreed to go in the first place."

Suddenly the whole day came into perspective. I touted that I was "doing it for the kids," when I had made the entire day all about me. I felt like an asshole.

I asked the kids if they had fun and there was a chorus of "yes," which turned into each of them talking over one another about what part was the best.

I said, "I guess it's a good thing they didn't notice my mood."

"Why would they? The kids don't care if we're miserable, remember?"

No doubt.

We went back to the beach house, had burgers and lit fireworks. I drank several glasses of wine and felt completely justified in doing so. Even though I'm still unwinding from the stress of the day, at least something good came out of it. The kids had a blast. And I learned to NEVER AGAIN trust Blair when she's organizing an outing.

See ya tomorrow, Lesson Four. I'm due for a shower... and possibly an apology to Shawn.

7/05/10

Even after yesterday's pooch-screw, I still haven't been able to manage a good anti-goddess profile. I've been staring at a blank page all day it seems.

It's only four-thirty, but I've decided to celebrate my lack of creativity with a nice, cold Shiner Bock, my favorite of all non-committal beverages. Why do I call it non-committal? Because unlike most wines, you don't have to commit to a certain type of food to pair it with. Why is it my favorite? Because it's delicious. *duh*

I recognize four-thirty is premature to start drinking, but I don't think I'm numbing any fears right now, so it's okay. Besides, the kids are outside playing and I'm sure as soon as Shawn's done mowing the lawn, he'll gladly join me for a beer to justify such an early cocktail hour. And you know what they say, "It's four-thirty somewhere."

• • •

What do you know? It ends up Shiner Bock was exactly the liquid inspiration I needed!

Once the warm and fuzzy buzz kicked in after my third beer, I helped myself to a pound of pita chips while I sat at the kitchen table with my workbook, waiting for Shawn and trying to figure out what possible "roles" my fears could play.

Hmm… think, think, think… I need some hummus with these chips… hmm…are pita chips good with guacamole? What am I thinking? Everything's good with guacamole! Fear, fear, fear…laziness…separation… being fat…oh God, I don't want to think about THAT right now—

where's my beer? Okay…fear…dude, I'm already getting puffy from the salt in these chips—that should be fun tomorrow…an hour of cardio at least… Let's see, fear, fear, fear…

With detective skills like these, I can't believe every CSI team in the nation isn't pounding down my door to beg for my assistance.

Hey, genius, how about we assign an anti-goddess to this whole "I have to be skinny AND eat everything" bullshit, eh?

I need to feed the kids and get them to bed. I'll put some thought into it and come back later when I can have a solid character profile.

• • •

OMG, I'm hilarious. I don't even care if no one else thinks so.

So here are anti-goddesses numero uno y dos. At first I thought maybe the fear of being fat and the fear of lacking fulfillment through food could be wrapped up into one character. Then I realized that wouldn't make sense because, while they're both fear based, they're completely different personalities. Here we go, anti-goddess #1.

Skinnie Cooper*

DESCRIPTION: Gaunt, gray in complexion and as joyless as a rectal exam, Skinnie's the saddest of the bunch. She obsesses over every calorie, every pound, every dimple and skin fold. Nothing is ever good enough, beautiful enough or strict enough. She constructs the ideal meal plan and exercise regimen every night and begins each morning assessing what she ate the day before with loathing and guilt, demanding the victim "do it right today."

ACTIVE POWERS: Masochism and denunciation of self-image

WEAPONS OF CHOICE: A mirror and florescent lighting

WEAKNESS: Any Lifetime movie starring Tracey Gold or Ally Sheedy

*Fatty McFat-Fat**

DESCRIPTION: Twin sister and arch nemesis of Skinnie Cooper, she's easily recognized by her "food baby" belly and beer-stained sweatshirt. The mere thought of deprivation sends her running to the cookie jar, but honestly, she runs to the cookie jar at the mere thought of *anything*. Being the parasite that she is, she loves nothing more than a good binge to really show her host how much she cares.

ACTIVE POWER: Master of persuasion

WEAPONS OF CHOICE: Imported beer, tortilla chips, Reese's Peanut Butter Cups, fried shrimp, good wine, bad wine, French fries, French toast, French bread…

WEAKNESS: the Athleta catalogue

*Warning: These two sisters work in tandem most of the time, contradicting each other and confusing their host.

[Example of common banter between the two of them:

SC: "Donuts, huh? That should pair nicely with those muffin tops you've been sporting."

FM: "What's wrong with muffins? Muffins are delicious! In fact…muffins sound pretty good right now."

SC: "How about failure? Does fat, greasy failure sound good right now?"

FM: "If it tastes anything like bacon, then, yes. Failure sounds amazing."]

So there's that. I have to give it to the author, I'm surprised. Strangely, I feel freer. Doing this has lessened the power of those fears somehow. And yet, I'm beginning to feel uneasy by that slight sense of freedom. What the hell is THAT about??? It's late and I'm done for today.

7/6/10

I've been trying to keep my list of common fears at the forefront, so I can spot them to write about when they pop up. I think sketching out the profiles of my first two anti-goddesses helped me to find an entry point into this lesson because I've discovered yet another.

Let's begin with a prelude.

There's a morning regimen I've adhered to for the last eleven years or so. It looks something like this:

STEP 1: Go to the bathroom.

STEP 2: Immediately after peeing, I weigh myself, since stepping on the scale post-urination is the lightest I'll be all day.

STEP 3: Mirror examination. This is when I inspect my reflection for any blemishes, blackheads, fine lines or new freckles. If none are found, I typically toss in a negative comment for good measure. "God, I look like death in the morning. I need to start taking more vitamins."

STEP 4: Root check. It doesn't matter if my hair color got touched up the day before. I check my roots to search for any gray hairs that might've sprouted since the last root check, performed approximately fifteen hours prior.

STEP 5: Dental exam. Why not find at least one more thing to pick apart? Seriously, I have the whitener and bleaching trays. Why don't I use them? I look homeless and British. Then I say something super UK like, "Chip, chip, old boy!"

STEP 6: After I'm done tearing myself down, I go to the kitchen and pour myself a cup of coffee the auto brew so nicely prepares for me each morning.

STEP 7: I sit down at the kitchen table and write out a list of daily chores on my nifty "Holly's To-Dos" stationery pad.

There are actually more steps, but I'll end it with the one that's relevant to this lesson. On to my point, I figured out my third anti-goddess while sitting down to begin the seventh step of my daily morning ritual. Here's what I worked out:

Holly's To-Do List:

–8 loads of laundry (fold AND put away)

–tidy house

–wipe down kitchen counters and clean oven

–change the sheets

–sweep off the front porch

–call Mom

–get oil changed

–buy groceries

–make tortilla soup for dinner

–organize kitchen drawers and pantry

–weed the flower beds

–go through unmatched socks and make puppets for story time

This chore list might seem like nothing to Martha Stewart, and that's fantastic for her. I envy her zeal for productivity. However, for me, a mere mortal, I found myself getting stressed by the weightiness of my list, except for that last entry. That one made me laugh. Puppets for story time? Seriously?

Anyway, I don't know why, but I looked at the list I made yesterday on the previous page, only to find a roster of the same kind of crap. I continued to backtrack through my notepad and found *all* the preceding "To-Do" lists were exactly the same. All work and no play make Jack a dull boy.

Seeing this as rather bizarre, I suddenly thought, *Holy shit! I wonder if this is another anti-goddess.*

I got curious about all the other notebooks scattered throughout my house that I've written in. I pulled them out one by one, and as I flipped through them, I found list after list after list. Chores, life goals, you name it, there was a list for it. Skimming through each one, I realized the similarity among them is that they are ALL complete horse shit. I make lists of tasks I have absolutely no intention of beginning, much less completing! Why? Because making a list makes me feel like I've accomplished something. How asinine is that? I distract myself with lists that appease the guilt I have for being lazy (which is another anti-goddess, I know, but let's pace ourselves).

I feel like I got a cosmic slap upside the head, I really do. Here we go, anti-goddess. #3.

Twisted Lister

DESCRIPTION: Sufficient only on the surface, Lister implants her prey with a false sense of success and accomplishment through endless "To-Do" lists that will never be fulfilled. (<u>Note</u>: She strangely prefers pen to pencil; pens feel more "official.")

ACTIVE POWER: Distraction through over-analyzed planning

WEAPON OF CHOICE: The seemingly productive To-Do list

WEAKNESS: The inability to find a pen

Since I realized laziness is a type of fear in Lesson Three, it made Twisted Lister's character easy to develop. Nevertheless, since Lister is but a symptom of laziness, I feel it's only fair to now give credit where credit is due... Anti-goddess #4.

Babette Lay-Zee

DESCRIPTION: Cousin to Twisted Lister, this monster could really pack a punch if she felt like it. Instead, she persuades her victim not to bother. She comes across as comfy and carefree on the surface, but don't let the Capri pants and neckerchief fool you. Beneath her "Ooh-la-la" façade is Jabba the Hut with eyelashes.

ACTIVE POWER: Intoxicatingly smooth voice used to tantalize her victim with counterproductive distractions and the disingenuous promise of "later"

WEAPONS OF CHOICE: Food Network, aimless "To-Do" lists borrowed from her cousin and her most powerful weapon: Amazon.com

SECRET WEAPON OF CHOICE: Workout clothes: The act of looking sporty alone convinces the host she's done enough activity for the day

WEAKNESSES: B-12 and Jillian Michaels

In the immortal words of Metallica, sad but true.

Well, duty calls. It's lunchtime for the kiddos and Shawn's about to take off for a three-day trip. I feel like I just got him back. *frown*

7/7/10

I think Lesson Four has found its momentum. Let me begin by saying today has been a trying day with my dear, sweet children. Zoe and Ryan are at each other's throats and Tyler keeps complaining about how annoying they are. I explained to him that pointing out the obvious, while seemingly helpful on the surface, is actually as annoying as the screaming kids.

I was cussing at toys and breaking up fights by 9:48 this morning, so I gave my sister a call for distraction purposes. It's what I do when there's some immediate circumstance I don't want to deal with.

"I'm telling you, dude. That's why I had one kid. I don't know how you do it with three," Libby says to me.

Two hours and a pot of coffee later, this is the biggest pearl of wisdom I got from a woman with a degree in communications: *Reverse time and only have one child.* Got it.

Once I was able to get lunch on the table, the kids seemed to quiet down. Food and a movie—it works every time. I headed to my room for sanctuary while the pack was distracted. I shut my door and flopped across my unmade bed. The stress felt similar to my day at the beach but on a smaller scale. I lay there motionless, contemplating mixing a drink and resenting the fact that Shawn's away on business and never has to deal with shit like this. *I wonder how his golf game is going today, fucker...* Then my thoughts went back to that drink. *Hmm, vodka soda doesn't sound bad. Although it is pretty early... I guess a Bloody Mary would be more appropriate.* Then it occurred to me that mixing a drink of any sort so early in the day wouldn't be appropriate at all. *What's wrong with me? This has to be related to fear,* I thought to myself as I considered my fear of being out of control. *DING* Anti-goddess #5...

Mommy Fearest

DESCRIPTION: A pore-refining mask and wire hangers are the least of this bat-shit, nut job's concerns. She's more interested in convincing her host that she's doing a terrible job because she can't keep her kids under control. She balances her impatience with guilt for having none.

ACTIVE POWER: Selfishness and an insatiable hunger for quiet, alone time

WEAPON OF CHOICE: Her thunderous roar lets all little ones within a five-block radius know that it's NOT okay for children to act like children

WEAKNESS: "Mommy, can you read to me, please?" It gets her every time

After about 204 deep breaths, I returned to the kitchen to hang out with the kids. Zoe and Ryan started arguing again, so I went back to the bathroom to take another 204 deep breaths and rejoined them when I was through. I didn't flip my shit for the remainder of the day. Yes, I had several glasses of wine once five o'clock rolled around, and I experienced a few high moments from overly oxygenating myself due to deep breathing. BUT I remained calm, which is more than I can say for most days.

I'm hittin' the sack. Until the next anti-goddess attacks, I bid you farewell, dear workbook.

7/8/10

Ah, date night, I've missed you terribly. Shawn came home from Tulsa yesterday, which was much earlier than expected. We called our sitter at the last minute and went out to eat, just the two of us. Before he got promoted and started traveling so much, he used to take me to the city every week for a romantic dinner. I've always looked forward to it because we have a blast and I get to dress up—something I don't do a whole lot anymore. And as I've explained in previous entries, I like to play dress up.

It's this whole process beginning with music and champagne while I do my makeup and hair. Then I assemble my outfit, go brief the babysitter, pop another bottle and then wait an additional twenty-five minutes for Shawn to finish getting ready because he's TO-TALLY the chick in our relationship sometimes. I call him a metrosexual all the time and it really pisses him off, which is basically why I do it. By the time we leave, I'm usually halfway hammered from drinking on an empty stomach, but does that stop me from drinking more at dinner? Don't be silly.

Anyway, since he's been traveling so much, we haven't had a date night since April. It goes without saying, I was really excited to be able to go out with him last night and catch up. We had a great time, as always. And as always, we ended up being "the loud table" that catches dirty looks from the quieter tables surrounding us. Whenever I get drunk I think I'm even *funnier* than normal, so my uproarious laugh can get out of hand. Last night was no different. The good thing is Shawn thinks he's hilarious too, so we spent the whole night at the restaurant laughing at our own jokes, like old times.

After we got home, I paid the sitter and sent her on her way after I tried to convince her "I don't usually get this drunk." We've had that same conversation countless times and she always acts likes it's funny rather than pathetic. And of course, she'll never complain. I can't count when I'm drunk, so I usually give her whatever money Shawn has in his wallet. The next day he's always like, "Dude, where's all my cash?" Whoopsie…

So, back to the lesson. I discovered anti-goddess #6 last night, and she's a real problem—mainly because she doesn't affect just me. I'll explain…

It makes sense to conclude a successful date night with some luvin' between man and wife, right? Especially when said man and wife haven't had a romantic night in months. But even with distance making the heart grow fonder, one has to have the perfect balance of certain ingredients in order to produce a well-rounded "mood." A little wine (a lot of wine), sexy lingerie (a training bra and underwear with shot elastic), sexy music (Shawn's humidifier) and last but not least, enthusiasm ("Oh yeah, we're supposed to have sex now…"). I'm getting tingly just thinking about it.

We took our places and Shawn was about to call "ACTION!" when I suddenly yelled, "CUT!" and shut down production before the cameras could start rolling.

"Sorry, babe, I'm really full and my buzz has turned into 'sleepy'… rain check?"

He always understands, and so do I when he goes to take an extra long shower.

I lay there in bed feeling guilty and wanting to be in the mood, asking myself, "What's wrong with me?" Doing my math, I realized it's been almost a month since I've made love to my husband, and I was baffled. It's not like the sex isn't good, and Shawn is beautiful. Yes, because he has a good heart, but even if he were an asshole, he'd still be totally hot (maybe even hotter to a masochist like me). He has a great body, dark hair, BLUE eyes, perfect teeth. If Robbie Williams and Matt Damon were to miraculously conceive a child, that child would grow up to look exactly like Shawn: gorgeous. And on top of that, he thinks *I'm* sexy. Yet there I was…completely uninterested in pleasuring him or in allowing him to pleasure me.

It's so much WORK.

[Enter stage right, anti-goddess #6]

No-No Libido

DESCRIPTION: The guilt for being frigid is no match for this commanding, life-sucking force of blah-ness. Although she longs to be sexually ripe and adventurous, she's tightly bound to Babette Lay-Zee, who keeps her host from being interested in sex, especially once she's already showered. There seems to be some underlying force that keeps No-No from thinking outside her box. (Note: No-No Libido does *not*, however, prevent said host from making perverted jokes.)

ACTIVE POWER: Rejection of body, sexual urges, husband's flirtation and intimate advances, and any new additions to the "routine"

WEAPON OF CHOICE: An attachment to getting in a solid nine hours of sleep

WEAKNESS: The movie *Showgirls*—KIDDING!

Sadly, even in light of this discovery, I still rolled over and went to sleep. I don't know why. I wonder if I can find a workbook on discovering my inner slut.

7/10/10

Libby called me today to tell me that she and her husband, Eric, are taking a mission trip to Guatemala with their church.

"Fuck *that*," was my initial response.

After I dodged a lightning bolt, I asked her to tell me about the details of the trip and all that jazz.

"We'll be gone for two weeks! I'm so excited because I'll get to live just like the villagers and really get to experience Guatemala."

"You realize it's going to be a lot like camping," I said to her. Libby hates camping. "You hate camping."

"Not when it's for a good cause. Eric's going to do dental work on the villagers who need it, and I'm going to do arts and crafts with the kids."

I immediately felt like a lesser person and changed my tone.

"That sounds awesome, Libby!"

"I know! I have to get all kinds of vaccinations before we go, which I'm not looking forward to. Oh, speaking of, I was wondering if I could borrow your Rosetta Stone so I can learn Spanish over the next month."

Yes, I drank the Rosetta Stone Kool-Aid, okay? On a whim a year ago I decided I wanted to learn Spanish, so I bought a program. I took it out of the box and put it on a shelf to collect dust in my office. I figured someone ought to get my money's worth, so I told her I would mail it to her.

"Have you checked it out yet? Is it a good program?" she asked me. Like she doesn't already freaking know the answer to that.

"Yeah, it's awesome," I said, right before I changed the subject. "So what's going on with Perez Hilton today?"

"Well, let's see," she says with delight in her voice. It works every time.

The kids are ready to go inside. Maybe we'll go to a movie to-day... right after I open the Rosetta Stone box and make it look used.

7/12/10

HOLY FREAKING GEEZE!

Have you ever been told a joke and pretended like you got it, only to bust out laughing days later when the meaning of it finally occurs to you out of nowhere?

"Oh my god! I just got it!"

Well that's pretty much what happened to me about four min-utes ago while folding socks, less the punch line and laughter. It's ALL about the comfort zone! Yes, I've said it before, but now I really get it. My comfort zone houses all my anti-goddesses, all my fears. But it's *me* that holds the key to unlocking it. So, if you really think about it, I'm the one responsible for it all. I plant the seed of doubt. I stir up shit amongst my fears. I distract me from freedom by choos-ing to stay "safe" inside my comfort zone. How in the HELL did this not occur to me before?

It's like there's been this big covert operation going on inside my head and I blew the lid off the conspiracy! This lesson's been mov-ing at a pretty steady pace, but I feel like the whole thing came full circle in a matter of minutes. In fact, I'm leery to trust something that came together so easily. Then again, if epiphanies were revealed slowly over time, they'd be called "developments."

Peace out, Lesson Four. I'm going to go do something uncomfortable.

LESSON 5

Negative Habits

It's never easy for one to admit their own negative behavior, but the sooner we come face to face with unconstructive habits, the sooner we can eliminate them from our lives and begin to grow. In Lesson Four, you made a character list of your fears in order to detect them more easily. As discussed, fear infiltrates our everyday lives through negative thoughts and emotions. These negative thoughts and emotions manifest themselves in our behavior, our habits. Such habits become so ingrained, that even the most destructive behavior seems "normal"; it becomes a part of us. The thought is, "This is who I am." It's all a part of the illusion. Unfortunately, the more negativity we harbor, the more of it we bring upon ourselves. It's a vicious cycle. Some people are well aware of their destructive way of life. Others are in complete denial and would remain in denial, even if it were brought to their attention. That's okay; they will come around in their own time. As for YOU, my sister, I can only assume that you are ready to shed your afflictions. Why else would you be here?

In Lesson Five, you are to examine two things: negative habits in your life that you are ready to free yourself of, as well as those you may not be so eager to cut loose. Our habits are tied to our comfort zone, and the thought of breaking down those barriers can be scary. But it's imperative to know and accept that true growth *cannot* occur without change.

As you reflect and write, pay mind to the emotions you experience when faced with letting go of your "bad" habits. Do you find it to be exhilarating or terrifying? Why? How do you expect your life to change once the insanity of self-destruction is exposed, and you no longer wish to be a part of it? This is a beautiful, beautiful thing, dear one. If you are ready, you are giving yourself the *gift* of a fresh start, a clean slate. Imagine the possibilities! *BLESSED BE!*

7/13/10

I can honestly say turning my fears into a cast of characters has been more helpful than I was willing to give it credit for. Even though I'm not crazy about the thought of being the "Octomom" of neuroses, Lesson Four was the most fun so far. I love bringing irreverence to an otherwise serious process, and it was a plus to benefit from that, for once.

However, if anyone's going to overlook the silver lining and focus on the black cloud, it's going to be me. The downside to profiling my fears is that now all of my negative behavior has been highlighted in Technicolor, a side effect I wasn't expecting. Man, oh man, if my bad habits were grains of sand I'd be that gigantic desert in Africa whose name escapes me at the moment.

I'm not one to enjoy feeling exposed and uncomfortable. I think I've already covered that. I must, however, admit to my curiosity at this point. I'm only at Lesson Five and I think I've already learned a lot about myself. This begs the question: What's next? I'm scared to find out, yet I want to find out. Hell, I NEED to find out.

With that being said, let's get on with the lesson. I'm not blind to the fact that overindulging on anything isn't good. I already know my obsession with overly processed food is an unhealthy one. I also know that drinking surplus amounts of alcohol every night will NOT be found on any "Healthy Lifestyle" checklist. They're bad habits. Got it. So, how do I feel when I think about letting go of both of them? It's like taking a downer and an upper at the same time, release and recoil.

The release feels good, but I find the recoil to be confusing. Why would I want to hold on to something that clearly hurts me? My immediate response to this question is, "I don't!" But don't I? If I REALLY wanted to be free of my bad habits, to quit getting drunk and begin only feeding my body the whole foods it requires, then wouldn't I do it?

When I think about it in different terms, it seems like it should be so simple. For example, I know touching a hot stovetop will burn and hurt like hell. I don't want to do that, so I make the decision every day to be careful in order to keep myself from getting burned. It's common sense, right? If I scorched myself on a continuous basis without ever learning from it, I would either have to be an idiot or consider the possibility that I'm a masochist. I'm failing to see the difference between the literal and hypothetical at this point.

Yoda said, "Do or do not, there is no try." I understand the meaning of that now more than ever. Quit trying to stop hurting myself, and just STOP doing it. Got it, Yoda.

Bad habit #1: Stop poisoning my body with excessive alcohol and crappy food. Am I ready for this? It *sounds* great, but the thought of it stresses me out. The anti-goddesses don't like it, that's for sure. Who would I be without these habits? I don't know.

I probably wouldn't have as much fun in life, but I imagine I'd feel better physically. If I were taking better care of myself, then I wouldn't constantly be obsessing about calories and getting fat, which would make me more of a pleasure to be around, I guess. Without that continuous struggle taking place in my head, I wouldn't be as tense, and I suppose I would have more of myself to give, allowing me to be a more available mother and wife. So we can assume that more than my life would be changed. It would affect Shawn and the kids, too.

The hard part will be staying aware all the time, and ole Fatty McFat-Fat comes at me pretty strong when she's awake. She's scrappy and has more stamina than I do. When she starts bitching at me, she doesn't let up and I grow tired of listening to it.

"Feeding your cravings shows you so much love! How will you feel nurtured when you're depriving yourself?" Fatty argues. And she's compelling.

But I know just because she's a master of debate doesn't mean that her argument is healthy.

I already feel like I want to back out of this. I should've brought something else up instead, like…bad habit #1: not flossing after every meal.

Speaking of meals, it's time to make dinner or order out.

7/14/10

I had lunch with the girls today. So far I suck at quitting bad habit #1. Let's leave it at that.

7/16/10

Shouldn't my problem with this lesson be so obvious to me? It's my comfort zone! This exercise has been hard to do because I woke it up with my attempts to make positive change. Ever since I acknowledged the fact I'd be happier if I quit overindulging, my comfort zone's been telling me how much it's going to suck the next time I want something sweet to eat, or the next time I "need" a drink, or worse—the next party I go to where I'll be exposed to BOTH vices.

My comfort zone says, "You're not going to have any fun, and then you're going to be disappointed in yourself when you cave in, which you inevitably will do. It happens every time. Why put yourself through all that?" This is what's going on inside my head every time I try to do this lesson, but it isn't so obvious at the time. This message manifests itself as an underlying sense of anxiety. If I'm not paying attention, I feel stressed out and don't know why.

So out of spite, I've been doing my best to adhere to my plan of no alcohol and clean food. And while my success has been undeniably nonexistent, I take solace in knowing that I'm at least aware of it when I'm screwing it up.

I'm pouring a glass of wine—not supposed to be doing that. I'm bringing the glass to my lips. I'm smelling the currant, my mouth is watering— I should put it down. I'm bringing it back to my lips—not supposed to be doing that. I'm about to take a sip—not supposed to be doing that, either. I'm taking a drink, not supposed—hmm, black cherry and cedar. This would be awesome with that goat cheese spread.

7/17/10

If bad habits were holes, I'd be Swiss cheese. Score!

That one is much better than the sand/desert analogy I came up with the other day. Of course, I'm aware there are many things holier than Swiss cheese, but it sounds better than, "I'd be a colander." That's just silly.

Moving on to another negative habit—it's one of my worst and Babette's specialty: procrastination. It's like crack. The shit be callin' me.

But what's really ironic is that it's my pet peeve with everyone else. I preach to Tyler almost daily about how he needs to stop procrastinating. Cleaning his room, doing his homework, he's constantly putting off his responsibilities and it frustrates me.

"Dude, just do it, do it right, and then you don't have to deal with it anymore." *Now I'm off to go avoid making my bed.*

Before I shift the focus of this lesson from "bad habits" to "why I'm a hypocrite," I'll absolve myself by saying I want my kids to be better than I am.

"It' too late for me. Save yourselves! Go clean your rooms while I run away from mine!"

Bad habit #2: I need to stop procrastinating.

And while I do plan on explaining how this would improve my quality of life, I'd like to point out that I'm proud of myself for removing the harsh judgment. "Stop procrastinating" sounds much more constructive than "stop being a worthless lazy ass," even though the latter feels more natural. Enough said.

My life would change dramatically if I stopped putting things off for later. How? Well, for starters, things would get done. What a concept!

Whenever I come across something I've been putting off, I experience major feelings of guilt. If I would just suck it up and get to work, I could avoid this entirely. And you know, now that I really think about it, there's no way the pain in the ass of doing menial chores is worse than the looming, black cloud of an unfinished chore list. On top of that, I could have a sense of accomplishment, like, EVERY DAY! This might be common sense to some people but to me this is profound shit!

7/20/10

Over the last few days my bad habits have been on my mind more than anything. Have I quit drinking and sworn off Mexican food? No. In fact we got take out from the local Jalisco last night, which I enjoyed with two beers. So in actuality, I put off cooking dinner and then ate crappy food *with* alcohol. But on a positive note, I usually make myself miserable on their decadent flour tortilla chips and guacamole salad (washed down with three or four margaritas). Last night, however, I paid attention to my body. After each bite, after each chip, after each drink of ice-cold Mexican beer, I questioned, "How am I feeling? Am I full? Should I stop yet?" When my body said, "Yes, you're full, you can stop now," I did. I had too many chips, but still. I always ignore what my body tells me, so the fact that I had the wherewithal to ask is a big step. In less than two months, this is real change and I feel good about it.

Also, this week I've been making my To-Do lists in the morning and am doing an okay job of finishing them. As stated in a previous lesson, I always start the day with rock star motivation and make a list that's way too long. That's always been my M.O. I try to make myself feel better with making grandiose plans of productivity, only to fall short (typical Lister).

I realized today what I need to do is start this change slowly. Instead of making a To-Do list that's twenty-five items long, I'll make one that's six or seven items long...or even three or four. Get used to that amount, and then bump it up gradually until that level of productivity is the norm.

I don't know if it's because my two main bad habits are the focus of my energy and it's making it hard to spot any others, or if I don't have as many bad habits as I thought. Other than talking about people, yelling at my kids and spending money frivolously, nothing else comes to mind to write about for this lesson. More habits may pop up as the days, weeks, months go by, and so I'll plan on writing about them if and when I discover them. Until then, I feel really good about this lesson and I'm eager to watch myself change. Good stuff.

Alright Lesson Six, you're up.

LESSON 6

Instilling Positive Habits

Out with the bad, in with the new! This lesson is self-explanatory: What good habits do you want to instill in your life? You've identified the negative behavior that needs to be addressed. What *positive* behavior would you like to replace it with? Make a list of five healthy habits, but no more than that (I don't want you piling too much on your plate). No matter how grand it may seem, don't limit yourself. Write it down even if the thought of following through with it makes you uncomfortable or scared. I do not, however, want you to be so uncomfortable that you skip this lesson altogether! If this seems overwhelming to you, take baby steps and write down only minor changes to begin with. As you introduce those positive habits and build strength, you can move on to more significant change. What we are doing is beginning the process of removing blockages and breaking down your comfort zone so your Inner Goddess can freely soar to the surface and shine through the way she is supposed to. As we have learned, facing our fears is the best thing we can do to transmute that negative energy into positive, but there are different approaches. If you are a tortoise by nature, you should avoid trying to keep up with the hare!

That being said, it's important for you to know I do not want you to write a list of fantasies. For example, if there are good habits you've always dreamt of assuming, but never had the genuine intention to adopt, then you were fantasizing. That's okay, but it does not apply to this lesson. Desire doesn't become reality without inspired action, sister, and the same stagnant behavior will not produce change. You need to be committed to the process.

Once you have your list made, I want you to write a plan of execution. What steps do you need to take in order to successfully integrate these new patterns of behavior into your everyday life? And similar to the lesson about negative habits, I want you to explore *why* you would like to adopt these positive habits, and how you expect your life to change once you have begun. It's important to understand the light as much as the dark, so again, be thoughtful and honest with yourself. Sometimes we wish we were a certain way for unhelpful reasons. Knowing what motivates us is significant. Get excited, this is going to be fun! *BLESSED BE!*

7/23/10

It's hard for me to write about positive habits when PMS is on the horizon. Every time I think of any action that's remotely positive, I throw up in my mouth a little. Does "pre-PMS" sound like a copout? I don't fucking care if it does, so how 'bout them apples?

I don't think locking myself in a closet is an overly dramatic course of action to take at this point. Who knows? It could be nice: some music, a flashlight and a crossword puzzle, a pillow, maybe some trail mix.

I find it interesting this is the exact state of hormonal turmoil I was in when I began this workbook. I have returned to "I Hate Everyone Land," and I've been crowned queen. I have a sash and everything. It's great.

The upsets my hormones can make from day to day are mind-boggling. Take yesterday, for example. I felt amazing. I finished up with the laundry, took the kids down to the pier to feed the ducks, paid bills online without shopping afterward (which is a big effing deal), colored with my daughter, reconnected with a friend on Facebook and baked a delicious lasagna for dinner (my grandmother's recipe, no easy feat).

Today... *UGH* Today I'm rendered helpless by a lazy haze of bipolar emotions, throbbing cramps, a bloated belly and the irrepressible craving for banana pudding.

I know exactly what good habits I would like to instill in my life. I've already mentioned the lists of them I've been building for years now, thanks to Twisted Lister. Every time I feel down on myself, I add one more item to the file. Even though I know I'll never apply it, it makes me feel accomplished to recognize my flaws and daydream about fixing them. It's one of the many ways I can sustain the love/hate relationship I have with myself. How I missed that bad habit in the previous lesson is completely beyond me.

Anyway, back to the matter at hand. Since I don't even feel like exerting the effort to read my list of goals and aspirations, I think it's safe to say I'll be even less likely to pursue them. Because of this, I'm going to put this lesson off for a few days. I need to get to a place of clarity, and where I am right now ain't it.

I know I said in Lesson Five that I'm going to quit procrastinating. Well, I'm putting that off, too.

7/25/10

I'm hormonally challenged. That said it is quite possibly the worst time to try and quit any bad habit, much less ALL of them. In the previous lesson, I decided to stop getting drunk and eating junk food. However, this was before my hormones went all wonky, so I haven't exactly begun to act on that just yet. My eating and drinking habits over the last few days could be closely related to that of the archetypal frat guy—a black hole appetite and very low standards. Beer, Cool Ranch Doritos, oatmeal cream pies, peanut butter and chocolate by the pound, you do the math. Skinnie Cooper isn't letting me live this down, and the guilt trip's been intense. My cycle always begins with a binge, immediately followed by a rededication to clean living. This time's no different.

So while it has become blatantly apparent to me that I should reference my menstrual cycle before I make any plans for major change, I have also learned the best time to strategize good habits is when I feel like crap. Much like I do now, needless to say.

It's time for a fresh start! I'm ready to wake up tomorrow an entirely new person—one who cringes at the thought of processed carbs and remains unfazed by the allure of an ice-cold stein of Guinness Stout.

I want to start waking up at five-thirty–NO–four-thirty every morning! I want to begin my day with a vigorous workout, followed by a fresh juice cocktail of spinach, kale and wheatgrass. After my daily exercise routine and Zen-in-a-glass, I'll prepare a homemade breakfast for the rest of the family. I can see it now...

Organic fruit salad served with wholegrain, blueberry pancakes. Fresh eggs gathered from the laying hens I've always wanted to have. Perhaps we'll get a Jersey cow for milking and I can make homemade butter and ice cream from the cream we don't use. Okay, so first I'll milk the cow and gather eggs, then I'll work out, have my juice, and make breakfast for the family.

After this, I'll get started on my housework directly. The chores for each day will be regimented, ensuring an organized execution of my To-Do list. Along with a well-organized plan for maintaining a tidy home, I will have activities planned for the kids: arts & crafts, nature walks, fishing. No more TV, computer games and cell phones!

I'll cook a five-course dinner and we'll sit down to eat it as a family, as stated, without TV. After the kids have been read to and put to bed at eight-thirty sharp, I will spend quality time with my husband that will result in crazy lovemaking and a quick shower. By ten o'clock, I will be ready for bed and sober due to my replacing the usual evening toddy(s) with chamomile tea. As I nestle into fresh sheets, I will drift off to deep, dreamless sleep knowing my laundry is done, my house is clean, I have no food choices to regret, my kids' brains have been properly stimulated and my husband has been sexually fulfilled. Life will be perfect.

I know I've already discovered my need for control, but if this could be a normal way of living, control wouldn't be a factor. It would take care of itself because of all the structure! I wouldn't even have to try to be in control, it would happen naturally. BRILLIANT!

To sum it all up, here are my new habits and freshly reconstructed day:

4:30 a.m. wake up

Milk the cow*

Gather the eggs*

1-hour workout

(*I forgot to mention I would have to gather fresh produce from the garden I intend to have)

Juice

Make breakfast for the family

Organize household chores, performing allotted chores on assigned day

Perform kids' activities that don't involve techno-gadgets

Cook dinner—no more take out*

Replace nightly cocktails with chamomile tea*

No more TV during dinner

Post-dinner kitchen tidy

Plan kids' daily activities for the next day (immediately following the kitchen tidy)

Read to the kids every night

Sex at least 3 times a week*

*items subject to change

I really don't have a game plan as to how I'm going to go about infusing these new habits into my everyday life. Is there such a plan? I'm going to DO IT. When the alarm goes off, I'm going to get up. When it's time to do housework, I'll do it. What else can be said? I know the lesson said no more than five habits, but I'm eager to get some changes happening mucho pronto. I'm ready to be this person! I'm ready for tomorrow. BRING IT!

(I'm taking into account that I don't actually own the milking cow and laying hens yet, nor do I have a fruit and vegetable garden. I'm building in room for forgiveness there. Everything else is a go!)

Now I'm off to go spend time with my kids and do my best to emulate Donna Reed sans the pearls!

7/26/10

Good news? I totally woke up at four-thirty today. Bad news? I fell back asleep during my, "It's the first day of the rest of your life" pep talk. It went something like this:

"OK! This is IT! Get up and get started putting those new goals into zzzzzzzzzzzzzz..."

Note to self: Remaining supine with my eyes closed will result in a bouncy arousal only if the bed spontaneously comes to life and spits me out. Who saw this coming? Anyone? Bueller?

So the day starts out with me feeling guilty for totally pussing out on my first goal. After that, my grandiose intentions seemed to crumble before my eyes. By the time the thought of working out even crossed my mind, the kids were all awake and wanting breakfast. Cheerios. Exactly the homemade feast I'd envisioned!

Juice? At least ten percent of it was. Thank you for your honesty, Sunny D.

Housework? Pass.

Kids' activities? Ask SpongeBob and Xbox. They babysat today.

Dinner? Grilled cheese. From a restaurant.

TV with dinner? Who can eat without a steaming side of Ryan Seacrest? Not me, good sir. Not me.

SIGH

I'm beginning to think I may have set myself up for failure here. I guess I understand why I was only supposed to shoot for five positive changes. Hell, even that seems like a lot at this point.

I really thought I was stronger than "baby steps." I hate baby steps. Let's effing get there! It's the same thing with weight loss. I don't want to transform myself over the course of a year. I want it NOW. Not, "do these crunches and you'll start to see a difference in eight weeks." No. I want Six-Minute Abs. "Six-Minute Abs for the Soul," is that available? That would be fantastic.

I swear, if the author at any point in future lessons mentions a word about Rome not being built in a day, I'm wiping my ass with this workbook.

7/27/10

So, after I spent all day yesterday beating myself up over my inability to commit to anything other than marriage and social engagements, I realized last night that my negativity was counterproductive. Instead of picking myself back up and trying again, I wallowed in how much I suck. Yet again, another poorly thought-out strategy, but par for the course.

It was about seven-thirty when I caught onto this (around the time I would normally be pouring another glass of wine or something like it). I was explaining to Shawn how I can't seem to do anything right. Just the conversation he wants to hear when he gets home from a business trip, I'm sure.

"Seriously, dude, I don't know what my problem is. How hard is it to make a decision and stick to it?"

His shoulders slumped at the sound of it. "Holly, really? How many times are we going to have this conversation? It's the same thing every time!"

"Well, I'm sorry, Captain Dedication! I'm not like you, okay? I'm not the kind of person that tackles every goal I set out to achieve."

"I know! And I'll never understand it! Why make a plan if you have no intention of executing it?"

"Um, excuse me, I *do* intend on executing stuff."

"You're smart and capable, Holly. You spend too much time feeling sorry for yourself and beating yourself up. I tell my sales team all the time, 'if you keep telling yourself that you're going to fail, then those are the exact results you're going to continue getting.' It really is that simple."

He's a real motivational speaker, this guy. Since I wasn't up for one of his lectures I threw out some condescending sarcasm to shut him up.

"Thank you, Tony Robbins. I got the point."

Shawn started laughing, "Tony Robbins…that dude's got giant teeth."

This is the good thing about arguing with my husband. All it takes is for one of us to start laughing and it's done. He hugged me and said with a squeeze, "Stop beating up my wife, okay? It's fucking annoying."

This made me feel somewhat better. I gave Shawn the finger for that bit about being annoying, then I started thinking about the few things on my list I hadn't screwed up yet. Most of what I intended for the day went south, but I could still replace my alcohol with chamomile tea, I could still read to the kids before they went to bed, and I could still make love to my husband…

The tea was very satisfying and the kids enjoyed story time. Two out of three ain't bad. Let's move on.

For now, I'm working on abandoning my need for instant gratification and sticking with what I followed through on last night. I'm going to continue to replace my nightly drink with chamomile tea, and I vow to read to the kids every night. How will I handle it when faced with a situation that could mess up my groove? Most likely I'll cave and beat myself up for it later. But that's not where I am right now, so I'll deal with what's in front of me. Chamomile, I'm practically snoring from the relaxation of it all.

7/29/10

Yesterday there was a short in the transformer that powers our area and we lost electricity for about two hours. It's times like these I start thinking about things I take for granted: TV, computer, lights in the bathroom when in the middle of using the john, those sorts of things.

Of course, I was relieved, albeit startled as hell, when the house sprung back to life. Every TV and bulb exploded with sound and light, interrupting a dark and calm silence. It was a complex reaction, "AAHH!!! Oh…well it's about time!" After I shut down the ruckus, I walked around the house, resetting all the digital clocks as the kids rejoiced in front of the TV like a tribe of fire-worshipping cavemen.

The idea of cavemen made me think about the settlers long ago, and how one of them might react to seeing a TV or digital clock. Would they be amazed or would it inspire another witch trial? Pondering this eventually led me to think about technology in general, and how it has changed humanity. Nowadays, we're so connected to one another, and yet so much more isolated, really. I can send anyone in the world a text message from my phone, but at the end of the day, it wouldn't be a real "connection," would it? After all, they're words sent from thousands of miles away. At least a handwritten letter has someone's energy in it.

Anyway, I soon thought about my kids and how their lives are so much different than mine was at their age. Gaming stations, the Internet, cell phones; it's a different world with new gadgets, new distractions and new addictions.

Last night in bed, I realized how appropriate the timing of all this is. In light of this lesson and new habits, I thought I'd try an experiment and go a day without technology. Just for a day, no TV, no cell phone, no web surfing…

Tomorrow, I thought. *Tomorrow this house is going back to the Dark Ages.*

Well, either it was a stupid idea or it wasn't important enough to remember when I woke up this morning. As soon as my ritual in front of the bathroom mirror was complete, I headed straight to the coffee pot, went to check my email and flipped on the TV, right after

I sent a text to a friend about what I had just seen on Facebook. I am a rock (that could either apply to my solid convictions or to my density).

What was I thinking about technology yesterday? That it's fantastic? I'm pretty sure I was thinking it's fantastic.

Is there such a thing as Bipolar Goal-Setting Disorder? Last night I was genuinely motivated to do a "technology fast." Now the thought of following it through sounds about as appealing as brushing my teeth with Cheez Whiz. Sure, I could do it, but why would I WANT to?

Despite my lack of enthusiasm *now*, I really do want to give this a try some day. Maybe it would be better this weekend when everyone's home and we can all go do family activities together. It will be easier then (I like how it makes me feel better to write that out, even though I know for a fact we won't do it).

7/30/10

I haven't nixed the technology yet—shocker—but bedtime stories have been a real hit with the kids. Of course, after talking to Libby today, I kind of feel like a shithead for not already having this routine in play.

"You didn't read to your kids at bedtime *before?*" she asked.

I scrambled to protect my image. "Uh, yeah. Just not *every* night like I am now."

Nice save.

Along with being less of a crappy mom, I've focused on cutting back on alcohol, and waking up earlier in the mornings. I'm still not up early enough to get my workout in before the kids are awake, but the boys go back to school in a few days, so it will soon be a non-issue. Man, summer is already done. Where did it go?

I'm acclimating myself to earlier hours in the most gradual way possible. Along with shifting my goal from a ridiculous four-thirty to a more reasonable five-thirty, my plan is to shave off fifteen minutes a week until I'm eventually down to my desired hour. This way I'm not experiencing the shock of rising before dawn when I'm used to getting up long after. Again, with school starting up in two days, this will be another moot point.

I've been semi-successful with the wine/chamomile tea swap, although when I say "semi-successful," I mean not very. But I'm taking baby steps, right? (By the way, I'm completely aware that I'm so much more willing to take it slow when it comes to waking up early and reducing alcohol than I am with anything else. "Spiritual perfection NOW! Five a.m. and no drinking? Hey, hey, hey, let's not be brash.")

It hasn't been super easy, the endeavor to drink less. The positive thing is I haven't experienced any cold sweats or shaking, so I've got that going for me. Chemical dependency doesn't have a dog in this fight. I almost wish it did. It would give me a better excuse than "I really like to drink." Although on second thought, "I'm an alcoholic" isn't really something I've ever aspired to say with sincerity. I should think before I make stupid comments like that.

In any case, I find myself switching to tea instead of pouring another glass or popping another bottle. This provides balance between satiating a "thirst" and practicing moderation. If I tell myself, "I can't have this," then Fatty goes nuts in my head. It gets turned into a taboo, and then I obsess about what I'm being deprived of. Not fun.

I figure if I allow myself a drink, the monster can be quieted, and I can have the clarity of mind to ask, "Do I need another drink?" Some nights I say, "No. I'll have tea." Other nights are not so successful. "Yes, I do, so shut up." However, I haven't exceeded two drinks in one night since last week. Progress? Yes? I actually think I've lost a pound or two, but that may be in my head.

Anyway, they say it takes three weeks to turn action into habit. I'm hoping in approximately two weeks, my concerted effort will become second nature, and then at that point I'll be ready to introduce something else. I can tell you one thing, I won't stop swearing any time soon. It's fun and there's nothing like a good F-bomb to really drive the point home.

8/1/10

The kids are back in school and for whatever reason, I decided today would be the non-techno day. I actually went through with it! Why? Because I'm an idiot.

This was the longest day of my life. THE. LONGEST. DAY. OF. MY. LIFE.

I've never been more bored than I was today. It was like fishing. No, it was more boring than fishing. It was like watching someone else go fishing. That's how effing boring it was. All I could do was housework and read. However, I did come across one positive loophole. Viewing the washer and dryer as technological tools prohibited me from using them.

"I can't do laundry! I made a commitment to myself and I *must* stick with it!"

I colored and played "birthday party" with my daughter for what felt like thirty-two hours. After I was full of imaginary cake, we moved on to other things outside. This dragged on forever. Then the boys got home from school, which is where things got tough. How sad is it that when I broke the news to them, they automatically assumed they were being punished?

"WHY MOM? WHAT'D WE DO?" After forty-five minutes of incessant complaining, I lost it. "BECAUSE WE NEED TO BE MORE SPIRITUAL, DAMMIT! GO OUTSIDE!" Oh, hello, Mommy Fearest.

After I calmed down, I headed to the front door to go practice what I was preaching. Before I turned the knob, I looked through the sidelight to catch my children sitting on the porch, moping. They were hunched over and pouting.

"This is so stupid. I don't know why we have to do this," I heard Tyler say.

"I want to watch SpongeBob," Ryan added.

"SpongeBob is stupid."

"I'm telling Mom you said 'stupid.'"

"Shut up, Ryan."

"I'm telling Mom you said 'shut up.'"

This pissed me off all over again, so I had to wait a couple minutes before joining them.

SERIOUSLY? Are they so conditioned to being enslaved to the TV that they don't even know how to play outside?

After a few minutes I didn't know who I was more annoyed with, my couch potato children or the person who spawned their "addiction." My kids are way too young to take full responsibility for their habits. At that point, I knew I was doing the right thing by forcing them to think outside the idiot box. It also made me see that I'm not the only one with a comfort zone. I went digging through the toy closet and found an unopened box of sidewalk chalk, a bottle of bubbles and a kickball. Weak, I know, but I had nothing else.

The boys weren't too thrilled, but Zoe goes bananas over bubbles, so at least SHE appreciated my efforts. However, within ten minutes she had poured most of the bottle of solution in the grass and the bubble wand wouldn't reach the bottom. Soon she was taking on the negative energy of the other two. Ryan was trying to make do with his chalk-drawn race track until Tyler pelted him in the back with the kickball. Awesome. No matter how loud I shouted that they stop fighting, they continued. Watching them go back and forth reminded me of our dogs, who are brother and sister. Sometimes I really think they're going to kill each other when they fight. *DING* I was suddenly inspired to handle the situation in the exact way we have to handle our dogs when they're at each other's throats.

The boys were pretty pissed by my hosing them down with cold water, but it was quite relaxing for me, I have to say. Like watering the shrubs, "Oops, there's a dry spot over there, shift here and—AH, there we go—sweet hydration." All I needed was a glass of wine.

About that time, Shawn came home. He drove up in the driveway and I could see his perplexed look through the windshield of his truck. I'm sure the image of seeing his sons being hosed down like rabid dogs by their mother was, without a doubt, unexpected.

"God in Heaven, she's finally lost it!" I can hear it now.

"Hi, honey!" I chirped as he walked out of the garage. "The boys were fighting so I thought I'd get them to stop."

Confused, he nodded and said "Well, it works on the dogs." Sometimes I think we're the same person.

The boys forgot why they were so mad and started laughing and playing in the water. Since they were already wet, they stripped to their boxer briefs and played in the sprinklers while Shawn and I split a bottle of wine at the picnic table. Zoe enjoyed the waterworks, too—that is, until her diaper got so heavy it became a hindrance to walk in. After that she was more interested in her juice box.

I made sandwiches for dinner since the stove is riddled with technology, damn the luck! We picnicked outside on the porch while the sun went down. The longest day of my life, yes, but that doesn't mean it was the worst.

The $22 question is will I continue this new lifestyle? No. More outside time? Yes. I'm sure there's a balance between the two, but I'm not going to try to figure it out now. Frankly, after today, I'm kind of over it.

8/5/10

With the kids back in school, some of the new habits have been much easier to adhere to, save for the whole "no technology" thing. F that!

Waking up early happens anyway, because the boys need to be up, dressed, fed and out the door by seven-thirty. Since waking up in a panicked rush is my LEAST favorite way to begin the day, I'm up at least by six-thirty getting breakfast ready and lunches packed. I do, however, still plan on gradually moving toward five-thirty. Why? I don't really know, but I'm going for it.

With it being Zoe and me at home between seven-thirty and three-thirty, getting in a workout is easier, too. She takes a nap after lunch, so there's my time to hop on the "mill." It doesn't always happen, but it is happening more than it did throughout the summer.

Housework is much less stressful now because there are two less people home all day. That means two less people pulling out toys and games, two less people dirtying up dishes, two less people spilling Kool-Aid on the couch when they know they're not supposed to have drinks in the living room anyway. *sigh* You get the idea.

My whole point in bringing this up is it seems that a few of my newly appointed habits have taken care of themselves. Obviously, I have to make the choice to practice them every day. BUT, with a change in scheduling, things have become a lot easier to make happen. Waking up early, working out, staying on top of housework, they kind of fell into place.

So, I'm thinking I might take on one of my bigger goals. I don't know which one yet. Possibly the garden. Whoa, I got stressed just thinking about that. Evidently I'm not ready for the garden yet. It's date night tonight. Maybe Shawn can help me out with deciding what to tackle next. He always has good ideas.

• • •

Shawn was a huge help.

"Can you work on becoming a nymphomaniac? I think that's a SUPER positive habit, babe." Ah, sweet inspiration.

Maybe I'll stick to what I've got right now before I move on to anything else. I know I should take my time with this process. I've always set myself up for failure in the past with ludicrous standards and expectations (refer to the beginning entries of this lesson).

Since that route hasn't proven successful so far, perhaps I should try a different approach this time. Hell, maybe *that's* my new habit: to practice pacing myself. No more crazy standards; no more disastrous frame-ups; no more going psycho every time something happens that wasn't on my plan. To pace myself, this will be the habit I work on *one step at a time.*

Rome wasn't built in a day, you know.

PART 2

Breaking Down Barriers

In the first section, we touched base with where you are in your life. We talked about your desires, fears, negative habits and goals. By this point in the workbook, I trust you are ready to begin the next phase of your transformation. In addition to the positive habits you have adopted, now we will begin to expand our minds, inviting new experiences into our world. With new experience comes new understanding, new perspective. Along with initiating new experiences, the lessons in the second part of this workbook deal with an even deeper level of self-exploration. If you are not ready to take the next step, that is perfectly okay. This is *your* transformation, *your* path. Feel free to continue journaling on topics we explored in Part 1 as long as you see fit. All I am asking you to do, dear sister, is make yourself a promise that you will see this journey through to the end. It is more than acceptable to move at your own pace, just as long as you KEEP MOVING! In the lessons to come, do yourself a favor and move slowly. Taking even strides throughout this process will allow you to ingrain new habit patterns, along with *true* evolution. Learn something about the woman you are, and open yourself to the woman you are *becoming*.

LESSON 7

Cleanse

If you have chosen to continue into Part 2 of the workbook, prepare yourself for new experiences, dear one. In Part 1 you worked to clear spiritual blockages. In this lesson, you will remove physical blockages in your body temple by flushing out the buildup of toxins left behind by the chemicals in food, air pollutants and, yes, negativity. You are going to partake in a total body cleanse, colon, liver, take it as far as you want beyond that. Do some research and find a cleanse that works for you and your budget. However, avoid programs that are particularly short in length and pill based, without a required change in eating habits. They typically are ineffective and not worth what you pay. Also, I would highly suggest a regimen that is no shorter than three weeks in length, since the body works in 21-day "repair" cycles.

In addition to ridding your body of contaminants, you are also to cleanse your pantry of any foods that are unwholesome. Overly processed products such as crackers, cookies, chips and sodas should all go. When in doubt, read the ingredients list; if you can't pronounce or define every ingredient named, throw it out! Your best bet is to stick to organic whole foods such as fruit, vegetables, legumes, whole grains and lean proteins (although a vegetarian diet is ideal). If you already follow this type of dietary lifestyle, kudos to you, sister! (I still want you to perform the total body cleanse, nevertheless.) If you are one of the many who find these food choices to be frightening, this lesson may be difficult for you. Take your time, this is a big transition. You may experience discomfort. I'm here to tell you it won't be the first or last time you'll be uncomfortable throughout this section of the book. Breaking down the walls of your comfort zone will not always be a walk in the park, but stay the course and you won't regret it! During your cleanse, journal daily about your progress and experience. What changes do you notice? How is your energy level? Is there a difference in your moods? Express the level of difficulty of these changes. Is it easier than you thought it would be? Is it harder? This lesson requires commitment, not perfection. If you fall off track, forgive yourself and hop back on. Just remember that you *can* do it. Have faith! You are going to be amazed at how incredible you feel! *BLESSED BE!*

8/7/10

This is actually something I'm really looking forward to. I can't count how many "cleanses" I've started and never finished. I think the longest I've gone was three days...on a five-day cleanse. I couldn't even hang for five days! I was almost there and I justified quitting by telling myself, "It can't be healthy to be this G-D hungry all day. This is bullshit."

Maybe the motivation of the workbook will help keep me focused since I failed to remain so in all of my previous attempts. I'll be the first to say, I'm a sucker for those infomercials about parasites and toxic fecal matter, but I'd be lying if I said my main intention had nothing to do with weight loss. "Ridding my body of excess pooh is SURE to be my ticket to slim-dom!" I guess the prospect of losing thirty pounds in five days wasn't incentive enough for me to stick with it. I can't take complete responsibility for my lack of commitment, though; some cleanses can be treacherous for those of us with a refined pallet. I bet my key to success in completing a cleanse is to find one that doesn't involve some nasty-ass sludge shake. The last cleanse-drink I tried was so thick and gritty it triggered my gag reflex with every reluctant sip.

I'll check around and see what I can find.

The organic thing won't be as hard. I've already been pretty good about buying whole foods. Of course, I say *buying*. I guess it doesn't count if I purchase steel cut oats for breakfast, only to end up eating the Cap'n Crunch I bought for the kids. Hmm. This might be more of a transition than I thought. Either way, I'm going to stick with it and do my best.

That is, of course, after today. I have lunch with the girls and I know it's going to be an indulgent one. Blair and her husband, Pete, have been struggling lately and it's only getting worse. They're both good people and it's not that they don't love each other, they're just poisonous together as a couple. When she called this morning and told me I needed to drive us today, I pretty much knew she had every intention of drinking, and drinking heavily, at lunch. It must've been a pretty big fight.

· · ·

I was wrong. It wasn't a pretty big fight. It was an *extremely* big fight. Blair and Pete are separating and she feels guilty because she's more relieved than devastated. She said the problem is there's no spark anymore.

"He shits while I'm in the bathroom. Is *nothing* sacred?" she fumed, throwing her hands up in exasperation. "No wonder I don't want to have sex. I feel like I'm married to my goddamned brother or something!"

By the time lunch was over, Blair was fully drunk and completely uninhibited. The drive home was a fairly quiet one, then out of nowhere she says to me, "I'm having an affair." I looked over at her as if she'd said what I thought she said.

"Don't look at me like that, Holly. You have no idea what I've been going through," she slurred.

I wasn't judging her. I knew for a fact Pete messed around at a sales conference last year in Vegas. I swore to Shawn I wouldn't say anything to Blair, and I meant it. If Shawn had gotten drunk and done the same thing to me, I wouldn't want to know.

Why separate? Why not make it final with divorce, I wondered. She explained she asked for a divorce and Pete won't give her one, but she doesn't want to tell him about the affair because of the kids. She's afraid he'll use it against her.

"Damn kids make everything harder," I said jokingly. I swear to God, I've got the worst timing ever.

She smiled then started bawling. My heart broke for her and I felt helpless; there was nothing I could do or say to make it better.

When I pulled up to her house, she sat quietly for a minute, as if searching for something to say. Her brown eyes were puffy and smeared with mascara, her rosy cheeks pale. She ran her fingers underneath her lashes and smoothed out her straight, blonde hair. She looked up at me and said, "I love you. Thanks." All I could say was, "Whatever you need, Blair..." She nodded, then said she was going to go throw up. "Good luck with that," I said while she flipped me off and shut my door. Poor Blair.

I hate to say it, but nothing gets me appreciating my marriage quite like watching someone else's fall apart. It sounds insensitive, but I can't help it. Something like that could so easily happen to Shawn and me, what with his constant traveling and my sex drive coming to a halt. After all, Blair began to stray because Pete withheld the kind of attention she needed. She's human...and so is my husband. Shawn's coming home early for Mrs. Gillman's funeral tomorrow, and after my conversation with Blair, I can hardly wait to see him. I can say beyond a shadow of a doubt, as soon as he walks through that door today, he's going to receive a very warm welcome.

8/9/10

Well, I said in Lesson Five if I came across any hidden bad habits I would write about it. I won't play it down, it's a fairly big one and being a good friend to someone doesn't pardon me in the least. The silver lining is that it's distracting me from thinking about Pete and Blair. Back to the bad habit.

I'm not going to act like I was completely unaware of my vanity until now. I've become really good at calling it other things, like "not letting myself go," or "staying on top of self-maintenance" but let's cut the shit. Looking good everywhere I go has always been overly important to me. Today, however, is the first time it occurred it me, "Gee, I'm kind of an asshole." I bet even someone super peaceful and nonjudgmental would agree. The Dalai Lama would be like, "Yes, you are an asshole."

Nothing inspires an evaluation of character quite like a funeral, right? A few days ago Mrs. Gillman, an elderly acquaintance of the family, passed away in her sleep. She was ninety-three and tired, so the news was more of a relief than an upset. I got the phone call and went through the usual suspects: "When? How's the family holding up? When are the services? At least she's at peace now."

Once the customary details were addressed, the second most pressing piece of business at hand was, naturally, "What am I going to wear to the funeral?" What can I say? I'm a true humanitarian at heart. God help me, it wasn't twenty minutes before I was standing in front of my closet contemplating possible outfits.

Too flowery…too bright …too red. Why is it poor etiquette to wear red to funerals?…Too sparkly, although it would be kind of funny to show up in full club wear. That's wrong, don't make jokes… THERE'S that top, how many times have I looked in this exact spot for this freaking shirt? I have GOT to go through my closet and get organized, this is ridiculous...Focus!

After a while of going back and forth, hanger by hanger, I settled for the classic boat neck, A-line dress. Oh, J. Crew, I'll never tire of your clean lines and Hamptons style. I knew I was taking a risk, stepping outside the box with a black dress and pearls, but that's how I roll. Then there's the subject of hair, which never takes much contemplation. Sometimes I waver, but typically I feel the best style for any melancholy occasion is a nice dramatic side part, coupled with a swept-back chignon. I refer to it as the "Bereavement Bun." It usually does the trick. It's sad, but the egotism of all this didn't dawn on me until I was getting dressed this morning.

You know, Holly, this isn't a fashion show, it's a funeral. This isn't about YOU or what you're wearing.

I agreed wholeheartedly and felt like an ass for having invested so much energy into my ensemble. At the same time, it was easy to self-criticize after I was dressed and felt confident in my outfit. I doubt it would've crossed my mind if I had nothing picked out and was scrambling at the last minute, but I digress.

We arrived at the funeral and snagged a place to sit near the back of the church. As the other mourners entered and looked for seats, I found myself evaluating every wardrobe malfunction, scanning these people up and down as if I were a judge at a dog show. My obsession with what *I'm* wearing is only one half of a whole. It so happens scrutinizing what other people are wearing leaves me feeling fashionably superior, thus making all the energy invested well worth it.

OK, let's see, well-prepared ensemble? Check. Accessories? Check. An attitude that exudes a lack of concern for how I look? Double check. Now all I need is a poorly executed outfit to trash and the circle is complete.

And complete it was, for who should choose a seat right in front of me but a grown woman donning the most gargantuan hair bow I'd ever seen. Manna from Heaven, it was pageant worthy. All she was missing was giant shoulder pads and I would've been catapulted back to 1987 instantly. It was as if I was standing first in line at the Catty Bitch Comments Buffet; I had my tray, fork and stretchy pants.

I decided to begin the feast of criticism with a juicy, "Well thank God she wore her black bow today." It paired nicely with the savory, "If it starts raining at the burial site, I'm totally standing next to her." On the side I helped myself to, "I swear to God if the wind picks up she better have a pole to hold on to." And to wash it all down, a robust, "Um, bless her heart."

Once upon a time, I would've considered that to have been pretty damn funny, not being able to keep those snarky gems to myself. But it doesn't feel so funny now. I sat there actually feeling kind of guilty, even after I absolved myself with "bless her heart."

I began to feel better because at least I wasn't as bad as old Henrietta Miller sitting behind me. She had been talking throughout the service and since she's mostly deaf, she practically yells when she speaks. "I mean, who does that, really?" I complained to Shawn. I couldn't help but overhear her, so it doesn't count as eavesdropping.

"She dresses fancy, don't she?" I heard her say. Ms. Miller's always been so sweet, so I couldn't help but be curious as to who she could be talking about in such a scathing way. "I don't know why she thinks she has to dress so fancy. Who is she trying to impress? That Holly always looks like she's trying to impress someone…always acting like she's *better*."

My mouth fell open. Sweet my ass! I guess it's a good thing I don't fucking care what that spinster bumpkin has to say about me.

"She's talking about me while I'm *right here*," I whispered to Shawn. "What a bitch! I don't think I'm better than everyone!"

"I know," he said, rolling his eyes. "Small-town bullshit, babe. Everyone's got something to say about everyone else. Don't let it bother you."

He grabbed my hand and gave it a squeeze, which was comforting, but only a little. I sat there fuming, kicking my foot as I crossed and uncrossed my legs. *Better than everyone? Whatever, dude,* I huffed. As soon as I heard "In the Arms of an Angel," I knew it was time for the tear-jerking slide show and I decided that slack-jawed yokel wasn't worth my time.

I sat watching the illustration of Mrs. Gillman's life and soon found myself obsessing about my own funeral. What would the casket look like? Which I guess is some sick extension of "what am I going to wear?" What self-portrait would be displayed next to the casket? Would someone put together some slide show choreographed to "In the Arms of an Angel" or some other death-related song I didn't like in life? What song would I want them to play to that slide show, because who am I kidding? I want the effing slide show. Would there be a good turn out? Who would show up? What would be said about me? Who would cry? Who would be relatively unfazed, while talking shit to someone else who was as equally unfazed? That old bag, I can't believe she said that about me... But more than anything else, when I tell people not to cry at my funeral, will they know what I truly mean is "you bitches better sob over that casket"? Because no matter how much I try to kid myself, there's this part of me deep down that really doesn't understand why I would want people partying at my freaking funeral.

"What's wrong with you?! MOURN, PEOPLE, MOURN!"

I got home and felt like a bad person. I had that coming, with karma and all.

Do I experience this every day? No. Being self-absorbed at a funeral isn't the bad habit brought to light today. What I did realize is my lack of compassion and the sense of worth I derive from things that have no worth. Clothes, physical beauty, popularity. Did I never mature beyond high school?

I feel ashamed and guilty, like I need to call someone and apologize for my behavior, even though no one was aware of it but me. I have a sense I should be thankful to see this now so I'll be aware of it in the future, but it doesn't make me feel any better.

I'm off to go get my kids from school.

8/11/10

After the yucky feeling of yesterday wore off, I was ready to submerge myself in this lesson. For me, I always turn to something wholesome to clean me up when I feel dirty. I'm not going to give any examples of past experiences. I trust the metaphor is enough to paint the picture.

Shawn's home for the rest of the month and I'm so pumped to be able to spend time with him! He's even taking the kids to school this morning so Zoe and I can hang around in our PJs longer. Aww.

I'm taking off for the city later to look for a cleanse. I'll write when I get back if I find anything.

. . .

After doing some extensive research (or going to the nearest health store and buying the only cleanse they had that didn't involve a wretched drink), I was able to find something suitable. It's a seven-day program, and in addition to about eight different herbs, I am to eat nothing but fruit every two hours. This includes avocado and tomatoes, which makes me super happy. At first I thought, "Guacamole every two hours? YES!" But then the herbalist told me it can't be more than one type of fruit at a time, so I can only make guacamole in my stomach once I eat some tomatoes two hours after I eat avocado. Which is fine, it wouldn't be the same without salt, chips and beer. I feel good about this cleanse. Who doesn't love fruit? How hard can it be?

8/12/10

Day one of the cleanse: thus far it's not bad. Bananas for breakfast, a bowl of strawberries two hours after that, juicy cantaloupe to follow in about ten minutes. I can't complain too much. Shawn's not super thrilled, though. I told him no date night while I'm "cleansing."

And speaking of complaining, God help me, the rest of the family is not doing well with the total organic makeover in the pantry.

"What kind of bread is this, babe? It tastes like woodchips and sponge. And what's wrong with this peanut butter?"

It's only been a few days since the switch, and I'm hoping comments like, "Wheat flakes? What are wheat flakes?" will soon come to an end. Some of the organic brands do take some getting used to, but it doesn't bother me at all. On the other hand, I have missed taking quick bites of the junk food my kids were eating. No one knows it, but I had a meth-like addiction to Fruity Pebbles back in '08. I was ashamed and kept it hidden well. Bedrock has itself a drug dealer and his name is Fred Flintstone. The shit should be outlawed. I'm not kidding.

Back to the cleanse. Since it's only the first day, there are no changes to report. I mean, I'm hungry, but that's not really so abnormal. Although I'm pretty surprised to feel hunger at all, considering one herb tablet is the size of a Honda. I swear, I have to take fourteen of them every 11.4 minutes, it seems. The supplements haven't had a chance to kick in yet, so there's nothing to report in that arena, either. The herbalist told me they're pretty gentle, which is good. I'd hate to be in the middle of a public place and suddenly have #2 making me its bitch. I plan on sticking fairly close to home for the next seven days, to be on the safe side.

Well, it looks like it's time for that cantaloupe. Until tomorrow, goddess.

8/13/10

I woke up STARVING today. Starving and tired and put out to not be able to taste the coffee I was making for Shawn. It smelled amazing. But so did my organic jasmine tea, which helped. What didn't help was Ryan's request for hot, buttery pancakes while I nibbled on apples.

How could I turn him down? My newest good habit that's being "instilled" is making the kids a homemade breakfast more often on the weekends. On top of that, my cute little Ryan has this lisp that is absolutely adorable. When he walks in rubbing the sleep from his eyes and says, "Mommy, will you make me thum pancakth pleathe?" I totally melt.

So far it hasn't been SUPER hard. I am noticing a change in energy, although I wouldn't say it's one for the better. I feel pretty sluggish and am dealing with a killer headache due to caffeine withdrawal, but the herbalist told me this could occur. She also said I might get irritable, achy and experience flu-like symptoms as the toxins get "stirred up" and come to the surface before flushing out. This is where the gargantuan pills come in. The herbs are what are supposed to "knock everything loose," but they're, uh, not working. I guess it takes time for them to kick in, I don't know.

I'm cooking sausage and peppers with spinach pasta for the family tonight. Why would I have started this thing at the beginning of a weekend? Oh goodie, it's time for my banana. *unenthusiastic high five*

8/14/10

Day three. It's getting more difficult to remain focused. I find my level of irritability growing with every hunger pang in my hollow gut and my brain is pounding against my cranium in protest of being cut off from caffeine. The herbs haven't begun to do their job and my stomach is so tight and bloated it's like I've swallowed a fucking balloon. I could pass for being six months pregnant, I swear to God! This cleanse isn't doing what I was expecting it to do. Moreover, I'm starving. I don't know if I've mentioned that yet.

I've heard it said the third day is always the hardest during any change of habit. I find this to be true considering I've never made it past the third day on any diet, cleanse or program of the like. More than ever, I now understand why. Because any regimen that involves deprivation sucks, that's why.

Everything's becoming gloomy, and my house is beginning to feel more like a prison and less like a home. I'm taking a lot of deep breaths and am refraining from using the F-word in between the syllables of each word I speak. I try to dodge sounding as though I suffer from Turrets as much as possible; however, such a task is grueling on this day.

My children have noticed an ominous calm has come over me. They keep their distance, wise not to trust my strange, yet composed quivering. Tyler asked me for a peanut butter and jelly sandwich for lunch. As I turned my head slowly to look him in the eye, he gradually backed away, avoiding the mistake of making any sudden movements.

The fruit has lost its flavor and these futile pills seem to be growing in size with each dose. I need your strength, goddess, as I grow weaker by the moment. Help me on my quest for a clean liver and unblocked colon. Hear my cries.

8/15/10

I hate my life and everyone who's in it. I'm so fucking hungry I've thought about eating one of my children. Tyler has the most meat. If I have to look at another piece of fruit I'm going to try and find someone to bludgeon with it. I have said that *childbirth* was the most excruciating experience of my life. I stand corrected. This is MISERABLE.

I cannot POSSIBLY imagine how in the HELL I'm going to handle another three GODDAMN days on this horrible DISASTER of a colon cleanse. I haven't even crapped. NOT FUCKING ONCE!!!! I swear I would scream at the top of my lungs if I wasn't using every SHRED of my energy in writing this STUPID FUCKING ENTRY!!!!!

I would quit. I would totally quit RIGHT NOW, but if I do, all of this is for NOTHING. The thought of going through what I feel right now for NOTHING pisses me off more than anything really dramatic that I can come up with. I hate fruit. I hate it so much, I want to walk into a restaurant and throw it at all the people eating the shit I can't eat. That's what I want to do with it, I want to chuck it at someone's head and make them think twice about eating a hamburger and French fries within a ten-mile goddamn radius of me. Juice THAT, goddess!!! Oh my GOD, I want to DIE!

8/16/10

Well, I feel somewhat better today. I woke up this morning, and strangely, didn't feel all that hungry. Perhaps the thought of fruit is so revolting, eating has lost its appeal completely. My headache's gone, but more surprisingly, my breakfast of honeydew melon didn't make me retch. I guess once the fury subsided, my taste buds opened back up, no longer fearing for their lives.

It's true. Once you get past the first three or four days, it really does get easier. I think day five may turn out to be okay...

I've gone through my fruit supply faster than expected and the kids are out of milk, so I'm going against my "sticking close to home" rule and venturing out to the store. In all seriousness, if I had been glued to the toilet all week I wouldn't be going. But since the herbs are STILL not doing their job, I think I'll be okay for a quick run to the market.

I can't explain how glad I am to be over the hump, so to speak. Two and a half more days and I'll be through. On a really positive note, my cravings for chips and beer have subsided. I guess that's the trick with these cleanse programs; they make you so miserable it completely distracts you from thinking about anything else! Hopefully these herbs will kick in soon and get rid of some of this bloating.

. . .

Well, if I had known that all I had to do was go out in public to make these herbal laxatives jolt into high gear, I would've done it in the freaking first place! The pill bottles should come with a warning label!

"WARNING: Contents of this bottle will send you shuffling to the nearest restroom with nothing but clenched cheeks and a prayer."

I literally had to hold my hand over my ass! I looked like a potty-training toddler doing the poopy dance. Luckily, I made it in time, but I had to leave my basket in the middle of aisle four. It's still there, actually. Motivated by my disgust for public bathrooms, I hurried home already unzipping my pants as I drove so that it would be one less thing I had to do before my ass exploded all over the place. I screeched into the garage, waddled as fast as I could to the bathroom, I don't even know if my jeans were pulled all the way down before the floodgates burst open. "Sweet, sweet relief..." That's all I could keep saying to myself. "Thank you, God, sweet Jesus...thank you." Seriously, dude, I made a Whoopee Cushion sound classy. After I finished raining down sulfur on my poor Kohler toilet, I asked Shawn to run by the store after work. Once he was done laughing hysterically, he agreed to go. Asshole.

The messed up thing is, I TOTALLY saw this coming and I STILL went to the store! Unbelievable! Uh oh. Gotta go.

8/17/10

How would I describe myself if I were to change my Facebook profile? I would most likely do my best to portray the image of a ketchup bottle that's almost empty, because that's precisely how I feel and sound every forty-five goddamn minutes.

The herbs? Yes. They're working quite efficiently now. Am I complaining about the fruit? No. No, I'm too busy shitting my brains out, thank you very much, you lying, herbalist bitch.

Gentle? Is that how she would describe Drano? The word "gentle" must mean something different in "Granola World" than it does in the world I live in, because these herbs only fit her description when they weren't causing me to shoot chocolate soft-serve out of my ass every half hour!

This has to stop at some point! It HAS to! There's nothing left, God in heaven! There's NOTHING LEFT!!!

8/18/10

Today was an adventure. NOTHING like yesterday or the day before, but it was no day at the spa. The trips to the bathroom were many and I may take a break from fruit after this. But thankfully, as the day has come to an end, the effects from the herbs have waned.

I took the last horse pill of the bottle and I'm about to go to bed on the final night of my seven-day cleanse. My colon is so clean it squeaks like a rubber ducky with every step I take. Seriously, I can say, beyond a shadow of a doubt, the possibility that there are any blockages left would go against the laws of physics. Ask Steven Hawking. I doubt he'll debate me.

I hate to admit it, but I actually feel kind of amazing. My skin is glowing, my hair is shiny and my skinny jeans are no longer cutting off my circulation, God love 'em. In addition to the sense of physical cleanliness, I'm really proud of myself for sticking with the program. If I can make it through THAT, the liver cleanse should be a breeze. It only consists of a daily "cocktail" of pure cranberry juice, apple cider vinegar and lemon. I'm supposed to drink it first thing in the morning and wait thirty minutes before I eat breakfast. If I have alcohol in the evening, then I need to have another cranberry mixer before bed. I'll start that tomorrow.

While I'm looking forward to returning to a normal diet, I don't want this feeling of cleanliness to go away. The good thing is there isn't a scrap of food in this house that isn't organic, so I think I'm getting off to a good start. Making it through the cleanse has, indeed, flushed the toxins and balanced me chemically. The thought of junk food and alcohol doesn't make me salivate right now. Am I saying that I'm never drinking again or that the local taqueria won't see another dime from me? Not necessarily. It might be a while before either one takes place, though.

I sense Fatty trying to add her two cents.

"What about your comfort food?" "What about the traditional bottle of wine you like to drink while watching *Project Runway?*"

I hear her. I do. She isn't as loud as she used to be. So, I'm grateful, very grateful, that I went through this. It was worth it. I'll never do it again, but it was worth it.

8/20/10

Well, I haven't moved on to Lesson Eight. The morning after my seven-day cleanse I chugged a pot of coffee then had BBQ and beer for dinner. I met the girls for lunch today and had a bottle of Veuve Clicquot as an appetizer, then washed it down with a nice sauvignon blanc and a spinach artichoke dip chaser. (A side note: Blair's feeling better. She and Pete are at least civil to each other and she and her boyfriend seem to be getting along quite nicely. Cheers.)

Anyway, I don't think my "fruit flush" took, because I'm drinking a glass of wine. And feeling like a big, fat loser. I finished the cleanse, felt great for about fifteen minutes, and the second I let down my guard I totally crumbled at the sight of ANYTHING that wasn't cantaloupe! Apparently the anti-goddesses didn't like this cleanse either.

I should've known seven days wasn't long enough... *UGH* A three week-long cleanse? THREE WEEKS??? How am I going to make it through twenty-one days when I seriously considered suicide before I even reached day *four?* My wine's low, I need a refill.

I forgot to mention the liver cleanse. The drink is so damn tart I swear I thought my mouth was going to turn inside out. The only saving grace here is my ability to take a shot with the strength and finesse of a veteran biker. As long as I have a glass of water within reach, the cranberry, vinegar and lemon juice shooter can go down quickly and be done with. *blech*

8/24/10

After I got over my resentment for this lesson, I once again decided to do some research on cleanses. Of course, this time I actually did do research instead of picking the first thing I came across. I must've gone through twenty books at the bookstore, and that doesn't begin to scratch the surface of what was available on this subject. I don't know what I was looking for. I followed my gut reaction while reading the book covers. Strangely, I probably picked the hardest one of all of them. No animal products, artificial sweeteners or additives; no sugar; no caffeine; no gluten; no ALCOHOL and last but not least NO JOY.

Why? Well, there are two possibilities. I'm either subconsciously falling into an old pattern of setting myself up for failure, or I have a serious dislike for myself. I genuinely don't know which is more accurate at this point, since they both feel pretty spot on.

With this in mind, let me focus on the positive aspects of this cleanse. Yes, this program has its share of "forbidden fruits," but it definitely has its very own silver lining, and that silver lining is Mexican food: corn tortillas and chips, vegan refried beans and rice, pico de gallo and the one thing that gets me giddier than a Hermès Birkin bag on eBay: GUACAMOLE.

On this cleanse, I can indulge in my favorite of all earthly creations, the almighty avocado. This Hulk-hued, velvety fruit of the gods brings me more peace than a margarita-induced coma. I truly believe there would be less war if people ate more guacamole, I really do.

So what's my meal plan for tomorrow? A corn tortilla with refried beans and what? GUACAMOLE. Lunch? See the above mentioned with, maybe a salad...that's topped with guacamole. Dinner? You guessed it! It'll be guacamole with a side helping of whatever pairs well with it. Just hook it up to my veins! I'm stoked. BEST CLEANSE EVER! Good stuff, good stuff.

Of course this starts tomorrow seeing I had a steak, pasta and wine for dinner. Now that my wine's gone, Ben & Jerry are keeping me company. Oh Cherry Garcia, lull me with your sweet, sweet song.

8/25/10

Am I really having guacamole for breakfast? No. Steel cut oats, walnuts, blueberries and almond milk. Not bad right? I don't need coffee. I think my resentment towards Shawn for drinking coffee in front of me will be enough fuel for the day.

It's 8:00 a.m., the boys are at school, Shawn headed out for the office and Zoe is still sleeping. It's very quiet in the house and all I can think about is the organic version of Cinnamon Toast Crunch that's in my pantry right now. Something tells me this is going to be a tough month ahead.

· · ·

It's later in the day and I'm beginning to realize how many animal products I use: butter, cottage cheese, parmesan cheese, chicken broth, milk, eggs, egg whites, whey protein powder, honey and something one would think is SO obvious but really taken for grant-ed, lunch meat. *eye roll*

"Oh, I'll make a sandwich...no, I won't, because I can't have lunch meat. Okay, I'll have a grilled cheese on gluten-free bread...oh wait... no, I won't because I can't butter my bread or have cheese...okay, I'll have that lentil soup I made the other day...huh, or not, since it has sausage in it and is based with chicken broth...CRAP!"

Oh, Google don't fail me now.

8/26/10

We can't live on salad for the next four weeks (not if I intend to remain married) so I looked up some vegan recipes that should get us through the next few days until my gluten-free vegan cookbook arrives. Again, it's too early to tell any changes in how I feel. I can say, however, when I told Shawn I was beginning another cleanse, his shoulders slumped and he looked a bit despondent.

"Christ, Holly, again?"

"Why are YOU acting put out?"

"Because you were hard to get along with on the last cleanse you did. You scoffed at everything I said and Tyler kept telling me that he was afraid you were going to kill him in his sleep."

"Well, that's his own damn fault for asking me to make him pea-nut butter sandwiches when he KNOWS I can't eat them!"

"Nice, MOM. How long is this one going to last?"

I was reluctant to tell him for obvious reasons. "It's a little longer than the first one."

"How much longer, Holly?"

"I don't know. It's like twenty-one days or something."

"Shit." He rolled his eyes. "Okay," he said right before he pretended to strangle me.

"Excuse me for wanting to get in touch with my Inner goddamn Goddess, Shawn."

"You mean she hasn't already emerged? With sweetness like that, I figured you'd be sporting a toga at any moment."

Whatever. I guess he's put out because he knows not only will I be unbearable to live with for the next month, he won't be getting laid either. Not unless he coats himself in peanut butter and rolls around in vegan chocolate chips. That's pretty much the only way it's going to happen.

8/27/10

This cleanse is flipping hard.

8/28/10

Hey, you know what's SUPER fun? Going to a party when you can't have anything that's being served. I really don't want to go and would totally bail on the whole thing if I hadn't RSVP'd a month ago.

Usually, when I get ready to go to any kind of get-together (or the like), I keep a steady stream of champagne flowing while I attempt to apply false eyelashes and dance to Lady Gaga at the same time. This ensures enjoyable prep time and a good buzz before the party even starts. Does chamomile tea get me shaking my naked ass around my bathroom while my hair cools on rollers? NO. What am I going to do when people ask me why I'm not downing liquor or bingeing on snack food tonight?

"Holly, these mojitos are amazing! Did you try the lobster dip?"

"No, you skanky bitch, I didn't because I can't EFFING have it, but thanks for rubbing salt in the wound. GOOD TIMES!"

8/29/10

Good news? I'm not hung over. Bad news? Everyone thinks I'm pregnant because I wasn't drinking alcohol or eating seafood at last night's party. Since Shawn "got fixed," I can only imagine what the other small-town wives are saying at this very moment. I guess my having an affair and being impregnated by some stallion's love child is a much better scoop than, "I'm doing a cleanse, no *really*, I'm doing a cleanse."

We got home at the end of the night and Shawn hugged me and said, "Good job, kid. I'm impressed."

I think that made the whole night worth it.

8/31/10

I haven't written in the last few days because I haven't felt like it. There, I said it. Today, however, I feel great! This morning I woke up at 5:45 a.m. with enough energy to go for a run. And even though it was tough in the beginning, the endorphins kicked in after about ten minutes and I managed to jog three miles, which is something I feel proud of. Shawn woke the kids, we got them breakfast, I finished two loads of laundry and mopped the kitchen all by eight-thirty. I want every day to start out like this!

The new diet has been trying, to say the least, but it's getting easier and tortilla chips have made it more than bearable. My vegan cookbook arrived in the mail this afternoon, and after flipping through it, I see some of the recipes actually look pretty good. *phew!*

I'm planning to make the vegan Pad Thai for dinner and I hope no one gives me grief over the tofu. Speaking of, it's time to get cooking…

9/2/10

My kids hate tofu. Shawn is growing resentful and starving for steak. Three weeks left.

9/4/10

I found another perk to this cleanse. Popcorn! What is it about that stuff that makes me so happy? Zoe and I went to the movies today and, considering the cleanse guidelines didn't specify "No MSG," I took down an entire bag of popcorn guilt-free! I didn't even miss the "butter product" I typically saturate the kernels with. Yes, I missed out on the M&Ms and bucket of Coke, but hey, you know what they say about choosey beggars.

9/6/10

I've never been a person who was curious about the taste of dog food. I know a couple of people who have tried it and said it tastes exactly like it smells. I'll take their word for it.

It's been eleven days since I've had any meat and I've been doing okay. That is until I gave my dogs bacon treats this morning and nearly had to drop the can and run away to keep myself from eating one. Just the sight of the rubbery pieces of fake pork was enough to get my mouth and eyes watering. Is it sad that I hesitated washing my hands so I could sit and smell the smoky, meaty scent on my fingers?

9/9/10

Two weeks down, halfway there! It's getting easier, although I miss having lunch with my friends. I've explained the situation and they understand why I'm avoiding our biweekly get-togethers. I left out the whole "goddess workbook" thing though. They probably would make fun of me, which is fine, since I would make fun of any of them for doing the same thing. We all have our roles to play and keeping up appearances is important to everyone, right?

White bean and kale soup tonight. Doesn't sound bad at all.

9/12/10

Could I still consider this cleanse a success if I clipped it off at three weeks? I mean, the author said no less than *three* weeks. Doesn't that imply three weeks is acceptable? I think it does. This way of eating is becoming a habit. I don't automatically reach for the cheese or butter to improve the taste of something. Checking for the "gluten-free" label on my food comes naturally. And most importantly, my mouth doesn't water anymore when I smell my dogs' Beggin' Strips. I feel I'm almost out of the woods here.

Even though the thought of a glass of wine does sound nice, I could take it or leave it. Along with that, the scent of coffee brewing in my kitchen no longer pisses me off. In fact, I think I feel better without it. Sure I've ingested an elephant's weight in tortilla chips and guacamole over the last two and a half weeks, and I think I've put on about three pounds from that alone, but my skin looks amazing.

I would say, on the whole, I feel pretty good. I work out some days, but it's more than I was doing before I began the workbook. I'm pretty happy with my results. I would even go as far as to say I might not go back to red meat. I won't stop cooking it for Shawn— he might leave me—but I don't miss it *at all*. I'm not saying the vegan lifestyle is for me. I love eggs, cheese and butter way too much! I think it wouldn't bother me to have a few meatless meals throughout the week. And since I've gone almost three weeks without a drink, it's probably a good time to knock that back to only social situations. Possibly. Maybe. Well, we'll see about that one.

Anyway, I think I'm good with the decision to make this program a three-week-long ordeal. I don't have any guilt with that. If I didn't feel confident in moving on, I wouldn't do it yet. But considering my family is more ready for me to be off this cleanse than I am, I think it's okay to cut it short. Shawn has begun to ask how much longer this cleanse is going to be, while the kids are asking their own questions. "We don't have to eat that weird white stuff again, do we? It feels like snot in my mouth."

Yeah, they didn't like the silken tofu, either. I think I'll surprise them with homemade pizza tomorrow night. Feelin' good, feelin' good.

9/13/10

Okay, it wasn't homemade pizza, but after the food they've been eating over the last few weeks, NONE of them snubbed the frozen variety. It smelled really, *really* good, but I refrained and made myself a big salad instead. *pat on the back*

9/15/10

No news today. About to make black bean burgers for dinner. Blah, blah, blah.

9/16/10

DONE! I'm so glad I did this. I can tell a definite difference between how I feel today and how I felt when I finished my fruit cleanse. When that was over, deep down I couldn't wait to get back to coffee, bread and alcohol. Today, I feel good about what I've accomplished. On top of that, I've continued to take the super-sour liver cleanse shot every morning and have grown quite used to it. I don't see any reason to stop doing it.

What surprises me is that I'm not even thinking about "normal food." I'm going to the grocery store today and I intend to buy some of the same food I've been eating, along with some different flavors of tea. I'm to the point where I truly enjoy my teatime in the mornings and evenings. I look forward to it because I feel as though I'm treating myself to something special, which is the same way I felt when I would open a bottle of wine or indulge in something sugary. I still get to feel pampered, but I've replaced that source of pleasure with something good for me. That's pretty cool.

Twenty-one days really is the magic amount of time to make a change. My pallet is cleansed, my thoughts are food-less and my digestive system has been regulated. I would recommend this program to anyone interested in making positive changes in their eating habits.

Okay, now on to Lesson Eight.

LESSON 8

Union

Now that your body is clean and clear, it's time to make it one with mind and spirit. The majestic practice of Yoga does just that. Yoga is an ancient discipline, one that dates back to 5,000 years! It has gained popularity in the West and has been a growing trend for good exercise, but it is so much more than a workout. The Sanskrit word "yoga" translates into bond or union. The physical practice is but a small aspect of yogic living and is used as an entry point into a higher state of consciousness, a tool, if you will. This "tool" will be the focal point of this lesson. It requires concentration of the mind, stillness and attention to your inner body throughout each pose (or asana). It also calls for awareness of breath and its marriage to each movement. Because your awareness is turned inward to the physical body and breath, your mind is still, free of clutter. This opens space for Spirit, your connection to the Divine, your Goddess Essence. At the same time, stillness of thought and heightened focus help to build a sharpened mind. The mind is much more efficient and powerful when used as a channel to *serve* your True Self, rather than an obstacle that suppresses it. Along with clarity of mind and spirit, your body temple naturally builds strength and vitality through practice. Your energy centers (called chakras) will open and balance. With this, there is literally a union of spirit, mind and body.

Since this is not a yoga book, I won't go into the history of this ancient practice, or the philosophies behind it. However, there are many schools of yoga: Anusara, Jivamukti, Ashtanga, Kundalini, to name a few, and I urge you to learn more about them.

For this lesson, take the next few weeks and integrate a physical yoga practice into your daily life. Do some research and find the style of yoga that's right for you. Begin with a twenty-minute daily practice, allowing this amount of time to grow as the weeks pass. How you choose to do this is your decision entirely. You may join a class, or get a book that explains each asana in depth. You may also get a video, although I would suggest taking a few classes with an instructor in order to gain perspective on how to perform each pose properly.

Over the weeks to come, I want you to continue journaling about positive changes in your life, in addition to how your yoga practice is going. If you already practice yoga, then write about why you began and what it does for you. You could also try different styles and write about your experiences there. Once you feel it's time to move on to the next lesson, write a reflective entry on how yoga has changed your life for the better, if at all. I'm willing to bet it will! Get excited about this new venture—it is one to be enjoyed! *BLESSED BE!*

9/17/10

This should be interesting. I've tried yoga several times over the years, wanting to experience that "connection." I've had friends tell me how much they love it. I've read articles about the health benefits. I've seen celebrities who attribute their wicked bodies to it. Despite my wanting and efforts, yoga doesn't "do it" for me.

There's a yoga studio in the city. I checked out their website and they offer several different styles. I guess what I'll do is try each one of them and decide which one works for me. Yippee.

9/19/10

So this is my first day on the yoga train, and the only class the studio offers that works with today's schedule is the hot yoga. I wasn't exactly sure what this is about, so I called Shannon, a friend of mine in LA who's been doing yoga since college. She's always talking about Bikram Yoga on Facebook, so I figured she could shed some light on the subject.

"You won't like it, it's so fucking hot," she said.

This was a huge turn off for me, since hot environments kind of piss me off. And when I say "kind of," I mean "nothing pisses me off as instantaneously." This being the reason why my friend so subtly told me I might find the class less than desirable.

She explained that Bikram Yoga is an hour and a half long class of twenty-six poses, practiced in a 105-degree room, on average (sometimes hotter). When she told me this I directly responded with, "Okay, so that's a NO." All discomfort aside though, she told me I should do it anyway because "when you're done you feel amazing, like your insides just got a hot shower."

I wasn't sold until she shared with me, "This is what I always do the day after I drink or eat too much. It's like a cleanse. I sweat all that shit out."

I saw a picture of Shannon in a bikini on Facebook this summer and remembered the surge of insane jealousy at the sight of her sculpted abs and arms. I was promptly back on board.

"I could probably deal with a little heat, I guess."

After my conversation with Shannon, I decided to give it a go, calling Mother's Day Out to reserve a spot for Zoe, then calling the studio to reserve a spot for myself. I felt good about that. Over the last hour, however, I've grown more and more intimidated. I can tell all of my anti-goddesses are having an emergency meeting right now. The only one who seems to be okay with this is Skinnie, who expects yoga to be a great tool for weight loss. The rest of them are pissed.

"You're going to hate it!"

"You'll be all sweaty and uncomfortable and everyone's going to be good at it but you, and you're going to look stupid!"

Most likely, they're right, but even though I don't want to admit it, I know I'll never grow if I never try to prove them wrong. I'm supposed to be breaking down barriers anyway, right?

With that being said, it's time to go. I'll write later.

• • •

It's later. I'll begin by saying, retrospectively, I'm very glad I went today. I didn't think I was going to make it to the end, but now I figure if I got through today's class, there is NOTHING I can't do.

One thing I learned before I stepped into the seventh circle of hell was that I should never confuse Bikram Yoga with "hot yoga."

I was quickly corrected after saying, "Hi, I'm here for the Bikram Yoga class."

The girl behind the front desk was petite, blonde and looked like she belonged on the cover of *Yoga Journal*. In the most passive aggressive way possible she said, "Oh, you mean *HOT* yoga?" She gave me one of those "Aw, you must be new" looks when I asked her if there was a difference. I already felt like a fish out of water. The last thing I needed was for someone *else* to point it out.

"Excuse me, fish? Yeah, you're out of water."

I was about to turn around and go, but as soon as I felt the collective ominous presence of my anti-goddesses—*See? I told you*—I knew I had to stay. I gritted my teeth and made my way to the large, hot room that smelled like stinky ass and incense. I couldn't help but wonder why anyone would *carpet* a room where people sweat so profusely multiple times a day. Unless I was prepared to steam clean that bitch after each and every class, I would stick to something that was less Petri dish-like, but hey, that's just me.

I spread out my mat and towel in one of the few available spaces, pretending to know what I was doing by taking a few stretches and side bends. I looked like someone who was about to go for a jog. I also pretended to be unfazed by the room's pungent odor. I swear it smelled like sweaty balls (for the record, I'd like to state that it *never* got better). The instructor floated into the room, shut the doors and glided to the front of the class. In a soothing voice, she greeted everyone and then pointed out the new student joining them today. Yep. That would be me.

Please don't ask me to introduce myself. Please, PLEASE don't ask me to introduce myself.

"And what is your name?"

DAMMIT!!!

My heart pounding, I squeaked out my name with a puny wave that *screamed*, "Hey, I have no confidence!" After the class of thirty-five people all turned to look and welcome me, the instructor went to her iPod, turned on some sitar remix and the practice began.

Beginning with (very loud and awkward) breathing, I started to work up some heat, but it was no big deal for the first six or seven breaths. However, by the time the actual workout began, that "heat" turned into Dante's EFFING Inferno. I was ON FIRE. I can say with every degree of accuracy that I have NEVER been that hot in my entire life. EVER. It was hard. Really, REALLY hard. There was a point where I was so sweaty I couldn't hold my pose because my elbow kept slipping off my knee. And as if that wasn't enough, my anti-aging daily moisturizer melted off my face and into my eyes. To dispel any curiosity, yes, it burned. The instructor continued walking over to correct my alignment, making me feel singled out, yet again. As irritated as I was, I might've punched her in the back of the head if she hadn't been so nice and nonjudgmental. After each correction, though she never stopped addressing the class as a whole, she would smile at me as if to tell me, "Don't force it. Be patient." I wanted to ask her if she, by any chance, was the author of this workbook.

I kept looking around the mirrored room at all the limber people who had clearly done this before as they moved into each pose with grace. How could I not compare their obvious experience to my total lack thereof? And I found it to be irritating that the chick next to me was still kicking my ass even though she was shorter and outweighed me by at least fifteen pounds. The instructor kept complimenting her form. "Very good, Monique, that is a *beautiful* chair pose." I did my best to keep from rolling my eyes every time ole Monique was praised by the teacher, but let me tell you something. I have the maturity of a twelve-year-old boy when it comes to bodily functions, so when the dude in front of me blew ass during our eighth sun salutation, I knew my poker face was wiped clean. As if that room needed to smell any worse? I was trying so hard not to laugh I looked like I was gagging. I thought I was going to bite through my bottom lip when the instructor said, "That's very natural...good release...very natural." Yes, farting is perfectly natural...and funny as friggin hell.

I never thought it would end! It was the longest ninety minutes I've ever experienced. There were at least five separate times during the class when I looked up at the clock, only to discover it had been a mere two minutes since I looked at it last. Each time this happened, I fought the powerful urge to grab my mat and walk out while flipping everyone the bird. The instructor must've caught onto my "I'm about to flip you off and run" vibe because several times during the practice she briefly opened the door closest to me, allowing a cool breeze to rush in for relief. Bless her merciful heart...

When the class was over, I lay there with a newfound gratitude for air conditioning, feeling as though I'd had my ass kicked. At the same time, I wanted to punch the air Rocky Balboa style and tell my anti-goddesses to SUCK IT!

I'll round out the entry by saying I found the class to be a challenge. However, despite the level of difficulty, Shannon came up with a perfect analogy for how I would feel afterward. I really do feel clean, refreshed. Had I known I would feel this great upon completion of the class, I wouldn't have had such a shitty attitude throughout the entire thing.

Before I left, while feeling inspired and euphoric from the class, I purchased a book on yoga philosophy that also has a sequence with in-depth descriptions and modifications. Since I'm an hour away, driving to the studio every day isn't feasible. Next time I come, I'm signed up for the "power yoga" class, which is an hour and a half, too. I'm beginning to understand why these people are in such phenomenal shape; another nonstop hour and a half? Crap.

Even though I plan to try different styles, I do intend to participate in the hot yoga again (I bought a package of ten sessions). The difference is the next time I go, I'll experience the CLASS instead of the misery of the heat. Good stuff. I'm off to bed. Something tells me I'm going to sleep very well tonight.

9/20/10

Yep. I slept like a baby in a milk-induced coma last night. However, I woke up this morning to discover I can't move. I can't chew. I can't blink. I can't freaking BREATHE without feeling the soreness of some muscle I didn't even know I had. My legs ache so much I thought I was going to cry when I sat down to pee this morning. I literally had to use the doorknob to hoist my broken body back up to the standing position. Don't ask how I managed to get my pants back up afterward. So while I'm feeling rather well-rested, all this energy doesn't do me much good when I'm too handicapped to expel it.

I had planned on trying out the sequence in my new yoga book after my breakfast settled. BUT considering I've missed three calls on my phone because it's on the other side of the house and I can't shuffle my crippled ass fast enough to answer it in time, I don't foresee yoga happening today. Luckily playing tea party with Zoe doesn't take much effort.

Ten sessions. No refunds. *ugh*

9/21/10

Today is power yoga day. I'm still sore as hell from the hot class two days ago, but I paid for today's session, so I have to go. I'd be lying if I said I wasn't afraid. Oh yes, I'm very afraid. I'm beginning to think the reason yoga brings people peace is because it consistently takes them so close to death.

If I can move later, I'll write about my experience. If you don't hear from me again, you'll know the class didn't go well for me. In that case, tell my family I love them.

. . .

I am Jell-O. I have enough energy in my limbs to write this. Why, Goddess? WHY?

9/22/10

I think it's fascinating to find I'm not sore this morning. I was expecting to wake up and not be able to move after yesterday's session of fast flowing, acrobatic torture. I suppose the two different styles of yoga cancelled each other out, eliminating the overabundance of lactic acid built up in my muscles. I have a class tomorrow morning and I'm not really looking forward to it, to be honest. I wouldn't consider myself to be having fun with this lesson; it's so damn hard. And talk about something that's out of my comfort zone! I know myself well enough. I can say that if I'm not having fun with this, it's probably not sustainable. I'd like to think yoga could become a part of my everyday life, but I don't think it will.

I'll stick with it through the rest of the eight sessions in my package, but more likely than not, I'll give it a rest after that.

9/23/10

Three down, seven to go. I wonder what Lesson Nine will be about...

9/26/10

Over breakfast I flipped through the yoga book I bought from the studio the other day, and the more I read, the more I got to thinking. I know me, and if I half-ass this lesson, I will always wonder if my spiritual growth had been stunted by my writing yoga off, only because it was hard. Simply put, if I move on to Lesson Nine prematurely, it could be a hindrance to the effectiveness of this workbook.

So, in the spirit of being dedicated today, I decided to practice the sequence of poses in the book I bought from the studio, and I happen to know for a fact I did most of it incorrectly. How do I know this? Because it wasn't very hard, that's how. I've learned if you think yoga isn't physically challenging, you're doing it wrong.

The introduction to the book, however, made me feel good about beginning a "personal practice." It explains yoga is indeed a *practice*. One meant to be done every day with the intention to perfect each pose, and with the purpose to "grow and connect to Spirit." This gave me an A-Ha Moment.

If I wanted to learn how to play an instrument, it would be completely unrealistic to expect to know how to play it perfectly the first time I tried it. Putting it in terms of a "practice" instead of a "workout" really changed my perspective. It takes the competition out of it, I think.

Before when I did yoga, I always felt like I looked silly, or I wasn't as good as the person next to me. Or more commonly, I could see my cellulite through my tight fitting spandex pants, meaning everyone *else* could too, and they must be judging me. But since it has nothing to do with anyone else, and everything to do with me and *my* journey, I feel as though I'm DOING something instead of UNDOING something, *building* instead of *fixing*. It's not a calorie burn, it's a practice.

I'm sure if the author of this workbook read this she'd probably say, "HEY, no shit. Start reading the lesson plan, genius." Yeah, yeah, yeah.

So I've decided, even if it's a few "sun salutations," I'm going to start doing yoga every day. Who knows? Maybe it will grow into a full-blown practice.

9/30/10

Okay, maybe it's me, but after only eleven days of doing yoga, my body is beginning to change. I was getting out of the shower today (after yoga at 6:00 a.m., thank you very much) and I noticed muscle definition in my arms that definitely was NOT there before!

I've been to power yoga twice and hot yoga twice and everything else I'm doing on my own at home, at least thirty minutes a day. It's obvious I'm enjoying it now because I wouldn't be doing it otherwise. I plan on buying a membership to the studio when my package is spent. What I'm really excited about is I'm seeing positive results in my body when that wasn't even my goal! Okay, yes, of course it crossed my mind once or twice that this might have benefits in the weight loss arena, but that wasn't my motivating factor.

I'll eventually branch out and try other methods, but I think I've pretty much found what works for me (for now). I like the "power" style because it's so intense. It makes me feel mighty. I like the hot style because it feels like a cleanse (and not the kind that sends me running to the bathroom in the middle of the grocery store, m'kay?). I find myself looking forward to the classes and my time at home because there's something that feels almost sacred about it. I may not LOVE it while I'm on fire in the middle of a pose, but I do love how amazing I feel afterward. I can definitely see this becoming a regular part of my life, for sure. Of course, Shawn has his own hopes for my yoga practice.

"Hey, doesn't yoga make you really *flexible?*" he asked with bouncing eyebrows. Perv.

10/1/10

Oh, October. I welcome you with open arms. All hail the Libras!

10/4/10

Right, so note to self #1: Do NOT do hot yoga right after having eyelash extensions done. When I left the studio my eyelids looked like they were molting.

Note to self #2: Do NOT drink alcohol within five hours of hot yoga unless properly rehydrated. I poured myself a glass of champagne while cooking dinner and half way through got drunker than Lindsay Lohan on a Tuesday morning. I had to dump it out, and that's REALLY saying something. I don't buy cheap champagne and pouring my glass of bubbly gold down the sink was a definite first for me. What's more, I was only bummed about wasting money. I wasn't all that put out about having mineral water instead. Anything feels special when sipped out of a champagne flute!

Oh, and yoga was awesome today. I'm becoming familiar with the poses and able to follow along. I'm also getting to know the studio staff, particularly the class instructor, Lindy. She seems to have a very healthy outlook on life. I'm sure her Inner Goddess is like, super present all the time.

10/9/10

HAPPY BIRTHDAY ZOE!

I'm off to get stuff for her birthday party this weekend, i.e., pizza and cake, nothing major. Shawn made me promise when she was born that I would hold off on the extravagant princess tea parties until she's old enough to appreciate them. BOOO!

On a side note, I'm down almost a full dress size and my arms look friggin awesome. I feel amazing and my energy is through the roof! Every positive habit I set out to instill, I've done. I'm waking up super early, working out, getting the kids breakfast—okay, maybe not a homemade breakfast every day, but still. I'm on top of my To-Do list, we sit down and eat as a family without TV and I've limited my drinking to the weekends. Holy crap, I'm practically PERFECT!

I realize I didn't mention a garden, laying hens, a milking cow or frequent sex. I'm working on it.

Lunch with my girls today after birthday party shopping. Looking forward to it.

. . .

Well, all the ladies commented on how good I look, which totally made my day.

"Thank you, thank you," I said proudly. "I'm down fourteen pounds since summer!" Of course they all buzzed, questioning my diet and workout regimen. "I've been cutting way back on the junk food and I started doing yoga, which is why I'm passing on the sangria today," I explained. "I plan on doing my practice later on today, and if I drink, I know I won't be up for it."

My buddy Casey made fun of me, throwing out some comment about Kool-Aid and joining a cult. I told her she's my least favorite friend but I don't think it fazed her. She shrugged, poured herself more wine and then gushed over how good it tasted.

"Oh, you're missing out. The aroma alone is heaven."

Yes, I'm sure the aroma of the $12 pitcher of sangria was breathtaking. *eye roll*

Blair's doing better. Pete still won't give her a divorce, despite her copping to the affair. She's on the brink of inviting her boyfriend over for dinner, but I told her having sex with him on the kitchen table while Pete's eating would be in poor taste.

"So fucking what?"

I suspect she's getting desperate because she seemed pretty serious when she said it. I couldn't help but laugh at that one. I think she's going to be okay.

10/12/10

HAPPY BIRTHDAY TO ME!

Thirty-five and still getting carded, baby. *That's* what's up!

10/14/10

Everything's good: yoga's great, I'm feeling good, getting ready for Halloween, my FAVORITE holiday. Shawn and I have a date night this evening to celebrate my birthday, but I'll probably take it easy on the wine since I've got yoga tomorrow morning. That's about it for today.

10/15/10

This morning I actually knew how much I paid the babysitter last night. *smiley face*

Zoe's birthday party is later on this afternoon. I've been thinking about that bright pink cake since yesterday!

10/16/10

Zoe's party was great yesterday. It was low key, family and some friends—like I said before, nothing major. We hung outside all day, grilled steaks for dinner. I had a few drinks of Shawn's beer and that's about it. I figured if I was going to wake up this morning and do yoga, I probably shouldn't load up on crap, which has been a growing trend for me lately.

At some point between falling asleep last night and waking up this morning, some kind of "shift" occurred. I truly don't know where it came from, but I think I made the decision to quit drinking.

It's a commitment I've made countless times in the past without ever genuinely planning on following through. I'm not alone; we all know it's easier to swear off the booze after a night of bingeing on top-shelf margaritas and bull blasters.

"Please, God, be merciful! I'll never drink again, I promise!" But once the hangover wears off, I find myself rummaging through the kitchen drawers looking for the corkscrew.

After all, Jesus DID turn water into wine, so I trust he understands the need to take advantage of an excellent Beaujolais Nouveau before it's past its prime.

I've never been able to make it stick, no matter how good my intentions are.

For some time, I've known and admired people who are able to have just ONE drink, no matter the occasion. My mother-in-law, for example, has one, sometimes two glasses of wine at a sitting, that's it. She could be at Sunday dinner or a big party, it doesn't make a difference. I've shared many bottles with that woman and I've never seen her have more than two. Typically, the majority of the bottle is enjoyed by me and so is the bottle after that. Her story is she got really, REALLY drunk twenty years ago and never wanted to experience that again, so she hasn't.

I have a friend, Jana, who doesn't drink AT ALL. I didn't know this about her until I offered her a beer during a BBQ last summer.

"No, thanks, I don't drink," she replied after I, assuming she drank as much as the rest of us there, handed her a bottle as I snagged one for myself.

I wasn't sure what baffled me more, her *purposefully* not drinking, or the fact that I hadn't noticed this about my friend before. Either

I was bad about getting too drunk to pay attention to my friends or, simply put, I was REALLY self-absorbed. Both are possibilities in this case.

Sadly, she thought I was joking when I quickly responded with "WHY?" like she had told me she wanted to kick my dog. I mean, it was a passionate "*WHY???*"

After my puzzled look clued her in on the seriousness of my question, she explained she doesn't like the way it makes her feel.

"Anything that makes me feel like shit can't be good for me," she said.

I felt embarrassed, and honestly, jealous. I admired her self-respect, and deep down, I wished I didn't like alcohol, either. So I made fun of her and told her she was a giant puss.

It's not that I get tanked every day. I'm not a "drunk." But because I don't drink whiskey from a coffee mug for breakfast doesn't necessarily mean I don't have a problem. It comes down to this: I find it hard to stop once I start. I'm that way with Oreos, too. Thank you, Fatty McFat-Fat.

With some of the physical pain and humiliation my habit has brought me over the years, it's unfathomable I've continued drinking at all.

FLASHBACK #1: We went to a wedding in Austin a few years ago. After the reception we went barhopping with some friends on Sixth Street, the strip where all the "go-to" bars are…if you're in *college*.

I remember the wedding ceremony and dancing to "Rock You Like a Hurricane," ALONE in the middle of the dance floor at the reception. The rest of the night is foggy.

The next morning I rolled over to find Shawn giving me this "I know something you don't know" smile.

I whispered, "Dude, I think I talked shit to a cop last night."

He raised his eyebrows, held up what I thought was a peace sign and said, "Two."

WHAT?

"Yeah," he said. "The first one wouldn't let you into the bar because you didn't have your ID on you, so you started demanding to speak to his *manager.*"

"Oh my God…did I know he was a cop?"

"Well, if the badge and gun didn't convince you, I don't know what would've."

"Oh Jesus…" I buried my face in my hands.

"Then," he continued.

"No, please stop."

"THEN, when you got too close to an arrest taking place outside of the bar, a different officer ordered you to get out of the way and you said you would move 'just as fast as my Jimmy Choos will take me.'"

I tried to recollect the slightest memory of the preceding night's events. No dice. Then I threw up.

FLASHBACK #2: I love Jason Mraz. A lot. I'm not willing to assassinate anyone to get his attention, so no worries there, but if Jason Mraz were Cocoa Puffs, I would be cuckoo for his delectable, chocolaty goodness. To be honest, if I weren't already married with three children of my own, I would selflessly and gladly offer my womb to bear his spawn. CUCKOO!!!

Well, Libby and I got the chance to go to his concert a few summers ago and I couldn't have been more elated. I scored pit tickets and totally manifested backstage passes to the "Meet & Greet" before the show. I give thanks to the Universe and all of its natural laws.

It was amazing, and I was SO ecstatic to be there, living that moment. As soon as we were done chatting with him and taking the obligatory pictures, I made a beeline for the beer garden. I had butterflies in my stomach the size of condors, and for whatever reason, I felt an excessive amount of beer was exactly what I needed to calm me down.

When he came onstage after the opening act, not only was I calmer, I was WASTED. I mean blurry vision, staggering, spilling and crying. Oh my God, I was CRYING like a twelve-year-old girl at a Justin Bieber concert. My favorite musical artist...a concert I had anticipated for months... I don't even remember what songs he sang.

FLASHBACK #3: Last fall we took the family back home to Pasadena for my aunt's fiftieth birthday party. It was a peach of a time. They went all out for this thing: white tents, hula dancers, DJ, dance floor. Open bar. By the time the night was over, I was pole dancing on the tent's support beams. I tried blaming my lack of balance and constant falling on my four-inch wedge heels but I don't think anyone bought it. Luckily there were plenty of people who were as drunk as I was and my relatives judge only in silence. Shawn missed most of the show because he was inside catching up with old college buddies who stopped by, but unfortunately, my oldest son saw the whole thing. He watched in silent horror as his mother danced like a stripper to Heart's "Barracuda." Tyler wouldn't come near me for the rest of the night. Worst walk of shame *ever*.

There's a surplus of occurrences that should've caused me to snap to and realize that getting SO intoxicated isn't worth the potential damage I could do to my family, friends, body. My once-in-a-lifetime opportunity to sleep with Jason Mraz. DAMMIT!

sigh

Anyway, I've had this urge to drop the drinking altogether for a while now. After the cleansing effects of Lesson Seven, my habit has lessened drastically. On top of that, getting into yoga has made me stop and think about what I put into my body. It's also made me ask, "How fun will power yoga be tomorrow if I'm hung over?" I can't deny how good I feel now that I don't drink a bottle of wine every other night. Since I've already cut back so much, I think I should cut it loose completely and see where it takes me.

I woke up this morning knowing something was different. As I stood at my sink brushing my teeth, it came to me as naturally as following up with mouthwash.

"I think I'm going to quick drinking, yeah, that feels right."

I decided to write it down before I did anything else. I feel good about the change I'm about to make, and I suppose journaling is my way of making a declaration. It's seven a.m. on a Saturday, I'm about to do my first sun salutation of the day, and I've decided that I don't drink anymore. No more empty promises to God. No more regrets about giving my kids a reason to disrespect me. I'm done drowning my Inner Goddess.

I don't know if this transformation is because of yoga, but since I'm supposed to write an entry explaining how yoga has changed my life before I move on to the next lesson, we'll just go with it.

I'm ready for you, Lesson Nine. Do your worst...or best. I guess tough guy shit-talking doesn't really apply here. Namaste.

LESSON 9

Meditation & Affirmation

What do you consider to be the ideal quiet time? Are you a person who has a few moments to herself each day for inner reflection, or does the thought of sitting send you running for the hills? If the latter is more "your type," you might find this lesson to be a challenge. Not to worry, dear one. All that's required of you is a single moment and a deep breath. I'm talking about meditation.

Many people have a skewed idea about this revered practice and what's involved in it. They picture a robe-clad yogi, clear minded and perfect, sitting for hours in full lotus on a mystical mountaintop. Is this image familiar to you? You're not alone. The truth is, however, meditation is a lot like beauty; it's in the eye of the beholder. Sitting still with a silent mind is absolutely the truest form of meditation, but there are other methods that can bring about a calm inner state. A serene walk in the woods, a prayer to whom you serve, a quiet jog through the streets of a busy city, writing in your journal or simply taking a single breath can *all* be methods of meditation. It's what you make of the moment that brings about the personal meditative state, *not* the action. The meaning of the word is simply to partake in contemplation or reflection, whether it lasts five seconds, five minutes or five hours matters not. Ideally, through practice, complete stillness of the mind is the aim; however, this can take years to achieve.

There are several great entry points into your practice of meditation. One is through positive affirmations, or mantra. This can be a phrase, word or truth to either center your focus on or to repeat with gratitude and enthusiasm. This fosters positive thinking, along with creating new thought patterns and habits. For example, "I am so grateful to serve as a channel for my Inner Goddess who creates, loves and lives through me!" Or "I exercise because I love my body temple and I love the challenge!" It can also be combining your breath with a word or two (i.e., inhale "peace," exhale "release"). Another method of meditation is through observance of the thoughts. Instead of getting swept away by the story being told in your mind, simply observe what's going on, as if you were listening to the story, without identifying with it. Many spiritual teachers refer to this as watching the clouds pass in the sky; the clouds come and go, but the sky remains still and unchanged. In this scenario, you are the sky, and the thoughts in your mind are the clouds.

Find time to do this daily. I recommend beginning and ending your day with this, but do not feel limited! Practice whenever need be. As time goes by, and your ability to focus becomes sharpened, begin to introduce *complete* stillness to your meditation. Simply move awareness from your words and place it on your breath, the tingling in your toes or the beating of your heart. Throughout this lesson, your mind may wander; this is okay. Don't judge the thoughts or yourself. Be patient. As stated, true meditation takes *years* of practice.

Write about your methods and why you chose them. Include in your entries the effects this newly introduced practice is having on your journey. Whenever you can infuse complete awareness and stillness into your life, it will strengthen and enhance your sense of connection to your Inner Goddess—your True Self. This is where pure love, joy, peace and energy live, in the stillness inside of you. Invite it forth and share it, dear sister.

Move on to Lesson Ten when you feel guided to do so. *BLESSED BE!*

10/20/10

Ah, meditation. I've tried it before and it never turned out the way the self-help books said it would. Here's how it went: I would start out sitting in a relaxed position, focusing on my breath. Thoughts crept in, judgment ensued and I, invariably, ended up lying down and taking a fantastic nap, the embodiment of Zen in its truest form.

One time this past spring, I sought out a spiritual therapist while in between self-help books. As I yearned for a new fix, I went to her to see if she could teach me how to meditate, since I was having no luck doing it by myself. The logic behind this was, "Maybe it's like having a personal trainer. I always worked harder in the gym when I had a trainer, so maybe I'll be more willing to focus and be still if someone's guiding me through it." It sounds reasonable even now.

When I met this therapist, I was very optimistic. She *literally* had a scarf tied around her head. I mean, seriously? How could this have failed, I beg of you? After she sat me down, she dimmed the lights and set the mood with incense, wind chime music and candlelight.

I found myself wondering, *Are we going to meditate or make out?*

After the mental image of THAT set in, I was definitely ready to focus on something else, ANYTHING else. It's not that I'm sexually closed-minded; she wasn't my type.

With a mellow voice, she told me to close my eyes, "banish" my thoughts, and then she began to guide me into a meditative state. I dreamt about shoes the whole time. Once the sequence came to an end, I realized I had gone through the whole damn thing without paying any attention to what she was saying. Hoping to experience a smidgeon of "stillness," I thought, *SHIT! Stop thinking, HURRY!*

Our session came to an end and she opened her eyes, eager to hear about my journey. She asked me with a dreamy smile and a bedroom voice, "How was that for you?" My response? "AWESOME!" She seemed pleased. I, on the other hand, was irritated to have spent $80 to choke on frankincense and daydream about Dior.

So Lesson Nine, MEDITATION, I'm afraid I may not do well. I'd like to consider yoga to be my time for aware stillness, but if I'm being honest with myself, it's not like my mind is exactly still during yoga. I'm not thinking about shoes or anything, but "Holy crap, holy crap, my thighs are on fire!" does frequently sneak in and linger. I don't suppose this is the type of mantra I should be focusing on.

At the same time, I shouldn't shoot the whole thing down because of past experience. I always used to think yoga sucked and now I love it. Why should this be any different? And I like the idea of meditating to a mantra. I've heard positive affirmations can have a lot of power when done correctly. The trick is the feeling and genuine belief you put behind it though, right? I can't exactly tell myself over and over, "I am Donald Trump," and expect it to magically come to fruition, now can I? BUT if I find the right mantra that really resonates with me, who knows? Maybe I can convince myself I don't like expensive shoes!

"I am repulsed by the capitalist fashion industry. I wear robes because I respect the earth, the Universe and my body temple."

Yeah, I think I'll have better luck convincing myself that I'm Donald Trump.

10/21/10

I went back and reread the lesson description, to see if there was any instruction or suggestion I might've missed when I read it yesterday. I found in doing this, sometimes I can gain a different perspective when I'm feeling stuck. It's truly amazing how I can read and interpret something once, then read it again and receive a different message entirely.

How did I miss this the first time?

Beginning each lesson with a sense of intimidation is pretty much the norm, but I felt a sense of relief when I went back and changed my intention from "remaining in a meditative state" to being peaceful "one breath at a time." Taking *one* silent breath is totally attainable, yet my first instinct was to set ridiculous standards for myself.

With all the personal growth I've done, I should be able to meditate like a Buddhist monk, no problem!

Old habits die hard and all that. It's interesting how many different ways my fear of imperfection and vulnerability infiltrate my life. It's like a sneaky virus. When I realize I need to be patient when learning a new skill, I then get down on myself for failing to have mastered fearlessness. Fear plays its very own part in my attempt to get over it. Clever. BUT, this lesson isn't about fear. It's about learning how to meditate. Not *mastering...learning.*

Something else that struck a chord with me as I reread the lesson plan today was the words, "love, joy, peace and energy." I like the idea of taking them in as I breathe and releasing the "bad" as I exhale. I can see the inhalation as an invitation to the positive, and the exhalation being the release of the negative. It sounds good, anyway.

170

I'm going to wait for Zoe to take a nap before I give this lesson a try. She may be perfectly content coloring right now, but I can guarantee as soon as I sit to meditate in silence, she'll come looking for me with her tea set in hand.

. . .

While Zoe was sleeping, I was able to take two solid breaths with my affirming words before outside thoughts crept in. My immediate reaction was irritation. "UGH!" And then a small voice from somewhere whispered, "Patience."

Generally the voice in my head is a bit harsher and a lot less forgiving.

"You failed. You suck."

This gave me the sense it wasn't the same voice. Either way, wherever it came from, I like this new voice much better.

10/23/10

After yoga this morning, I dedicated ten minutes to meditation. Yes, most of it was consumed with the day ahead. *But* this time I got *four* breaths into it before my To-Do list crept in. Progress is mine!

10/25/10

Okay, yesterday I could only take one silent breath in one sitting; but I gave it about forty-eight tries throughout the course of the day. That has to be *at least* three or four minutes of silence!

10/27/10

silent breath

Shawn's been away on business for the last three days, and when the kids are at school or sleeping, I've been lonely—this being why I was super excited to meet up with my friends in the city for lunch today. Also, I've missed the last two lunch dates, and being so absorbed in this workbook, it's been a while since I've seen everyone.

An abridged history lesson: These have been my girlfriends for years; our families hang out together, we party together, our kids play sports together. We have the same SUVs, the same beer preferences, the same bad habits. When we get together it's all about food, drinks and gossip. Never before has this struck me as negative or unhealthy. Until today.

The boys got off to school fine, but Zoe gave me hell this morning.

Right after I got her dressed all cute with a matching bow, she dumped chocolate milk down the front of her dress. When I started to change her clothes she threw a complete shit fit.

"BUT I WANNA WEAR MY DRESS!" she screamed at me. After ten minutes of arguing, I finally wrestled her into a clean change of clothes, and then broke a sweat as she stood in my bathroom with her jaw clenched, refusing me access to brush her teeth. I had to pinch her nose in order to get her to open her mouth for air! And boy, oh boy, do I love the dead weight of a three-year-old whose body has gone limp in protest of walking. With her school bag slung over one shoulder and my purse over the other, I finally said, "Screw it," and dragged her out by the hand (her giggling the whole way).

I was worn out and in need of another shower before I even got to the damn restaurant. This was the first time since my decision to quit drinking that I actually questioned whether or not it was a good idea. I was late when I finally arrived at Casa Garcia, so it was no surprise to find all the hens seated and working on the large, sweaty pitcher of margaritas in the middle of the table. As I headed their way, I looked to the only vacant seat. There was a full margarita in my place and my mouth watered at the sight of it.

"We decided to get started without you, so sit your ass down and catch up," Casey bellowed.

I tossed my purse next to my chair and dropped into my seat, definitely tempted to drain my cocktail like nobody's business. "Dude, it's been one of those mornings," I said, rolling my eyes as I reached for my drink. It was so cold in my hand, the touch of it was refreshing. I ran my thumb up and down the glass, wiping off the condensation as I contemplated what I was about to do.

Am I going to be mad at myself if I do this? I questioned, already knowing the answer. After a few seconds, I let go of the slushy margarita, wiped my hand on the white linen napkin in my lap, and picked up my water glass instead.

"Well, that sure as hell isn't going to help your stress level," Blair joked about the water in my hand.

"I actually have a terrible headache today," I said. "I'm going to hold off on drinking for right now and start with some water." I hadn't told any of them about my recent decision to quit drinking, so I suddenly felt like I needed to start making excuses as to why I wasn't going to partake. Someone called me a "puss" then got right back to the juicy scoop they were in the middle of before I interrupted.

After ordering, eating and sitting through the conversation for a while, I realized I wasn't having any fun *at all*. Not because I wasn't drinking and bingeing on fried cheese, but because the overall vibe of the table was so dark. Bitch, bitch, bitch. If someone wasn't talking shit about someone else, they were complaining about their husband or their kids or their thighs. Except for Blair, of course, she's down three sizes and glowing from all the crazy sex she's having with her nameless boyfriend twenty-eight hours a day.

I sat quietly and listened. At one point Blair, who was sitting next to me, nudged my leg under the table and gave me that, "What's wrong?" look. This got the attention of Marissa, my friend on the other side of me. Soon, all four of them were looking over and one of them said, "Yeah, Holly, what's going on?" There was a chorus of "Are you okay? Did something happen? Have you started taking those diet pills that make you 'blah' again?"

I had no idea what to say. *I don't want to eat this shit food and the only thing you women do is complain.*

It sounded okay in my head, but I had a feeling it might come across as judgmental. For a split second I considered telling them about this book, explaining why I didn't want to drink or gorge or slam someone who probably didn't deserve it. Still, I was afraid they'd make fun of me, so I settled for, "I don't feel good. I think I need to head out. I don't want to bring everyone down with me."

I took some cash out of my wallet and put it on the table. As I did this, my friends buzzed, "Sorry you don't feel good. Let's set something up for next week. Blah, blah, blah." I apologized as I made the rounds, hugging everyone's neck and telling them to have fun with the remainder of their lunch. Their negativity suffocated me, and I couldn't wait to get out of the restaurant and into some fresh air.

I went and picked up the kids from school, doing my best to write it off as a one-time thing. Yet as the day has moved on, I've become more and more concerned. I know I wanted to change *me*, but I didn't expect feelings toward people in my life to change (even though I guess it makes sense). This is the group of friends I've run around with since we moved here from Pasadena. I love these women, and they've been there for me when I had troubles of my own. I don't want to cut myself off from my circle of friends, but at the same time, I don't want to continue to put myself into negative situations. And more than anything, I do NOT want to revert back to old habits and behavior.

I would love to share this workbook with my girls, but I know them. I caught hell for being weird with my pixie haircut last summer; I *seriously* doubt they'd be open to any of this "new age-y" goddess business. I'm hard enough on myself as it is. I don't need anyone else doubting me or discounting my efforts.

"Oh, that's just Holly looking for her 'Inner Goddess.' She's always doing loony shit. Remember when she cut all her hair off?"

I don't want to think about this anymore today. *silent breath*

10/31/10

HAPPY HALLOWEEN! The day was filled with sweet treats, classroom parties and costumes. Tyler was a zombie, Ryan dressed as his alter ego, Batman, and, as a nod to my workbook, Zoe was a goddess. She looked so cute in her little toga.

They should be sugar crashing about right now so bedtime will be a snap. I can't wait to raid their candy bags, tee hee!

silent breath

11/1/10

No dice on the good candy. My kids are smart and picked out all the quality chocolate before I had the chance to get any. Assholes. *silent breath*

11/5/10

This lesson's going pretty well. I have to keep reminding myself that every day is not the same. Some days I feel super focused, while other days, meditating is absolute *torture*. But the more I practice, the easier and more enjoyable the experience becomes, so I'm grateful for that.

The great thing about this exercise is that it's helped me to gauge the amount of growth I've actually achieved thus far. For example, this morning at breakfast, Ryan spilled a full cup of milk all over the floor and himself as he ripped the entire top off of a brand new box of cereal. We were already running behind schedule, and now there was a giant mess to clean up and he needed to go change his clothes. A few months ago I would have *lost it*, and I could tell by Ryan's reaction, that's precisely what he was expecting me to do.

"I'm sorry, Mom! I didn't mean to, I swear!"

At that moment, I was actually more irritated that he rendered the cereal box un-closable. I hate that!

I shrugged and said, "It's cool. I make messes all the time. Go grab a new set of clothes from the laundry room."

He looked as though he were waiting for the punch line as he slowly backed out of the kitchen. After he returned and the mess was cleaned up, I poured him a bowl of cereal and said, "See? No problem. Of course, next time, ask for help before you destroy the box of cereal, dude."

That was it. He and Tyler exchanged wary glances, wondering telepathically if this reaction of mine should be trusted.

"Should we make pumpkin pie this weekend?" I asked them. Their eyes lit up and we moved on.

This is an impressive change for me. Not as impressive as my newfound sobriety, though. That's a big effing deal.

11/8/10

Today's A-Ha Moment: Applying awareness to this lesson has dynamically changed the entire thing.

What?! Shut your mouth!

I know, I know. My "A-Has" are common sense to everyone else, but give me a break. I'm a newcomer to the realm of the obvious. Now back to the A-Ha.

Yesterday began as a "meditation is torture" day. That being the case, I reread the lesson plan and was inspired to try "tailoring" my meditation to the conditions of the moment. For example, I was feeling stressed, so I took a few minutes to inhale "tolerance," and then released "tension" with my exhalation. Before long, it was actually helping! I meant to write about it yesterday, but I never got the chance. Shawn got home from his business trip right before lunch. We hung out on the porch swing and I caught him up on what he's been missing over the last week or so.

Anyway, back to what I was saying. Because of my little development, I've decided to practice meditation in this way. When I feel anxious, I can inhale "strength and potential" and exhale "limiting beliefs." When I'm stumped, I can inhale "creativity and wisdom" and exhale "blockages." Since yesterday morning, I've been doing this each time something pops up that stirs any kind of negative emotion. And since I'm going to have lunch with my friends next week, every time I think about it, I inhale "openness and acceptance" and exhale "insecurity." I really like this approach and I'm pleased by how positively I respond to it.

This method totally helped me find my keys earlier today, no joke.

"Inhale *clarity*, exhale *panic*."

BAM, then it came to me! My keys were in my yoga bag. I don't know if it was the meditative breathing or pure coincidence, but I sure as hell know which one makes a better story.

11/9/10

This lesson has taken on a life of its own. I swear, I feel like a kid with a new toy. Every chance I get, every time it occurs to me, I close my eyes and try to be still. Sometimes I focus on a mantra; sometimes I focus on my heartbeat. My yoga instructor, Lindy, has mentioned something about focusing on the area between the brows, the "third eye." She said she sees colors when she does it. I haven't tried it yet, but I will. Hell, I'll try it right now! I'll be back!

• • •

This isn't exactly par for the course, but I actually *did* see small flashes of color during my meditation. It was like a subtle, purple strobe light.

This is a welcome change. Usually I would be excited about something new, only for it to flop and be disappointed, but this time it delivered! Although, I'll say, it was much more challenging to keep a quiet mind. My thoughts would interrupt and I'd have to "start all over."

I prefer the mantra method, but I think it's because "giving my mind a job" with a mantra is easier for me. Focusing on my third eye took much more concentration and silence. I'll stick with the beginner stuff for now, but I'm glad I tried it. It was pretty cool.

11/11/10

Fall is in full effect and it makes me giddy. It's my favorite time of year, opening the curtain for the celebrated holiday season and the fall fashion lines. Jackets and sweaters and boots, OH MY!

However, you wouldn't be able to tell that it's autumn by the looks of it. Fall foliage is fairly nonexistent here. We're surrounded by oaks that stay green all year long, so the only evidence of the season is some dead grass and a few Thanksgiving decorations throughout our neighborhood. And did I mention that it's eighty-three degrees outside? So despite my affinity for fall fashion, I don't exactly need a surplus of sweaters and jackets, living where I do. Anyone who's spent much time in South Texas knows we don't really experience all four seasons here. We have summer, which is sporadically interrupted by cold fronts during the "winter" months. The rest of the time, it's pretty damn hot. Someone who prefers cooler climates might find it challenging to stay comfortable. Like me. Then again, someone in South Africa might tell me to shut the hell up.

Getting back to my point, November is when the "cool fronts" finally make it to us, which gives even more cool points for fall, in my book, no pun intended. Cold-weather cooking is another favorite of mine and I can't wait to get to it! Pot roast with mashed potatoes, chili and cornbread, beef vegetable stew with crusty artisan bread. Good Goddess, I could go on and on.

What I'm getting at is, fall is here and I'm not upset about it.

Thanksgiving is right around the corner, and it happened to be the topic of conversation at the dinner table this evening: discussing holiday details, school programs and that sort of thing. With all this talk about Thanksgiving, it inspired me to ask my family what they're thankful for this season. We each took turns sharing our thoughts of gratitude, beginning with Tyler.

He was thankful for "Sports Center" and to have found the iTouch he falsely accused his brother of stealing, which he then apologized for. Sweet kid. Next was Ryan; wearing his filthy Halloween costume that he refuses to let me wash, he was thankful for lunch and to have the honor of being the REAL Batman. Quote: I'm thankful that I got to eat lunch today and that I'm the real Batman. End quote. Zoe was thankful for chocolate milk, although it's completely possible she confused "Sweetie, what are you thankful for?" with "Sweetie, what do you want to drink?" Then it was Shawn's turn. He was thankful for his healthy family, his job, his home and bacon.

After they each had their turn, everyone but Zoe looked at me, as if waiting to hear my answer. I sat there thinking, going through the list in my head of everything I'm grateful for. I had to smile. I realized I have so many blessings, I didn't know which one to choose.

So I decided to go with, "I'm thankful that I have *so many* things to be thankful for. I can't even decide which one to talk about!"

My kids, unfazed, nodded then switched their focus back to dinner. Shawn shook his head, "Nice, Topper."

Despite the newfound competition between Shawn and me over who's more thankful in life (which we both CLEARLY know is me), this evening really did give new insight into what I've learned up to this point. I think it's awesome. The more awareness I introduce into my daily life, the more joy I find. I guess I'm thankful for that, too.

Now I'm off to go wrestle Ryan out of his Batman costume. Sweet baby Jesus, that thing smells like a wet dog. *gag*

11/13/10

Lunch with the hens today. I'll write about it later. I'm nervous.

· · ·

So, I totally told them about my workbook. Yes, Casey gave me shit, but I expected that. I flipped her off and kept talking. Blair and Marissa both looked really intrigued, the rest of them listened, but at least they listened without rolling eyes or shooting each other glances.

"So *that's* what's been going on with you? We've all noticed you seem different lately. We figured you got back on Wellbutrin," Marissa admitted. "Why didn't you tell us about this in the beginning? We could've done it as a group!" They all chimed in to agree.

I felt guilty for assuming they wouldn't understand, and at that point I realized how great it would've been to be able to have four other women to take this journey with. I don't know if they all will go out and buy this book, but I can guarantee Blair will.

"Goddess, huh? That sounds sexy." God love 'er.

Oh, and by the way, her divorce will be final by the first of the year. Pete's devastated and furious. Blair's ecstatic. Shawn and I are Switzerland.

11/14/10

After yoga this morning, I decided to meditate on my Inner Goddess, my True Self the author keeps referring to. All of the love, joy, peace and energy living within me, I pictured it swirling around in my belly like a light show. With every inhalation, I imagined it growing bigger and brighter, filling more space. With every exhalation, I brought that light closer to my heart. After a few moments, I felt as though my whole body was glowing, humming like a high voltage current.

I don't know how long I was sitting there, but it was long enough to experience the sensation of weightlessness. I know it sounds cheesy, but that's the only word I know to describe it. I literally felt like I was floating.

When I opened my eyes, to my surprise, Shawn was standing in the doorway, watching me and grinning.

He said, "I don't know where you were, but it must've been pretty great because you've got the biggest smile on your face."

For the first time since my daughter was born, I cried because I was happy. With an overabundance of gratitude, I think I'm ready to move on to Lesson Ten.

Thanks, Lesson Nine…

LESSON 10

Goddess Essence

Part I: The Body Temple

What is your relationship with your body temple? Is she your friend or foe? Do you treat her like the miracle that she is, or is she more like a built-in garbage can? Would you say you really *know* your body, or is she a stranger to you?

In the first part of Lesson Ten, I ask you to examine this relationship with great detail. However, I want you to change the context. Instead of viewing your body as simply that, consider your temple to be a different entity altogether—a person sitting across the table from you, if you will. What would you say to this person if you were able to look her in the eye and express yourself? More interestingly, what would this person say to *you*? This may not sound like much of a challenge, but there are many who are extremely out of touch with their own skin, and what's more, they don't even realize it. You may or may not be one of these mentioned, but it's important for you to know either way.

Because of this, I introduced meditation in the previous lesson in order to loosen you up, so to speak. Think of it as the warm-up before the stretch. If you are able to go within to find stillness, then communicating with your body temple is much easier. Additionally, meditation has amazing healing powers when needed. If you find that your relationship with your body is in a toxic state, meditation can help cultivate your reunion. Your temple is what houses your True Self, your boundless potential, your Goddess Essence. It *must* be honored. If you are living while disconnected to your body, you are not *living* at all; you are merely *existing*. Write about what you experience throughout this lesson and now, more than ever, do not judge. Simply observe, write and move forward. Now would also be a good time to do something nice for your body. Get a manicure, facial, massage, whatever is appropriate for your budget. After all, every goddess needs to be pampered every now and then! *BLESSED BE!*

11/15/10

After the Zen-like high Lesson Nine left me with, I was so hoping Lesson Ten would deal more directly with astral projection or saving baby seals. *UGH* I really don't want to talk about my body. I've been working so hard to get past my obsession with all its imperfections; why would I want to make that my focus now?

I'm going to go color with Zoe; that sounds much more fun. I'll come back later.

• • •

What would I say to my body if it were a person? How about, "Hey, you think you could tell Metabolism to speed shit up?" Or, "Small tits AND love handles? W-T-F?"

What would my body say if it could talk to me? "You're an asshole and I hate when you feed me chili."

• • •

"Hey, knees, I'm only thirty-five, stop acting like I'm eighty."

"Hey, host, don't expect agility after years of sitting on my fat ass."

"Yeah, that's right, your ass IS fat!"

"Actually it's YOUR ass, so you're an idiot!"

"YOU'RE an idiot!"

"Leave me alone or I'll poop myself in the store again."

"Okay, okay...geeze."

Man, my attitude sucks on this one.

• • •

If my above entries have failed to convey the message clearly, I'll take the liberty and speak for them: I've been irritated by this lesson so far. I've given journaling three solid tries throughout the day and can't seem to shake my shady outlook. After thinking about it objectively, I find it interesting that this subject is striking my nerves so much.

I've been doing yoga and meditating, both which require a great deal of "body consciousness." I guess I've been focusing so intently on my new practices, my body issues haven't been at the forefront they way they used to be. That explains why I've been experiencing so much lightness, ironically.

I thought I was exorcising the demons, but obviously I was wrong. Have I only been *suppressing* them? Has Skinnie Cooper been hiding to give me false hope, or what? It's really deflating. I feel like I discovered something I *thought* was fixed is still broken. I'm sure I can expect this lesson to be based on coming to terms with something significant, which is why I'm writhing like a salted slug right now. I'm not stupid. I know something's up and it's making me uneasy.

I have a feeling now is when I'm supposed to put what I've learned to good use instead of falling back into old, familiar patterns, right? I guess I should change direction and come at this from a different angle, but how? Maybe the best way to go about it is to treat these emotions like clouds in the sky? Instead of identifying with the "story," perhaps I should observe it. If that's the case, I can see why the author would've put meditation before this lesson.

Okay, so let's go within. What's going on inside my head right now? What are my anti-goddesses telling me when I think about this exercise, when I think about my body...and accepting it exactly the way it is?

They're telling me the same thing my instinct tells me about base-jumping...

It's not a good idea.

I'm going to do my best to "be" with this one for while. I'll come back tomorrow.

11/16/10

After some soul searching and a good night's sleep, I've decided to embrace the lesson and do exactly what the author instructed. I'm going to treat my body temple to a spa day!

I've got a full mani/pedi combo on the books for tomorrow. Along with that, a full body seaweed wrap, in order to detoxify the body and diminish cellulite. A hot-stone massage, because it's awesome, and since nobody loves having the top layer of her face chemically removed more than this crazy broad right here, I'm having a peel done. Overachievement, thy name is Holly.

After my spa day, I'm going birthday shopping for Tyler, although it shouldn't take long. Money and gift cards are the only things he asks for. He's also mentioned something about "Microsoft points," but I don't know what the hell that is, so he's getting something I actually have the techno-savvy to purchase.

He'll be thirteen and I'm baffled that I'm the soon-to-be mother of a teenager. That whole decision to quit drinking wasn't such a great idea after all.

11/17/10

I'm about to take off for my spa day. What would my body say to me if it could speak? "Gee whiz, Holly, you're the *best* host any body temple could ask for!"

I know, Body...I know...

. . .

Well, I feel like a new woman. Yes, the hot-stone massage was much hotter than I expected and I will probably avoid that particular service on my next spa day. I yelped like a whipped dog when the masseuse put that first piece of flaming coal on my bare back. "Shit, that's hot!" I yelled. I could tell I startled her as much as she startled me. But even though I have a trail of third-degree burns running down my spine, the seaweed wrap was absolutely divine. Of course, I fell asleep on the table and woke myself up with my own snoring, but let's not get into that. My blush pink nails are almost as shiny as my freshly singed face, my feet have been scrubbed of icky dead skin cells, my muscles are all loosey-goosey, and if I didn't know any better, I would say there's at least one, maybe *two* fewer dimples on my ass than before the seaweed wrap. Relationship healed! Let's move on to Lesson Eleven!

11/20/10

Yeah, yeah, yeah, I know. I wish I could say it was worth a try, but that would be ridiculous. This is MY workbook. This is MY journey toward self-improvement. Despite my chicken-shit efforts, I know the only way out of this "self-image" rut is to dig my way out. I realize my attitude toward this lesson isn't improving, and I would venture to say it isn't going to, but I can't keep putting something off because I don't want to deal with the discomfort. On top of that, I know waiting around for my outlook to change all by itself is another distraction.

Clearly I had an A-Ha today, but before I get to it, I have a brief but important story. It may seem like I'm getting off point, but bear with me, it *will* come full circle.

After school today, Tyler was complaining of an ache in his elbow. "It doesn't hurt *super* bad, it's kind of achy and stiff," he said, while flexing his arm in and out.

After some diagnostic questioning, "No spills or athletic injuries?" I narrowed it down to growing pains. When my son asked what he should do about it, I said, "There's nothing we can do, really. You're going through a growth spurt and sometimes that can cause pain, it's part of growing up. You're going to have to grit your teeth and go through it, babe. It'll pass, don't worry."

I tip my hat to Motherhood and all the lessons she offers when needed.

Growing pains... I like that.

That's what I'm experiencing here: growing pains. I have a feeling I walked through a one-way door when I began this process. Sure, I could stave off the progress of my growth, but I don't think I could regress now even if I *wanted* to. It's similar to waking up from a nap. Your thoughts start to come to and you begin to hear the sounds of your surroundings. You may not be ready to get off the couch yet, and you can lay there with your eyes closed as long as you want, but you know there's no way you'll be able to go back to sleep. That feels like a pretty accurate way to describe this.

I could put this lesson off for as long as I want, but doing so will never cover up my knowing it's *still here waiting for me*. I may have been better at suppressing things when I began this book, but that's one of the many things changing about me.

It's late and I need to hit the sack. Ta-ta for now, Lesson Ten.

11/22/10

With a fresh perspective on this lesson, I thought I would take an unexpected approach.

I love magazines, but for "unhealthy" reasons. They usually entrench me in daydreams about "what it would be like to have this and that." The worst of all of these for me are fitness magazines. Dear lord, I subscribe to *at least* four health and fitness magazines. From homeopathic living to bodybuilding, I get them all.

Over my morning tea, I was inspired to pick up this month's issue of *Oxygen*, which never fails to deliver in the "*amazing* body" department. This one is usually a fantastic tool for self-loathing, but not today. Instead of beating myself up, ogling and coveting, I *admired*. The amount of work and dedication it takes to achieve what these women have achieved is unbelievable.

I asked myself, "What's the difference between their desire and mine?"

Surely their hard work began with a goal or a dream, like me. Other than their follow through and my *complete* lack thereof, what separated the similarity of what we wanted?

I don't know where it came from, but while pondering this question I suddenly thought to myself, *They probably don't hate their bodies.* And then it hit me. Maybe some of the women in this industry are motivated by *love*. In my case, I spent my life hating what I saw and wanting it to be different. Maybe they were *inspired* by what they saw and used that inspiration to push themselves to the next level. I doubt Ms. Universe earned her title from despising her body.

It makes sense. I want to love my body, but that can't be accomplished when such a desire is coming from a place of dislike. What I'm saying is I can't *hate* my body into a shape I love. If I wanted my kids to feel more accepted, would I continuously harp on their faults and tell them they have to change before I can love them? Of course not. That would be incredibly counterproductive, not to mention mean. What's the difference between that analogy and what I've been doing to myself for years? Not much.

So what would my body say if she could look me in the eye and speak to me? She would say, "Stop being such a bully. You would get what you want if you treated me better."

Touché.

11/23/10

HAPPY BIRTHDAY TYLER! *sob*

11/24/10

With tomorrow being Thanksgiving, on the eve of this great holiday, I decided to honor both the day itself and this lesson.

I would like to entitle this entry, *Ode to My Temple*. I tried to come up with something quippy that rhymed, but after fifteen minutes, I gave up and went with a title that sounded "deep."

Ode to My Temple

To my bodily functions, you mystify me. In fact, I don't even know all of your names or how many of you there are, hence the reason I lumped all of you into one unit to thank as a whole. I don't know how you do it, but you keep me fueled, breathing, moving and feeling. Don't mistake my lack of savvy for lack of gratitude; I don't know what I would do without you…other than die, of course.

Toes, you are my balance, and since I'm a Libra (new zodiac be damned), balance is very important to me. Thank you for keeping me straight and upright. Warrior Three pose would be impossible without you.

Feet, you take me where I need to go and never ask questions. I've heard your complaints and I'm sorry for the four-inch heels. I promise to wear more reasonable shoes in the future. Thank you for your hard work.

Legs, my dancers, my runners, my most abused. You bring fun to life, even when I talk to you so badly. I'm so sorry for the way I've treated you and the awful things I've said in the past. You are strong and beautiful and I thank you so much for everything you do.

BOOTY! Girl, you know I love you, don't stop SHAKING IT! *HIGH FIVE*

Belly, you sheltered my babies. I am *forever* in your debt.

To my breasts, providers of nourishment, I thank you and so would my children if it weren't weird for them to speak to you directly. Also, you ladies are the gateway to any sexual friskiness I might encounter, so my *husband* thanks you, too.

Shoulders, back and arms, I thank all of you as one because you're a team and work better together than ranch dressing works with, well, anything it's paired with, really. Thank you for your grace and for carrying the load every day.

Oh, hands, my creators. Whether it's making bread, writing a grocery list or running fingers through my daughter's hair, you allow me to craft and experience great things. Much of God's work flows through you. Thank you for being so receptive.

Neck, you've got some pretty vital stuff going on in there. *And* you are the hanger for necklaces and other great accessories, so thank you.

Head, even though your hair doesn't always cooperate and I sometimes question your contents, I know that what you're housing is a miracle. Thanks for keeping my noodle safe and for all those sporadic good hair days.

To my eyes, oh, where do I begin? My gratitude for you is unparalleled. If I had to save one sense and give up the other four, I would save the one that belongs to you. You are my window to the world and are truly a gift every day. Thank you.

Dear nose, don't take offense to what I said to eyes, because you're very important and as cute as a button, too. Your sense is bonded with nostalgia, more so than any other. A single whiff of a scent transports me to another time and place. Even when that time or place isn't one I want to visit, I still appreciate your undeniable power. I'll bake you some brownies to smell someday soon.

Then my mouth will get to *eat* those brownies 'cause mama loves her sweets! Mouth, I won't pretend that you're always my ally. You sometimes get me into trouble with the rubbish you put out, but that's more my fault than yours. I need to think before I tell you what to say. You allow me to taste, communicate, partake in karaoke, and most of all, you express my laughter. That's pretty awesome.

Ears, my iPod would be *useless* without you. And if I could no longer hear my kids laugh, that would be a tragic day, indeed. You keep me entertained and have probably saved my life at one point or another; I wouldn't know it because you get taken for granted a lot. Thank you for your contribution to my well-being.

New Daily Affirmation:
I am thankful for my body.
She is perfect,
She is loved,
And she is wise.

Happy Thanksgiving, Goddess.

LESSON 10

Goddess Essence

Part II: Your Goddess Center

The second part of Lesson Ten is of crucial importance. I trust you and your body temple are in a state of unity, allowing you to go deeper within. Over the millennia past, your Goddess Center has been turned into and considered a taboo. The message has been passed down through the ages that this miraculous center of power should be hidden, quieted and used as a tool for procreation and nothing more. You might have guessed by now the miracle to which I refer. Yes, sister, your Goddess Center is your vagina.

In Part I of this lesson, I had you examine, and if need be, repair your relationship with your body temple. In Part II, I ask you to go to the powerhouse of your body temple, the center of your miracle. Do you take care of your vagina and honor her power? Do you have a relationship with her, or does the mere thought of discussing her make you uncomfortable? Do you know what she looks like? Whether you answered "no" or "yes" to these questions, I want you to focus on this relationship and write about it. Look at her in the mirror and pretend she's a person, talk to her. What emotions come to the surface during all of this? Observe, write and be open. If you find the relationship between the two of you is strained, I request you work toward fixing it through journaling, meditation and deep reflection.

If you have suffered abuse of any kind, along with the therapeutic methods mentioned, I strongly urge you to seek professional help, if you haven't already. I want to reiterate the *extreme* importance of this bond, for it is the bond to your womanhood that is the foundation of your strength as a woman and as a goddess. There can be no flight if the bird feels separate from its wings. How can a goddess shine if she is detached from her light? Breathe deep, go within, and find peace... *BLESSED BE!*

11/26/10

Yikes. Well, I'd be lying if I said that I'm completely comfortable talking about my girl down there.

God knows what neurosis is due to my pretense that she's less of a body part and more like an accessory. When I need her, I pull her out, and when I'm done, I put her away. Other than that, she doesn't get a second thought from me.

So, if I had to describe my relationship with her, I'd have to say I don't have one. In fact, I don't even use the word "vagina" unless I'm using it in a derogatory manner.

Example: "Shawn, you are being a giant vagina."

Anyway, the subject, when taken in a serious manner, pretty much makes me want to, well, change the subject.

I'll take the rest of the day to ponder the state of separation between my "goddess center" and me. If I had to try and come up with an explanation for why I choose to ignore my privates, all I would get is a shoulder shrug.

11/30/10

I'm having a hard time. I did the whole "inspect myself in the mirror" routine and the word "uncomfortable" doesn't *begin* to do justice for what I was feeling.

I locked my bedroom door (after Zoe went down for a nap), peeled off the layers of clothing and just as I *oh so* reluctantly assumed the most awkward standing position EVER, the phone rang. Startled and exposed, I quickly answered as if to exclaim, "WHAT? I wasn't doing anything but standing here!" I didn't know what emotion was more prominent, the need to defend what I was doing or the guilt I felt at the thought of "getting caught."

At any rate, I found the whole ordeal to be very unpleasant. First and foremost, my girlfriend down there ain't pretty. After a few brief moments of inspection, I glanced up with a "gross" face, as if my own reflection in the mirror was some kind of corroborating witness.

You're right, she's ugly.

I felt incredibly vulnerable. It was the longest two and a half minutes of my life, and every passing second felt like an eternity. A lot like how I feel when I go to the OB-GYN, minus the florescent lights and probing.

The sight of my nakedness was so unappealing, I couldn't get dressed fast enough. *Just cover it up.* If not for this workbook, I most likely would move on, vowing to continue to disregard the privates, *along* with making sure the lights stay off during those intimate moments with Shawn.

However, a large part of this lesson is to reflect on the emotions that arise while examining my "vaginal relationship." Considering the marginal success of Part 1, and for the sake of following directions, I suppose I should ask myself some questions.

Such as:

–Why is the subject of my vuh-jay-jay so unnerving to me?

–Does this have anything to do with my sexual frigidity? Of course it does. That was a stupid question.

–Am I uncomfortable with looking at her because I think she's ugly?

–Why does her "ugliness" bother me?

—Does the way I view my vagina affect my body image, and is there a connection between the two?

—How does my poor self-image in terms of my "goddess center" affect my confidence all around?

—Why would I experience a sense of guilt and violation when looking at my *own* vagina in complete privacy? (That one's throwing me for a loop, I have to say.)

—What is my motivation for keeping her "separate" from me?

—Am I shielding myself from negativity I associate with her?

Maybe THAT'S the real question: What negativity do I associate with her and why?

• • •

It never fails to amaze me how asking one question can produce a whole laundry list of other questions, each one deeper than the one before it. I'm going to process this before I even attempt to come up with any answers. I guess I didn't see this coming.

12/5/10

I'm still not feeling "connected" to this lesson, but that shouldn't surprise me in any way. I've read over my list of questions a thousand times, but my "emotional dig" is coming up without results. It's frustrating because I feel I've done really well in most of the preceding lessons. Suddenly, things got so hard when it became all about my body. Why?

On a positive note, and I'd LOVE to change the subject, I had a yoga instructor approach me today about getting certified to teach at the studio. She told me I've come a long way in my practice in a relatively short amount of time, and that I should consider leading a class. It made me feel really good! I'm not interested, but it made me feel good!

12/7/10

I had the most obscure sex dream EVER last night. It's about five-thirty in the morning and I want to write it down before I go through my asanas because I know I won't remember all of it later.

So there I am in high school, and it's the first day back after summer break. First and foremost, I hate my outfit, of course, so I already feel embarrassed, out of place and can't stop asking myself, "Why in the hell did I wear this?" Denim overalls and a polo shirt? Dude. I'm aimlessly wandering the halls of my school and I remember it smelling like Band-Aids. My high school in Pasadena smelled like that, too. So weird. Anyway, kids are buzzing, lockers are slamming and the tardy bell starts screaming at me to get moving. I know I'm late for class but I don't know my schedule, and I don't know who to get it from, even though I could've sworn I knew it earlier. There's some of it I don't remember, and then all of a sudden I'm in some kind of seedy bedroom/bar. The lighting is red and really dim, almost like a darkroom used for photo development. I look around in confusion, and suddenly realize I'm being hit on by some faceless man. I remember feeling really awkward and turned off by the smell of ashtrays, but strangely turned on by him. There was some touching and kissing. I didn't want him to stop, I know. But then I'm back in the halls of my school again, except this time I'm naked and no one will talk to me. I was thinking, *I'm naked and no one is even looking at me and oh yeah, WHY AM I NAKED???* I kept trying to hide and there was no place to go. The dream moved on to something else and that was it.

With the "vagina lesson" on my mind, this dream seems obvious enough for my dog to interpret. Then again, dreams are incredibly ambiguous; it probably signifies my recent craving for French fries.

12/14/10

I met Blair for lunch and finished all the Christmas shopping with eleven days to spare. I think I earned some cashmere gloves! Not that I need cashmere ANYTHING in southern Texas, but I can wear them around the house and pretend it's colder than sixty-four degrees outside.

All of my family in California is coming to stay with us for Christmas, and on my fourth conversation with Libby today, we finalized all the details of their visit. And when I say "details," I mean menu items and grocery lists. I swear we could talk for an hour about Q-tips.

"So I was thinking we could do a breakfast casserole for Christmas morning, that's always good for a crowd. Oh my gosh, did I tell you about that recipe I saw for breakfast bread pudding?"

"You know, Libby, a bread pudding recipe does seem familiar."

"Well, I'll tell you about it again because its sounds absolutely phenomenal! We should totally try it while I'm there."

After we finished lusting over custard-soaked brioche, we talked about the status of my Inner Goddess. Libby told me she can tell a difference in my tone lately.

"I've been meaning to tell you that, Holly. You seem lighter, and you don't say 'fuck' as much."

"Really?" I wasn't so concerned with that. 'Fuck' happens to be one of my favorite words. "Well, I know I feel different," I went on. "I'm really enjoying it, Libby." I told her she needs to give this book a try and she gave me a "yeah, yeah, yeah." Anyway, I'm so excited my whole family is coming to stay with us. It's been over two years since they've all been here. And with Katy, my baby sister, being home from Spain on winter break, she'll be here, too. There's definitely a jingle in my step today!

12/19/10

I know I keep dancing around this lesson, but I haven't been ready to sit down with it yet.

I've called Libby and talked to her about it. I had lunch with the girls yesterday and talked to *them* about it. I even talked to Shawn about it. I'd be lying if I said it hasn't been on my mind nonstop. I can't seem to get past asking the same questions over and over. I know this is important, and I want to do it right, but I can say with all certainty, this is the hardest lesson yet. Part 1 was nothing compared to this, and I find it irritating.

It's my own mind, my own body, my own nether-region. What's the effing problem?! Is it that I genuinely don't know the answers to my own questions, or have I suppressed them so deeply over the years that the resolution can't be seen? Does my comfort zone HAVE to be an impenetrable fortress? Why can't it be something simple like a Red Rover line?

"Red Rover, Red Rover, let Holly's issues with her vagina come over." It would be so much easier. *deep breath*

I know, Goddess, trust and be patient. You're right, you're right, I *know* you're right.

12/21/10

Christmas is in a few days and with my family coming in tomorrow night, I'm not sure I'll be able to write much. Everyone and their dog will be here, except not literally. They know better than to bring their dogs to my house.

Living states away from them makes it really hard to visit as often as we'd like, so I'm really excited and looking forward to their arrival. Also, my family loves a good party, so when a bottle of champagne gets popped at nine-thirty Christmas morning, there are no judgments. There's a collective "WHO-HOO!" Gee, I wonder where I got that from.

Moving on, I'm also really looking forward to sharing this workbook with my mom and sisters. Libby already knows about it, and I think she's close to buying in, but Katy hasn't been filled in yet. Not that I plan on sporting a turtleneck and reading it to them by the fireplace, but sharing my experiences and what I've learned would be cool. Being as close as we are, I know they'll be able to appreciate the lessons, and maybe be inspired to do some "digging" of their own.

12/22/10

Well, there was a shift today.

I went to the city to pick up some last minute items for the arrival of my family tonight. Afterwards, I crashed a hot yoga class because I had extra time. I'll skip over messing around with a clever prelude; I'm going to dive in.

During class, I started crying right in the middle of my full wheel pose. I don't know why. On one inhalation I was fine and on my next exhalation, the tears welled up and I couldn't rein them in. I took myself into child's pose so I could cover my face, hoping to regain control of myself and rejoin the rest of the class. That didn't happen. I stayed there for the remainder of the session, embarrassed and silently sobbing.

As soon as the class was over, I collected my stuff and my pride with every intention to escape from the studio as quickly as possible. With my head down, I went to my designated cubby, grabbed my shoes and my purse and made a break for the front door. Before I could flee, I made the mistake of looking up, catching the nonjudgmental gaze of Lindy, my instructor. She smiled and waved me over to the front desk where she stood, greeting students arriving for the next class. I wondered if it would be rude to pretend I mistook her summon for a wave goodbye. I figured it would be, so I obliged and walked over to her.

Before she could say a word, I began to apologize for my neurotic behavior during her class. As she took me aside, she shook her head and said, "It's very common to experience emotions during certain asanas. The body holds memories in its cells, did you know that?" I shook my head.

"Yes," she continued. "It holds on to old injuries, old trauma, emotions and karma. This practice can help you to discharge that resonant pain."

She went on to tell me to be grateful for such a powerful release, and to let go of each moment as it passes so I can be open to the gift of the present. I started crying again, and despite my sweatiness, she hugged me. Then she said something so profound yet so simple, I'm still in awe.

She said, "My guru says we have to be grateful for pain and suffering. They are our teachers. They show us what areas of our lives need work."

It made so much sense, so I cried some more.

I cried the whole way home, thinking about what she said. *Suffering is my teacher. If I pay attention to it instead of trying to numb it out, maybe it can lead me to its root.* I soon realized I was crying tears of relief, even though I wasn't completely sure why. When I got home with this in mind, I decided to revisit my goddess center and her reflection. I don't need to answer all of the questions I asked the other day. They're only a diversion from seeing what's in front of me now.

I feel I should acknowledge mistakes made in my past. While I don't want to relive them, I sense the need to bring them to the surface, because my buried shame of those mistakes is manifesting itself in other problematic ways. Namely, I don't feel comfortable in my own skin most of the time, I would rather pretend to sleep than make love to my husband, I'm emotionally agoraphobic, and I long for powerful perfection on the surface because deep down I feel so insignificant. And broken.

To my Goddess Center,

I am so sorry.

I'm sorry that, in the past, I didn't honor how sacred you are, and I'm sorry I didn't respect you. I gave you away so easily to so many, at such a young and formative age. I didn't know what I was doing. I was ignorant, and lost, and I looked for validation in the wrong places—even when I knew my actions were causing me pain. My guilt and shame of those actions turned into apathy then negligence... I continued to get darker until there was no light left for you, as was my plan. If I couldn't see you, then you weren't there, and neither were the fears, disappointment and sense of abandonment I associated with you. I didn't know my denying you would create the monster that lives in me now. I recognize that in order to be the woman I want to be, I have to rebuild from the foundation, and I have to begin with you.

I no longer bind you to the shame of the past mistakes I've pretended to forget. I appreciate your miracle. I take responsibility and apologize for the pain I have caused our relationship and for the pain our separation has caused others. I free you of your burden and greatly anticipate the freedom that will eventually come to me through embracing the death of my past with each new moment.

Thank you.

Namaste.

12/23/10

This is going to be quick because I've got hungry kids waiting for pancakes in the kitchen, but dude, everyone raved over the changes they could see in me when they got here last night!

"Holly, look at you! Fourteen pounds? You were being modest!" my mother exclaimed, as she yanked on the waistband of my jeans.

Then my dad chimed in. "Don't go getting carried away with that weight loss, baby. You look like you could use a hamburger or something."

Is it wrong that I took his comment as more of a compliment than my mom's? I'll blame that on society and move on. Pancakes for everyone!

12/24/10

I love Christmas Eve, I really do. But God bless America, must the children ask what time it is every twelve minutes? I know they're anticipating Santa's arrival and all, but come on!

"Mom, what time is it?"

"Twelve minutes past the last time you asked me, Ryan."

"Okay...so what time is it then?"

eye roll Other than that, it's been a good day. I'm having a great time with my family, although I will admit, it's been hard not drinking. Right after lunch today, Libby popped open the bottle of Maker's Mark with bouncing eyebrows. The ice cubes clinked around in her highball glass as she brought it to her ear, giving it a shake.

"Mmm, I love that sound," she said. "It's like my own version of *Jingle Bells.*"

"Oh, Libby, drinking so early?" Mom feigned disapproval as she cracked open a can of soda in preparation to make a drink of her own.

"I'm celebrating the birth of our lord and savior, Mother. I see no reason to judge."

"You know that handbasket you're going to hell in matches your shoes perfectly, darling." I watched them toast to the holiday with jealousy, I have to admit. Whiskey doesn't sound all that good...but I wouldn't be mad at a glass of wine. Maybe I'll have some with pizza tonight. One glass wouldn't hurt anything...right?

12/25/10

It's Christmas Day and I watched my kids open more presents than any Wal-Mart could hold. "I think we may have overdone it," Shawn whispered to me, like he has every Christmas since we began having kids. "It's those damn dollar bins, they get us every year."

It's been a magnificent morning: great family, great breakfast, great coffee, great gifts and great children.

The sky is clear and the weather is cold, my favorite. The kids are playing with their cousins outside on the play set. Shawn's rustling, crunching and tearing his way through the bomb of wrapping paper that exploded during the gift exchange, as my dad snores through the clean up on the couch. My mom and sisters are in the kitchen prepping for lunch, and my whole house smells like heaven. Roasted root vegetables with maple syrup and sage, crown rib roast, hazelnut dressing, every dessert imaginable, and the best part of all, my Mom's sweet potato casserole. It's the most decadent dish in the history of fattening food, I swear! Her secret touch to the recipe? Butter. Then she adds a few bites of sweet potato and tops it off with brown sugar, pecans and more butter to cut the heaviness of the butter. God bless her cooking.

I sipped on a glass of wine with my pizza last night and found that after one serving, I was genuinely done. No need to worry about slipping back into old habits. I think I'm mature enough to be able to *experience* wine instead of mindlessly guzzling it, so I'm going to celebrate that with a gorgeous '06 Rubicon Estate that Libby brought from Napa, bless her heart. It's leathery and robust and has been a long-standing favorite of mine.

"Oh, are you drinking again?" she joked. "Hell, if I'd known that I would've brought something I'm actually *willing* to share." It's breathing in my kitchen at this very moment and the both of us are salivating.

My family is staying through New Year's, so I won't be writing while they're here. I'm sure come New Year's Day, I'll be ready to drive them to the airport, but for now, I'm as giddy as can be. In fact, if I continue to list everything that makes me giddy right now, I'll be writing until tomorrow brings me more things to be giddy about. I thought my gratitude for all this happiness was worthy of an entry.

My life is beautiful and so is this day. I'm declaring it. Merry Christmas, Goddess. See you next year!

PART 3

Personal Growth

Congratulations on a job well done, sister! You have made it to the third and final section of this workbook. Give yourself a moment and take in what you've done! It is with great honor and excitement that I bring the next series of lessons to you, because this is where the FUN comes in! In Parts 1 and 2, we dealt with spiritual blockages as well as the physical. You were asked to dig deep within yourself. Your being here right now speaks to your success. You could say we've gone through the "breaking down" phase, now we're ready to start rebuilding! The lessons ahead are all about personal growth, learning new things, *giving back*, stretching yourself *beyond* that comfort zone. You have cleared the path for your Inner Goddess, now let's invite her to emerge and watch her grow!

LESSON 11

A Day for Ritual

What a fun lesson this is going to be! Sister, in Lesson Eleven, you will begin to learn how to nurture the growth of your Inner Goddess. You might be wondering, "Isn't this what I've been doing?" Yes, of course it is, but in a different way. The preceding sections served as a tool to clear the air, so to speak. Where previously your True Self may have been overshadowed by emotional blockages, there is now clarity, allowing the Light inside of you to shine like a beacon. The lessons that led you here helped to nurture the spiritual "spring cleaning" you undertook. Now, after digging deep down and out the other side, we embark on a new path, with a fresh take.

And so, with excitement, we begin Lesson Eleven, the weekly goddess ritual. Times are busy, as we all know. Many of us hardly have time to eat real food that isn't served out of a window, much less remember to stop and smell the roses. Sadly, it isn't just the roses being forgotten. Between the insanity and rush of everyday life, we no longer take time to pay tribute to the power within us, to honor our connection to our Source. This is why I designed this lesson.

Your weekly goddess ritual is specifically for celebrating your Essence, to acknowledge your power and connect with it. You can get as creative with this as you like! You may choose to change it up from week to week, or you may be more of a traditionalist, sticking to one ritual only. You might choose to meditate on your Spirit with special music and incense. You may feel drawn to setting up an altar with particular objects that make you feel connected to your Inner Goddess. You might commit to having a date with yourself once a week to anywhere of your choosing. There is no right or wrong way to do it! As long as it's special and you feel centered, powerful, and renewed, your method is spot on! My only suggestion is that you remain as consistent as possible on the day of the week you choose for your ritual, such as every Saturday or every Tuesday—this way you're more likely to stick with it. You may know right away how you want to go about performing this lesson. Then again, you might not have a clue what to do. No worries! Start the process by choosing your ritual day, taking the next step from there. Just be still for a moment and you'll be guided toward your next move, I assure you.

Once you have selected your method, as always, I ask you to write about your decision and your motivation behind it. Additionally, continue to journal often about your journey and any special occurrences you might experience during your ritual, along with any changes you may encounter associated with your newly adopted habit. Connect with your power, my sister. Connect and you will never feel lost again…

Move on to Lesson Twelve when guided to do so. *BLESSED BE!*

1/3/11

What an appropriate way to begin the New Year! For the first time in no less than eight years, I wasn't hung over on New Year's Day, I went for a five-mile run on the treadmill at sunrise, I finally have reclaimed my house from my parents and siblings and I'm beginning a new chapter of self-discovery. I'd say 2011 is off to a fantastic start!

I really like the idea of a goddess ritual. Having a distraction-free evening during the week that's just for me sounds fantastic, which goes without saying. I have three kids and sometimes those three seem more like twelve. I've come a long way from where I began, but I won't delude myself. My beloved children drive me freaking nuts sometimes and I only say "sometimes" to alleviate the guilt from the fact that they drive me nuts more often than sometimes.

I know Sunday is going to be the best day for my ritual. Shawn's typically home on Sundays, and between yard work, hanging out with the kids, and the afternoon football game on TV, he stays pretty busy. I guess I could say he has his own ritual. With the house being quiet most of the day, it's the perfect time to capitalize on practicing this lesson.

I'm not sure what I want to do yet, but today is only Monday. I have all week to come up with something wicked cool for my Super Powerful Happy Goddess Fun Time. I'm going to start calling it that because I figure anything that sounds like a Japanese game show HAS to be awesome.

1/5/11

Should I perform a special meditation? Or maybe cook a nice meal? Neither of those things resonates with me. I don't know. I'll keep working on it.

1/7/11

I haven't come up with anything for my ritual yet; it's been a busy week. But I'm not worried about it, I'm sure something will come to me.

1/9/11

I swear I'd just gotten used to writing 2010. I should get used to writing 2011 in time for the world's end in 2012. It's truly scary; time seems to be speeding up with every passing moment. In fact, Sunday's here and I still haven't decided what to do for my goddess ritual!

I've hardly written all week and I'm feeling guilty for it, kind of like when I keep forgetting to call a friend back. I'll tell myself, "Crap! I need to call them tomorrow," only to repeat the same thought when tomorrow rolls around and I forget to call them AGAIN. Could it be that I'm as crappy a friend to myself as I am to everyone else? Probably. Oh well, that's another workbook.

Back to the matter-at-hand. As previously mentioned, I have yet to figure out what to do for my ritual. Since I have nothing planned, I think what I'll do is take a nice bubble bath this evening while the family is watching the football game and dedicate that time to plan my future rituals.

And it would be nice to actually bathe in my bathtub for once. It's this gorgeous claw foot style tub and the only one who uses it is Zoe.

She points to it and says, "It's MY bobble baff tub."

I always correct her and say, "No, it's Mommy and Daddy's."

But who am I kidding, really? It wasn't *my* idea to decorate the tub with stickers of *SpongeBob*. She's right, it's totally her tub.

I'll be back tomorrow to write about what I come up with.

1/10/11

In the bathtub last night, with my messy chignon, citrus-scented bath salts, dim lights and moderately sized glass of Shiraz, I realized I was only a Kenny G hit away from the most cliché of all "female relaxation scenarios." And I know WHY this cliché exists. Because bubble baths are EFFING awesome, that's why.

I don't know what was better: the silence, the warm and fuzzy buzz from drinking red wine while submerged in REALLY hot water, the silence, the scent of the salts, the silence or the silence. The whole thing felt like an *event*; from pouring the wine, drawing the water, sprinkling the salts and listening to them fizz, all the way to getting out and wrapping up in my super thick terry cloth robe. I felt pampered and renewed when I was done. THIS will be my weekly ritual, my Super Powerful Happy Goddess Fun Time.

I'm going to go all out: bath salts from the Dead Sea, aromatherapy bubbles, candles, fresh flowers, special music...probably not Kenny G...but something sensual, hypnotic, ethereal.

I may not always go for the wine, seeing as I was practically drunk by the time I got out of the tub, something I haven't experienced in several months, I'm proud to say. Maybe instead of wine, I'll go with some chamomile and a joint.

Oh my Goddess, if I could pull it off, that would be SO awesome! Talk about a relaxing bath! Of course, with MY luck I'd set the smoke alarm off at ear-bleeding volumes. The whole family would rush in only to discover no fire and a VERY startled mommy whose mellow high went to shit. I don't know if Shawn would be upset that I brought an illegal substance into our home or pissed at my inability to pass the Dutchie on the left-hand side. I'll revisit this possibility at a later time. For now, it's best if Mary Jane and I bathe separately.

Back to the ritual, I could even go as far as getting new pajamas to help extend "the mood" beyond bath time. I always feel special when I wear matching PJs, and I never do anymore. I've gotten so used to my oversized t-shirt and sweats that it might be nice to break up the monotony of the dowdy sleepwear I've grown so accustomed to.

I'm so excited about this, I can't wait for next Sunday!

1/12/11

HAPPY BIRTHDAY Ryan!

This Saturday we're having his birthday party at one of those inflatable play yards in the city. It couldn't be more ideal. We show up, play for an hour, open presents and have cake for an hour and leave. The employees do the set up and clean up. I will never host another party for anything at my house *ever* again.

Sure, our friends might wonder why we're having our next get-together at a children's play park, but if I'm okay with a playground full of oversized inflatable Jungle Gyms, they should be too.

1/13/11

I got to thinking about my ritual bath this morning and I remembered the herbalist shop where I bought that stupid fruit cleanse had a decent selection of organic bath essentials: oils, salts, soaps, lotions and more products whose purpose was a mystery to me.

I was hesitant to return to the shop out of fear I might deck the woman who sold me the "Really Gentle Ass Blow" herbs, but I don't have many health stores in my town. I wanted some more unusual bath ingredients to make my weekly ritual feel more earthy and goddess-like. At the same time, I didn't want to have to wait two weeks for shipping from some online boutique. Against my better judgment, I decided to go back and hope I was lucky enough for the quirky herbalist to have forgotten me. No dice.

"Oh, hi there, long time no see!" She said with the kind of excitement you'd expect from someone who owns a shop with few patrons. "How did the colon cleanse work out?"

I opened my mouth to say, "Fine, thank you." But at that very moment, I'm pretty sure I encountered my very first out of body experience. It was strange. The clock slowed, I stepped outside of myself, turned and as time began to pick back up again, I heard myself say...

"I shit my pants in the grocery store."

OH-MY-GOD.

Wide eyed, we both stood there stunned by what had been voiced in her peaceful haven for holistic wellness. It was, quite possibly, the most awkward silence I have ever had the displeasure of experiencing. I searched for an icebreaker.

"Bath salts?"

Brilliant, well played.

She said, "Yes...um, over there," as she raised her arm to point me in the right direction, avoiding having to say, "Next to the colon cleanse."

I don't even know what I bought. I shoveled whatever looked "pretty" into my basket so I could get the hell out of there with as little interaction as possible with anyone else. I wish I could say I had too much pride to turn around and leave, but since I told this woman I "shit my pants," I couldn't really claim to have a great deal of pride at that moment. But the real humiliation came during my check out.

"I'm taking ten percent off your purchase since the herbs gave you so much trouble. Can you tell me about your experience?"

I'm sure she's totally mature enough to talk about explosive diarrhea to any and all strangers, but I'm not. This was the part where, if I could've crawled outside of my own skin and run away, I would've totally done it. What was I supposed to say?

"My experience was emotionally scarring and you can stick that discount up 10% of your ass. And P.S. look up the definition of 'gentle.'" Not so much.

I thanked her, told her everything was fine and moved ever so swiftly out the door.

The two-week long shipping delay would've been worth it. Thank the lord for online shopping.

1/16/11

Happy Super Powerful Happy Goddess Fun Time Day!

I'm so pumped Sunday is here! I've already decided to make a special breakfast to honor the event: my high-protein "Green Goddess" smoothie, SO delicious.

The hubs is taking the boys out to do "boy stuff" for the duration of daylight, and Zoe and I are going to paint our toenails, watch princess movies and bake cookies (peppered with some housework, a few loads of laundry and a walk).

I've looked forward to this day all week long, which is funny because I used to DREAD Sundays. Before, Sunday always meant Monday was only a matter of rapidly passing hours away. The only thing I hated more than Sunday was Monday, because Monday signified the beginning of another tedious week of school or work, neither of which has EVER agreed with me.

Even since I've been a stay-at-home mom, Sundays have implied the "end" of something: the weekend, a great vacation, a big party the night before. I can see the practice of a weekly ritual turning "the ominous end" into "a joyous beginning," the birth of a new week instead of the death of a Saturday. Good stuff.

For tonight's bath, I'll be using some of my newly purchased oils and salts, along with a few candles and an album of classical cello I downloaded. I forgot the flowers and new PJs, but it's only my second time, so there's plenty of room for growth. I'll write tomorrow with results!

1/17/11

My goddess ritual was superb last night, as expected. The candles and music set the perfect ambience; and the organic bubble bath was a lovely vanilla-lavender scent that filled my bathroom AND bedroom with a warm and inviting aroma. The whole "master suite" still smells like a spa. I love it.

Sunday, as a whole, was a great day. I ended up with the two youngest kids while the "men" ventured out into the wilderness, but having Ryan join us girls didn't dampen a thing. He's very in touch with his feminine side, despite his draw to NASCAR. And while he wasn't interested in painting his toenails, he didn't object to princess movies and he'll NEVER turn down a cookie, even if it is frosted with pink icing. Notwithstanding a few fights between brother and sister, the day was flawless. I think this lesson is at the top of my "Favorites List."

1/20/11

I went to town today for power yoga and afterward stopped by the mall to look for some new pajamas or "jamamas" as Zoe calls them. I have no intention of correcting her because that's possibly the cutest damn thing I've ever heard.

I bought a couple of really cute soft cotton, cami/pant sets: one zebra print with hot pink polka dot ruffles, the other a shell pink with black lace trim. The second set is more my style, but the zebra set was so tacky and over-the-top, I couldn't refuse. In addition to the jamamas, I got some really cute lounge clothes. I figured I could make the whole day feel special beginning with a great breakfast, a cute and comfy outfit to wear while doing special activities and ending with a decadent bath. My goddess ritual DAY.

I also stopped by a new boutique that sells home décor and luxury toiletries. This shop had some gorgeous soaps, bubbles and these crystal apothecary jars filled with sparkly bath salts and beads. They cost a small fortune, but were so perfect, I had to get them. I also didn't have to deal with a timidly apologetic herbalist, so that was a plus. This Sunday's going to rock the freaking Casbah.

After I finished my errands I met the ladies for lunch.

"D'you ever figure out your vagina situation?"

Yes, Casey, I love your eloquence.

1/23/11

So, as I mentioned the other day, what began as an evening for ritual has turned into an all day event. I love it! In my soft cotton lounge pants, comfortably supportive cami and heavenly cashmere cardigan that flows with elegance as I walk, I feel like royalty.

The weather is a brisk fifty-five outside and not a cloud in the sky. I plan on making a pot of hot tea and bundling up on the porch swing while my kids romp around the play set in the yard.

I bought a large bouquet of tea roses and berry branches yesterday and plan on making a few mini arrangements around my tub for this evening.

Performing my weekly goddess ritual has taught me that I can make every day special; it doesn't have to be a big, ritualistic thing. Having a cup of hot tea after lunch, practicing yoga at sunrise (or at brunch-rise), reading to my children at bedtime; it's simply about gratitude and honor. It's about finding the joy in each of life's little facets, even the ones that are otherwise considered mundane. It's all a matter of perspective, I guess. Each day can be as joyous as you want to make it. Every day can be Super Powerful Happy Goddess Fun Time Day. KUMBAYA.

1/24/11

So maybe there's something to this bath and matching PJs thing. Note to self: When I wear sexy pajamas instead of sweats, I actually *feel* sexier. Good to know.

After my ritual last night, I totally initiated Super Powerful Happy Goddess Fun Time Sex with the hubs. Needless to say, it's been a while since *I've* initiated *anything*, especially right before my period. Typically around this time of the month I feel totally justified in avoiding sex at all costs, but something feels different. I think the vagina lesson caused a shift in me, I really do. Just like I asked what was behind my food cravings in the fear lesson, I have found myself asking what's behind my abstinence. *Am I genuinely tired or am I avoiding intimacy with Shawn?* More times than not, I recognize it has more to do with my issues with control and vulnerability than anything else. The good news is, the more and more secure I become with myself, the more secure I become with Shawn. Last night I felt sexy and I wanted to share that with him. It was almost like a gift. *"Hey, I have something I want to give you...ME."* A new concept, I can tell you.

Shawn looked pleasantly surprised as he watched me crawl across the bed toward him with a certain twinkle in my eye. He said, "I don't know what's going on with that 'ritual' of yours, but feel free to do it more than once a week, babe."

Aw, so supportive.

1/29/11

There was something really cool that happened today. I want to share it.

So, it's that dreaded time of the month; the four- to five-day time span when I'm lethargic, cranky and willing to excuse any and all poor food choices.

Peanut butter and chocolate make me happy every day of the year; hormones will never change that. As one would spread jelly on toast, I spread peanut butter on a chocolate bar. There is never a time of day, week or month when this treat doesn't appeal to me in the most powerful way. I emphasize *treat*, of course. If I ate this every time it sounded good to me, I could lease my ass to the local Drive-In, if they were ever in need of an extra movie screen. My ass would be huge is what I'm saying.

However, during my cycle this culinary match-made-in-heaven is used more like a supplement than a treat. Meaning, I take it as needed, as well as after every meal. This has been the norm for as long as I can remember.

Now, getting to the cool part, I realized today is the third day of my cycle and I haven't had my usual overindulgent serving of PB & C. Usually, I've had shameful amounts by now, especially if you count the three days of PMS prior to my period. This got me to wondering, when did I indulge last? After crunching the numbers, I realized it's been almost a month, not only since I've had peanut butter and chocolate, but since I've even *thought* about it. I called Libby to share this realization.

"NO SHIT?" she exclaimed. "Okay, what's the name of the workbook again? I wonder if it's available on my iPad..."

That's how big of a deal this is.

PB & C is the treat I go to when I want ultimate comfort. Alcohol, tortilla chips, neither of these gives me the warm and fuzzies the way peanut butter and chocolate does. I don't know what this emotional tie is about, or where it comes from, but I've always had it. And when I'm not eating it, I'm at least thinking about it. *God, that sounds good.* Yet lately, it hasn't crossed my mind at all.

I realized I haven't "needed" to turn to that for comfort, even on stressful days. The same goes for drinking and junk food, since I used to find comfort in those, too. Lately, if I partake in them, it's in moderation and I stop when I've had enough. Now, I know if I have too much of anything, it feels bad. And I *want* to feel good. Yes, Fatty rears her chubby head from time to time, but it isn't multiple times a day the way it used to be. That's real growth!

Before this, the illusive pleasure of overindulging was more real to me than *the reality of the pain it was causing.* Now, the reality of the discomfort caused by overindulgence outweighs the false promises of fulfillment. In other words, it isn't worth it anymore.

I have now reached the same point with my comfort food as I have with wine. Even though peanut butter and chocolate still own the #1 spot on my list of favorites, I can *experience* a bite, instead of mindlessly trying to fill a chasm.

I hope I'm not provoking any anti-goddesses by recognizing this. *keeping fingers crossed*

1/30/11

Lesson Eleven has been the most fun of all the lessons thus far. I am so, SO glad to have gone through this month, learning and instilling this new tradition. I can honestly say, even if everything I learn throughout this process is somehow forgotten (which it won't), my ritual day will continue to be an ongoing practice. It may not always be a bath. Maybe as I grow, my rituals will change, but they will never cease.

While I may not feel like I'm 100% ready to move on from this lesson (only because it's been so fun), I greatly look forward to the changes Lesson Twelve might bring.

With that being said, I'll close Lesson Eleven with confidence *and* gratitude.

Now I'm off! The Goddess's bath awaits her.

Learn Something New

If you enjoyed Lesson Eleven, which I'm willing to bet you did, you're going to like Lesson Twelve just as much. It's been said that you can't teach an old dog new tricks. Well, I don't know who coined that phrase, but I couldn't disagree more! It's so easy to convince ourselves that we know everything we need to know, or that it's not easy to learn new skills later on in life, or that we don't have enough time to dedicate to frivolous hobbies. All of this is true...for someone who is not ready or doesn't *want* to grow. If you've made it this far, you are NOT one of those people, sister! I commend you for your bravery and am proud of you for stretching out to reach new heights.

To begin Lesson Twelve, I want you to take time and make a list—length doesn't matter—of what you have always wanted to learn. You may have some items from a list already made in Lesson Six that can be applied to this. Due to personal growth from the process of this workbook, you may have some new items to add.

Either way, once you have made your list, prioritize it, beginning with the most important or most compelling to the least.

Your next step? You guessed it, start learning! Whether it's picking up a new language, learning how to cook, or wanting to become skilled with pastels, do some research, enroll in a class, buy the book. The method doesn't matter as long as you're being taught efficiently and learning. You can take as long as you want with this lesson. You may have one item you choose to master on your list. You might have several items that are associated with one another, and so you may decide to tackle them all at once. Maybe you want to master them all, one by one! There's no time limit, no pass or fail; it's you and what you decide to make of it. Write about what you're learning as often as possible and include the changes you see in yourself along the way. Is the experience everything you hoped it would be? Is this new skill or knowledge opening new doors for you? Set your intentions, envision the goddess you want to become, and then step back and watch her emerge! *BLESSED BE!*

2/2/11

Seriously? February? I'm amazed! I started this workbook in MAY! It's been over eight months since I've been on my path to sel-discovery and I feel pretty good with the results I've seen from these exercises. No, I'm not perfect, but what is perfect anyway?

Learning something new... I'm intrigued. There are *lots* of things I've always wanted to learn how to do. I've put them off due to laziness or some other slew of reasons that make up one big lousy excuse. Some of the stuff I came up with was on my "good habits" list from Lesson Six, and even some daydreams from Lesson Two. But I added a few new items, as well (Lister had fun with this one). So here we go...

I want to learn how to:

Play the guitar (it's always been a dream)

Sit in full lotus (it's so much harder than it looks)

Garden well (I kill *everything* I plant)

Sew (even if it's doll clothes for my daughter)

Be Present...truly and deeply Present

I recognize I listed Presence last, suggesting it to be the least of my priorities. It's quite the contrary. I would consider it to be of utmost importance. But since South Texas isn't exactly teeming with spiritual leaders, I'm unable take classes on Presence. It might be me, but I find self-professed gurus who offer online services to be a bit shady *and* laughable. No, I have a feeling that Presence is more of a practice, like yoga or anything else one might do to grow on a daily basis. This is something I'll have to learn one moment at a time on my own.

I chose to learn the guitar first because I am so deeply moved by music and have always had an affinity for the guitar in particular, along with guitar *players*—Mraz! For the longest time I've held an image in my mind of me sitting cross-legged on the porch, singing and playing music for my kids. However, more frequently I picture myself on a well-lit stage, rocking to my acoustic version of "With or Without You." Of course, all the while paying COMPLETE respect to U2 and impressing the critics with the super original spin I put on it.

"It's like a completely different song. She's brilliant!" I can see it now.

Yeah, I feel I would be doing this country a HUGE disservice if I were to ignore my urge to master this instrument as soon as possible.

Lotus can be guided by my instructor at the yoga studio, and again, practiced on my own.

Gardening...yikes, I may have to master the guitar first. I don't know what it is. I follow the directions; I feed, I water, then I kill. At the same time, I feel compelled to learn how to do it. It's been a growing urge to become as self-sustaining as possible and reduce my family's carbon footprint. I also love the idea of grabbing tomatoes off the vine for my dinner salad or stepping outside to clip fresh herbs. And I could make great gift baskets with surplus fruits and veggies. Then again, that might be one of those goals that only *sounds* like a good idea.

I already have some basic skills on the sewing machine, but I'd like to improve upon them. My mother is an excellent seamstress, as was her mother before her. I feel it's a legacy of sorts. She says it's all a matter of practice.

"Once you get the hang of it, it gets easier and easier."

I get it, but I'm scared shitless that I'm going to run my finger up under the needle, which is why I don't practice very much. I have a pretty high threshold for pain, except when it comes to burns and injuries that gross me out, like running a power-charged needle through the top of my fingernail. The image of that gives me the willies and makes me do the "cringe dance." Eventually I want to get over this and really learn how to sew, but it's not a gigantic priority. I think it would be cool to sew something for my little girl or be able to make my own outfit for an event instead of trying to find what I envision.

"Unbelievable! She sings, plays AND designs amazing couture! She's *unstoppable!*"

I know there are many more things I've wanted to learn how to do, but if I write them all out, I have a feeling it might seem daunting. I'm starting small at a light pace.

I'm learning the guitar first.

2/3/11

The more I've thought about this lesson over the last forty-eight hours, the more excited I've become about it. I have this "I'm actually going to do it!" feeling.

A while back I saw an infomercial for a musical home study program and decided to look into it. Finding guitar lessons in town proved impossible, and I figured if I'm going to do this, I'll have to teach myself. I checked reviews about this "Master the Guitar at

Home *Fast"* course, and they were pretty positive for the most part. I'm going to do more research, but I may buy it.

2/7/11

First of all, last night's bath was awesome. Secondly, I had a very interesting experience today while finalizing my decision on which guitar lessons to invest in.

I must say, I'm a bit surprised to have discovered another anti-goddess this late in the game, but man-o-man, she rose from the depths and showed herself with fury today.

I decided to go with the "Master Fast" program because it received the best reviews and it says "Fast." I'm a big fan of fast. I went to the website to make my purchase, bypassing the payment plan to receive my free upgrade (a book of sheet music ranging in difficulty from "Three Blind Mice" to Tom Petty's "Free Falling." I was confused, too).

As soon as I confirmed the purchase, my excitement began to fade. The newest edition to the anti-goddess sisterhood was about to make her grand entrance. I knew something less than positive was about to go down as an eerie *hush* came over me.

I sensed a change in the direction of the wind outside and the room's temperature dropped at least eight degrees, maybe nine, but no less than seven. I felt a sudden awakening of sorts, but oddly negative, like a dark entity inside me was emerging. The excitement of new possibilities had roused this hidden saboteur, this titan of destruction: Cruellica.

Cruellica

DESCRIPTION: Warrior-like in stature, she's a bully who can break any spirit. With her pointed teeth, she tears and devours the flesh of a new dream and draws strength from negativity with every snarl and scathing comment. Simply put, this bitch is a big ole meanie.

ACTIVE POWER: The ability to shred a goal to pieces, leaving her victim feeling weak and stupid.

WEAPON OF CHOICE: Sarcastic judgments and insults. "What a surprise! You've come up with yet another dim-witted goal you'll never reach. Does failure *never* get old to you?"

WEAKNESS: I have a feeling my Inner Goddess could take her.

As if being summoned from a deep sleep, Cruellica sat up, stretched her back, and immediately got to work. With zeal and vigor, she began weaving the tapestry of dream-crushing, judgmental sarcasm that would spawn the biggest buzz-kill experienced this side of the Rio Grande.

"Guitar lessons? *Awesome*," she sneered. "That will be exactly what you need to become the perfectly well-rounded person you've set out to become. What an addition to the collective you'll make. Now after you finish learning Spanish with Rosetta Stone, complete the 'Become a Personal Trainer' home study program, and master Microsoft Excel, thank *you* Video Professor, you'll not only be able to choreograph a kick-ass, fat-blasting workout, you can present it on a well-formulated spreadsheet and *then* write a song about the entire process in Spanish. You're a stack of unopened boxes away from having it all, Holly. Carpe diem!"

As soon as she said her piece, she returned to the pit from whence she came. I sat there, silent and dejected. She did her job, and she did it well.

For a moment, I stared at the computer. "Thank You for Your Purchase!" flashed across the screen, and I wondered if I'd made a mistake. Had I, yet again, spent money on some program I was sure to put on the shelf and never open?

All this time, I thought it was Babette Lay-Zee who was responsible for my lack of pursuit. I always chalked it up to apathy, but at this moment, I realized I was wrong. It was Cruellica. It has *always* been Cruellica. It was her venomous tone telling me my desires were stupid, and so was I for having them.

"Why bother?" She would demand. "You're not going to be good at it, and even if you are, what are you going to do with it? Nothing, because you don't have the confidence to apply a new skill. Just daydream about greatness. It's what you do best."

This is her platform. Or better yet, her craft.

I felt like that person in the big chicken suit who got jumped unexpectedly by a gang of angry children. Confused, disoriented and *pissed*. I haven't experienced self-sabotage like that in a while, so to say it caught me by surprise is an understatement.

I called Shawn and told him I had decided I was going to learn how to play the guitar, and I bought lessons through a home study program. He started laughing, "Okay, but you don't have a guitar."

Dammit!

He was right. It wasn't what I *wanted* to hear, but exactly what I needed. I got in my car, took Zoe to Mother's Day Out, drove an hour to the city and went into the first Guitar Center I came across.

I walked in, talked to the long-haired, inked-up dude at the cash register, and after an hour of consultation, walked out of there with my acoustic Yamaha GigMaker.

"Perfect for beginners."

My lessons should be arriving within the next three to five days. In the meantime, I'm going to set aside a few minutes every day to get acquainted with my new friend and maybe toughen my fingertips up until I can begin lessons. A few people have told me it hurts in the beginning when learning to play. I'm not concerned. I don't care if I *bleed*; I *will* learn. Why? To prove to myself that I can.

There was a period in my life when I would've made some comment like, "Suck on THAT, Cruellica!" But I wasn't as enlightened then as I am now.

2/9/11

So a few days ago I was irritated with my inner demons. However, it's safe to say my spiteful determination has returned to excitement. And as a side note, if I may say this to my journal and my journal only, I look pretty hot holding a guitar. I need to get my arms more cut and I could give Sheryl Crow a run for her money, right after I learn how to play really well, and sing, and write music and surf. Yeah, after I do that? *psh* Then I'll be some chick who's awesome at stuff and isn't famous.

Hmm... It seems less glamorous when I put it like that.

2/12/11

MY LESSONS ARRIVED!!! I'm so pumped, had to write. I'm going to practice now!

2/13/11

When people told me learning how to play the guitar could be a physically painful experience, I shrugged it off.

Maybe painful for YOU, I thought.

For some reason I felt I knew better than they did, and seeing how I've never played this instrument before, I have *no idea* where that sense of arrogance came from.

I practiced my guitar for the first time yesterday, and I did it for over an hour.

Every time I touch something with the three middle fingers on my left hand, I experience a startling sensation similar to touching a hot stove. And for the love of Mary, how do these musicians spread their fingers to reach each chord *without* looking as though they have acute arthritis in their hand? I can't imagine the look on my face was a thing of beauty while I tried unsuccessfully to keep my fingers in the right spot. I think I've developed carpal tunnel syndrome from contorting my wrist around the neck of the guitar for so long, I really do. Of course, Shawn says I can't get carpal tunnel in one sitting, but he's not the one who was rippin' up the fret board with "Three Blind Mice" all day, so until he becomes a master guitarist or a doctor, he can just shut up.

I always figured, with deep jealousy, that people who are amazing musicians were naturally talented, and to a certain extent, I still do. I know there are those who have "the calling" to do certain things in their lives: teachers, doctors, artists, spinning instructors. But there's no way there are many people in history who blindly picked up a guitar and were already good at it. No, no. Two words, PRAC-TICE. Much respect to you, Mr. Hendrix. I am in awe.

Although I'm marginally handicapped by the blisters form-
ing on my musically challenged phalanges, I can't help but feel
giddy every time I run my thumb across the tops of my shiny red
fingertips. Typically, I would be discouraged by the level of difficulty here. At the same time, I figure if I can perform the "Bird of
Paradise" pose in ninety-five-degree heat while dripping wet from
sweat, I'm not going to let a few blisters and a stiff wrist get in my
way.

In any case, there was something very natural about playing,
something almost familiar. I can't explain it. I'm sure I was a rock
star in a former life or something.

Soon these blisters will be callused over and there will be one
less dream I didn't pursue. "Three Blind Mice" will someday be "Free
Fallin'".

2/14/11

HAPPY VALENTINE'S DAY!

Shawn sent me flowers. I wish he could've given them to me in
person.

2/15/11

Lunch with the ladies was good today. They asked how the
workbook is coming along and I filled them in on the lesson. I had
to smile. The girls talked about what they would choose to learn.

"I've always wanted to know how to crochet," Marissa said.

"Crochet? What're you, sixty?" Good ole Casey. She always
knows how to crap all over someone's excitement. Nevertheless, even
the Mistress of Pessimism herself couldn't hide her intrigue. Casey

asked me in her own unique way if I really had seen positive results from this workbook.

"Does all that deep shit really work?"

"For everyone but you," I said.

I'm so glad I finally shared this with them. Who knows? Maybe I'll be able to help one of them through this process someday.

On an unrelated note, Blair rode home with me after lunch. She wants me to meet her boyfriend "Jaysin."

"Is he young enough to be in the generation of trendy misspelled names?" The lack of expression on her face spoke volumes to me. "Is he younger?"

"Not SUPER young… He's younger than me, but it's not like… ridiculous," she said in a way that screamed, "DON'T JUDGE ME!"

"Okay, how old, or young, rather?" I prodded. I was fully prepared to begin living vicariously through her, so she had my FULL attention.

"Twenty-four…or three, twenty-three," she stuttered. Something told me she wasn't being *completely* honest and I have no poker face. "OKAY! OKAY! Twenty-two! Christ!" I couldn't help but laugh.

I asked her why she felt she needed to lie to me. "Like twenty-three is so much older than twenty-two? You're such a dumbass."

She began to tell me all about him. How they met, what he does, how great the sex is. "Which is weird because usually you would expect younger guys to be less experienced, right?"

"I wouldn't know, Blair. I've never had sex with a child before."

She didn't want to laugh, but she did. She asked if it would be awkward to go on a double date with Shawn and me, to which I responded, "VERY." Shawn and Pete are good friends and if she thinks *I'm* giving her a hard time about dating MTV, she should wait until she hears *Shawn's* two cents.

"Oh yeah, you're probably right," she said.

I told her all the youthful sex she's having is clouding her judgment. Then I asked for more details on all the youthful sex she's having.

I learned that these kids today are, well, pretty creative.

2/20/11

I'm a week into my lessons and really enjoying them, but I wish I could sit down with a real person who could teach me. I feel I could get so much more benefit out of it. No matter, I'm not allowing this to sway me in any way. I haven't deviated from my daily thirty-minute practice. In fact, I'll pick up my guitar and sit on the porch while the kids play, to be able to practice more. I'm hooked. On top of that, even only a week into it, I feel accomplished. I wonder what the next month holds.

2/22/11

Shawn's back and we have a date night tonight. Sadly it's been over a month since our last outing. The traveling had slowed down for a little while, but January and February have been hectic for him. It reminds me of when he first got promoted to the director's position. I hardly saw him for two months after that. I'll never forget it. Zoe had just entered her Terrible Twos, and Ryan was having problems adjusting to kindergarten (daily calls from the elementary school principal are always fun). Tyler was beginning to ask questions about sex because of a stupid YouTube video he saw at a friend's house, and I had no idea what to tell him because I've never been a pre-teenaged boy. I was spinning a lot of plates by myself while Shawn was taking clients to dinner and closing deals on the golf course. He put money in the bank and mowed the grass when he was home. Everything else fell on me and I resented my husband each time I saw him packing his suitcase.

Yeah, go chase your dreams, asshole… I'll be here…cleaning up spilled milk and having the sex talk with Tyler by myself.

It was really hard. Mainly because my form of coping with abandonment issues was to wallow in self-pity, which is a terrible way to cope, just so you know. But something I realized in the midst of all this self-help stuff was that resenting Shawn for doing his job has gotten me nowhere. I can either sit around feeling sorry for myself, or I can find something else to do that doesn't make me feel like shit. Is it really that simple? Yeah, actually, it is.

This is what it comes down to: I love Shawn more than I miss him, and being pissed at him all the time is only going to drive us apart, like Blair and Pete. I would rather avoid all that. Although, wouldn't it be funny if when Shawn retires we end up fighting more because we can't stand to be around each other so much? I've heard of that happening.

2/23/11

Date night fell through due to a babysitter with a stomach bug. *sigh*

Oh well. Better luck next time.

2/24/11

Last night was my goddess ritual. For whatever reason, I was inspired to change things up a bit. I think it has to do with my recently adopted hobby. I decided to practice my guitar out by the water, where I could possibly integrate two practices, music and meditation.

Shawn was hanging with the kids, so I bundled up in sweats, poured a glass of wine, grabbed my six-string and a blanket and headed out to the pier. The sun wasn't quite set, but its light stretched from behind the purple clouds; the sky had turned from blue into shades of orange and pink. The pastel horizon and the vast space above it reflected on the water in front of me, sharing the heavens above with the earth below. I felt humbled and awestruck.

I experienced a silence unlike any other I had ever known. After a few minutes, the world around me took on a different form, like any object does when you look at it long enough. It was as if all that was around me became whole or one, connected. It was different from the one-dimensional "nature" I'm so used to seeing, where all is separate from one another, individually labeled and compartmentalized.

Every now and then, puffs of my breath floated up in front of me and I'd realize how cold it was outside. I didn't feel it. From time to time, I'd remember the wine glass on the pier next to me or the guitar in my lap. Each sip I took warmed my chest and every random note I strummed vibrated the space I sat in, bouncing off of me, the pier, the pond, the crystallized water particles in the air, the crickets, the ducks, the evening itself.

My original intention for my goddess ritual was to practice on the pier. I don't really know how much I played, a note here and there, that's about it. It didn't seem to matter though. Guitar or no guitar, whatever I was experiencing, I was one with it. I felt balanced, gracefully empowered. Peaceful. It was one of the most beautiful evenings I've had the honor of knowing.

This morning I'm changed, as if I woke up after crossing back over from another world. As I look out the window, the view is different and doesn't seem as supernatural as it did last night. I feel like I've discovered something new, and yet I'm unable to put my finger on what it is.

Without analysis, without wonder or expectation, I will remain open to whatever change is going on inside me, and I will do what my inner guide tells me to do from now on. If I can be led back to what I saw and felt last night, I will follow my goddess wherever she wants me to go. Good, good stuff.

2/27/11

HAPPY BIRTHDAY SHAWN!

For the occasion we're having friends over for bar food and cold beer. I'm antsy because Pete and Blair were both invited. I'm sure they'll stay on opposite sides of the room and there won't be any drama, but still... it's awkward. Surely she knows to leave Jaysin at home.

2/28/11

phew She left Jaysin at home. Still, she talked about him the whole time, so she might as well have brought him with her.

Most of the night, while the guys played darts in the garage, we women huddled around Blair in the kitchen to hear about her new boyfriend and their adventures. I'd heard most of it already, but as soon as she mentioned "the swing" she had recaptured my undivided attention. That is, of course, until Shawn came in and told me he needed to take Scott Brown to the emergency room because he got a dart stuck in his back. I swear to God that actually happened. As you can imagine, I was baffled as to how something so random could've happened to this guy. Or in other words, "What idiot was throwing darts like that? It's not a goddamn Nerf ball, Shawn!"

Evidently one should never mix competition, excessive amounts of beer and any object that's sharper than a cotton ball. Men are so fucking stupid.

3/2/11

P.S. Full lotus hurts. I'm getting there, and am trying to refrain from self-criticism. It's hard because I have achieved poses that *appear* SO MUCH more difficult than sitting cross-legged!

Lindy told me my body might be holding on to old injuries in my ankles, making it more difficult to gain flexibility in them.

I said, "I've never had an injury in my ankles, though."

She smiled. "Just see yourself doing the pose, and someday you will."

I told her she needs to start saying things in backwards order so I can call her Yoda. Frustration I sense, but achieve the pose I will.

3/4/11

Not much going on today. Zoe walked into my room while I was in the middle of my downward facing dog pose. She asked me what I was doing and when I told her it was called "yoga," she responded with, "I want some yogurt, too!"

Oh Bill Cobsy, you couldn't have said it better. Kids really do say the darndest things, don't they?

3/5/11

I have successfully taught myself the opening sequence to Ingrid Michaelson's "Take Me the Way I Am." It took some doing, but I can now play it in correct rhythm without stopping to find the right chord. Tyler, who's adjusting to being a teenager too easily for my taste, came into my room today, most likely from hearing me play the same thing over and over.

"Cool, what else can you play?" he asked, flopping himself across my bed.

I sheepishly said, "Well, 'Three Blind Mice.'" Proud of myself, I explained I've only been playing the guitar for two weeks.

He replied with a shoulder shrug and the most unimpressed, "Oh."

Ah, I remember him before he turned into a teenaged asshole. The look on my face must've conveyed my sentiment because he promptly backpedaled with, "Uh, good job, Mom."

He left my room laughing after I called him a butthead.

"No one says butthead anymore, Mom."

"That's because they're not cool like me!" I hollered after him.

I guess his growing laughter at my comment suggested he disagreed. Damn teenagers.

3/9/11

I'm unsure when to move on from this lesson. I mean, I have yet to master the guitar, of course, and lotus is a work in progress. Sewing isn't a huge priority to me right now, and it goes without saying that I'm practicing Presence every day. I've justified putting off the garden because it's technically still winter. In all actuality, I'll probably get to it when I purchase the milking cow and laying hens. *eye roll*

I'm unsure if the goal of the lesson is to learn something new *completely*, or to get the ball rolling and then move on.

I feel the urge to move on, but at the same time I want to make sure I'm doing this right. I don't want to rush anything. Maybe I'll meditate on it and see if I'm guided to stay or go.

3/11/11

I practiced my guitar while sitting in full lotus. I'm moving on. Thank you, Lesson Twelve. Peace out.

LESSON 13

Get to Know the World

Are we having fun yet? Saddle up, sister, because Lesson Thirteen is ALL ABOUT fun! With the help of technology today, the world and all its beautiful cultures are literally at your fingertips. No matter your budget, whether it's a website on Irish traditions, a meal at an Ethiopian restaurant or a trip to Tokyo, you can easily expose yourself to new ethnicities, learning more about your brothers and sisters around the globe!

Just as you chose a day during the week for your goddess ritual, I want you to do the same in Lesson Thirteen: dedicate time (weekly, biweekly, monthly, it doesn't matter) to learning and experiencing the diverse cultures of this planet. This can be as lax or extensive as you like! Do you have a fascination with one culture in particular? Submerge yourself in it and experience all you can. Learn the language, taste the food, educate yourself on the history. Perhaps you would like your approach to be broader. You may want to diversify and try a new region each week, that's great, too! As always, write about your experiences and don't forget to HAVE FUN!

Move on to Lesson Fourteen when you're ready. *BLESSED BE!*

3/11/11

Uh, yeah, we talked about this in Lesson Two. I can think of a few cultures I'd like to visit: the French, the Italian, the Spanish, the Greek, the Hawaiian, pretty much any location that's stereotypically associated with good food, good wine, beautiful people and paradise.

I think I'll visit all five fabulous locations. With the help of all my travel miles, the world is only a blackout date away!

Zoe and I have errands to run. I'll come back later.

• • •

This lesson's really got me daydreaming about what exotic locations I would visit if I could get someone to watch my kids for two weeks. Tuscany, Scotland, Cabo, Chicago. Out of curiosity, I decided to go ahead and check my travel miles, "Who knows? I could get lucky."

After tallying my accrued points, I was thrilled to find I actually have some options! Either I can go and experience the culture in Shreveport, or I can allow an express jet to whisk me away to an often overlooked and underappreciated El Paso. Now, both of these locations have some very interesting people who, I'm sure, have a fascinating way of viewing the world. Without judgment or snobbery, I say, "No, thank you."

Since an onsite visit to *anywhere* of interest is off the table for a while, I suppose I'll have to take a more practical approach. Maybe I could go to a travel agency and pick up a crap load of brochures? Then again, if I were a travel agent, I would be irritated by that.

"Oh, no, thank you. I'm not here to receive services the Internet has rendered practically obsolete. I came by to get some literature on a bunch of places I'm not going to visit. Have a good one!"

That would be funny but most likely only for *me*.

3/12/11

So, after some consideration, I had a list of five different countries and cultures I felt emotionally drawn to (I wanted to dig deeper than food and wine). I planned to dedicate a few hours a week to learning more about these places, their people, customs, history, etc. I thought it would be cool to put together some sort of collage or "vision board."

I thought about India because of its color, its richness in yoga, spirituality and the sense of tradition it seems to emanate.

I thought about China and the beauty of the awe-inspiring Sacred Mountains whose peaks reside above the clouds. I've never been drawn to mountain climbing until I saw pictures of Mt. Emei in the Sichuan Province. The pictures alone took my breath away, inspiring a sense of amazement and reverence. Learning there were more Sacred Mountains (four associated with Buddhism and five associated with Taoism), I thought it would be such a great adventure to visit all of them.

With a heavy heart, I thought about Africa and its many troubles. The disease, the poverty, the lack of water and sanitation, the kids who don't get told they're loved every day. I'm no doctor or teacher. I don't know how to build a school or give vaccinations. I don't know how to design irrigation fields or harvest rice. I certainly don't possess the spiritual savvy to tell a village who to worship or how. Nonetheless, I don't think you have to have a PhD when it comes to helping out. If I have no constructive skill to offer, I'd still love to go over there and give everyone I meet a high five.

"What's up, Rwanda? You're awesome, that's what! *HIGH FIVE*"

I can't deliver babies, but I *can* make someone laugh...

After that, to lighten my mood, I thought about Latin America. Honestly, any culture that can produce such booty-shaking music is near and dear to my heart. I say this because no one LOVES to shake their booty as much as this booty shaker right here. In addition to that, chips and guacamole would hardly be possible without the culinary expertise of this fine culture. I say unto the people of Latin America: MUCHAS GRACIAS!

Lastly, Italy—and don't bother pointing out that I'm supposed to be digging deeper than food and wine because I totally am! Think of the history, the Roman Empire? Come on, that was major. And the architecture and agriculture; those people can really grow some stuff, huh?

Moving on, after I had my choices in front of me, I began organizing a research project of sorts—at least that's what it felt like. Picking regions of the countries to study, looking into the everyday life of the people, reading up on festivals and their meanings, studying historical events and that sort of thing. After some time passed, I started to notice an underlying sense of stress. I felt like I was in the middle of an important homework assignment that counted for a large percentage of my grade. I soon became aware I wasn't having fun; I was trying to orchestrate a final product to turn in.

When this struck me, I thought, "Oh yeah! This is for me, not my GPA."

So I decided to scrap the research project and focus more on having fun, first and foremost. I know me, and if I'm having fun, the entire lesson will be about appreciation and the joy of the experience, instead of something I feel I'm supposed to learn.

I'm lucky to live where I do because my community is very rich in Latino cultures. Regarding those that reach far beyond my county line, it's a different story. I'm not 100% certain how to go about immersing myself in them in a fun, "non-researchy" kind of way. I figure I'll do what I've done in the past: meditate on it. It hasn't steered me wrong so far.

3/14/11

Many thanks to my inner guide. Once again she has given me results!

What better way to get in touch with my Latin brothers and sisters than to take up Salsa dancing? YES! I can't believe this wasn't obvious to me earlier when I was writing about shaking my ass!

Shawn won't be able to join the dance lessons due to his work schedule, so I guess I'll have to partner up with some oiled-up Latin hottie named Fernando. Damn the luck! Damn the injustice!

Onto a different culture, I found an Indian restaurant in the city I'm going to try on Friday after yoga. Lindy said they have the best gobhi matar she's ever had. After I stared at her blankly, she told me to trust her and order it. Okie dokie.

As far as China and Africa are concerned, I'm stumped. I'm looking into reputable charities for the Africa relief effort and am planning on eating at the Golden Dragon Restaurant for lunch today. Not because of this lesson, but Zoe likes their fried rice and I freaking love the steamed veggie dumplings, mouth watering FO 'SHO.

Italy: I think it would be cool to learn about the different wine regions and have a tasting to experience the attributes to each region. I bet Blair would be in on that, too.

I like the idea of dedicating a few hours a week to familiarizing myself with other cultures, and I accept that it doesn't have to be some super organized, regimented "to do." A new recipe, exotic restaurants, National Geographic specials, Telemundo, whatever strikes my fancy that week is what I'll invest my time in. If it's a foreign film, it's stepping outside the box.

Salsa lessons start on Wednesday. I CAN'T wait! *ARRIBA*!

3/15/11

I'm super pumped! I found someone who teaches guitar lessons at the city college! It works out perfectly because I can schedule lessons before or after Salsa and still be able to make it back in time to get the kids from school! It's like the Universe WANTS me to be as badass as possible! *FIST PUMP*

3/16/11

Salsa lessons today at eleven o'clock. I'll write later with feedback! YAY!

. . .

I'll start by saying I'm grateful to have had this opportunity. Unfortunately, I have to tell the truth, it wasn't *exactly* what I was expecting.

First of all, my instructor was a doughy white dude named Eugene, so immediately my lustful thoughts of Fernando and his leather pants were dust in the wind. *poof*

Secondly, I was disappointed to have not broken a sweat *at all*. I had this image in my mind that my body would be glistening head to toe from all the lusty gyrating and repetitive hip thrusts. *However*, since I was the only one in the class below the age of sixty-five, things were paced slower than I was anticipating. Step forward, step back, step forward, step back. No ass shaking. None.

No matter, I will not be discouraged. These hips are destined to swing their way to merengue bliss, I can feel it! However, I think they'll have to do it in a Zumba class.

Sorry, thanks anyway, Eugene.

3/18/11

Yoga was great today. My lotus is "blossoming" nicely, and I was able to recruit my instructor, Lindy, and two ladies from class to assist me in my culinary experiment over at the Taj Mahal Restaurant. (No one from my usual lunch group was interested in Indian food, so I told them all to kiss my ass while I went to go be more enlightened than them.) I was glad to have my yogis there because of their familiarity with the place and the cuisine. I sat back and let the ones who knew what they were doing order for me.

I wrote it all down so I could effectively "report" on it. We started out with some appetizers, including a potato dish called aloo ke sooley and these chili cheese rolls called chakri. Next was a cucumber koshimbir, a salad. For the main course, we spilt the gobhi matar (Lindy's favorite), which is a cauliflower and pea dish, another vegetarian entrée consisting of turnips, carrots and pickling spices whose name was way too long to write, and then to be cliché, a chicken curry. Before the order was finalized, our server, Amar, gave us a friendly warning that the chef is known for his curry.

"It might be a bit spicy for some," he said.

I can eat Altoids by the handful so I wasn't scared of a little spice.

Most of what I ate was interesting. I know when I say "interesting" it seems to suggest I didn't like it, but I mean it in the most positive way, really. The combination of seasoning and textures was so different—experiencing such new flavors was strange, but in a good way. It's kind of like seeing a new color, I guess. At first you don't really know what you're looking at, but you like it and you find it interesting to have not seen it before.

I enjoyed, for the most part, everything I ate. Until I got to the curry, which is HANDS DOWN the most *nuclear* effing thing I have EVER put in my mouth. Right after I subtly exclaimed, "JE-SUS GOD!" I thought I was going to choke, but the uncontrollable sneezing fit that followed allowed the much-needed air to rush in quite efficiently. I'm not kidding; my reaction was so violent, surrounding tables began to take notice, and I had to excuse myself to the bathroom! I literally wanted to cut my tongue out of my mouth because at that point, I truly believed it would've been less painful. AND since I couldn't find an ice bucket big enough for my entire HEAD to fit in, self-mutilation seemed like a viable option. There are gang initiations gentler than this curry, I'd put money on it!

When my sneezing stopped, I dried the tears from my face, smoothed my hair and returned to a table of three women who CLEARLY had been laughing their asses off, and oh yeah, had NOT eaten the chicken. The only thing I could say was, "I need a fucking milkshake," which only made my friends laugh harder and louder.

I might take a break from curry, but I can actually see myself going back to the restaurant. The food was good and the service was excellent, despite some slight translation issues. Come ON Amar, a BIT spicy? Sweet Mother! Four hours and a bottle of Maalox later, my stomach is STILL torn up from it!

All that aside, it was a good experience, and it makes for a semi-humorous story to tell once the scars have healed and I've forgiven those yogi bitches for setting me up. I better get some free yoga sessions out of this, that's all I'm saying.

On an unrelated subject, even though I won't be returning to the geriatric Salsa class, I set up guitar lessons for Wednesday. I'm really looking forward to it.

I'm off to go laze on the couch. I'm not feeling too great.

3/19/11

Well, well, well. I must say, had I known Indian food was so good at cleaning out one's insides, I would've saved my money on those Godforsaken herbs and hit the curry from the get-go.

I've had to run to the toilet no less than eight times since seven o'clock yesterday evening. I had planned on going to a Zumba class at the gym in town this morning, but since I'd like to avoid history repeating itself, I think I'll stay home.

Call me nuts, but I can't help wondering if everyone who's done this workbook got the shits as often as I have. I don't know what the future lessons hold, but if they require ingesting ANYTHING, I'm not doing it.

3/23/11

Guitar lessons were awesome today! I was actually able to get some critiquing on hand placement, which is exactly what I wanted. The instructor is really nice; his name's Seth. He's very patient and super talented. I guess it would make sense to take lessons from someone who knows what they're doing. *duh*

The only thing that set me back was his youth. He's twenty-one. When I walked into the room and shook his hand it was hard not to say, "You're a child. Nice to meet you." I found it uneasy taking lessons from someone fourteen years younger than me. It got awkward when I told him, "I still get carded when I buy wine at the grocery store, dude. You don't have to call me 'ma'am.'"

Yeah, I immediately felt stupid after saying that. But he was really cool and dismissed my apparent complex.

On a side note, Shawn finds the whole thing amusing.

"Should I be worried that my wife's going to get swept away by some guitar-toting youngster?"

"First of all, he has acne and weighs about 110 pounds. Secondly, I can't believe you just said 'youngster.' Have you been watching 'Matlock' again?"

"Whatever, Mrs. Robinson."

I regret having shared ANY of this with him. *eye roll*

3/24/11

You know what I did while folding laundry today? I totally watched a "*novella*" on Telemundo. Yep, I sure did. It's called "Sophia." I don't know what any of the actors were saying, but I can tell you there's some serious drama happening on that ranch down in Mexico.

3/25/11

Tonight is foreign movie night. I was inspired to look up the top 100 foreign movies and then got the idea to watch at least two a month until we've watched them all. "We" being Shawn and I, of course. I seriously doubt the kids would be interested in watching anything with subtitles. On the other hand, in light of his recently developed interest in the opposite sex, it would be funny to see Tyler's reaction to chicks with hairy armpits.

Moving on, I also thought it would be cool to plan dinner according to the cuisine of the country the film is from. French movie, French food. I don't need to explain further. Tonight we're watching "The Bicycle Thief," an Italian film made in 1948. This title popped up on several "Top Foreign Films" sites I went to, so it must be good. I'm also looking forward to the spinach manicotti and eggplant parmesan that's going to accompany this Italian film, along with the lovely zinfandel I'm pairing with it. This might change movie night as we know it.

3/29/11

I downloaded a playlist of Brazilian café music. I love it. Love it! It reminds me of that Spanish soap I'm getting hooked on. I'm not sure what they're saying, but it looks like Consuela is having an affair with Alessandro. Ten pesos says she gets pregnant. I'm totally calling it.

I downloaded French music, which I'm crazy about. Some of the songs I would love to learn how to play, so I'm going to take the playlist to Seth. He told me whenever I find a song I want to learn I can bring it to him and he'll write up sheet music for me. I love that kid. I should introduce him to Blair, LOL.

Anyway, the last few lessons have gotten more and more fun. We enjoyed our foreign movie night so much last Friday that we decided to make it a weekly thing, if and when Shawn's in town. He'll be gone this Friday, so I'll be watching "Amelie" alone. Boo.

I know I'm not on my way to earning a doctorate in anthropology, but I feel I've grasped the appreciation of getting in touch with other cultures. Albeit through movies, food and a few steps of salsa, a small experience is still an experience. And Blair *is* coming over next week to drink Italian wine with me. I didn't research the region, but I'm sure we'll discuss it. Uh huh.

No, I haven't traveled beyond this country's borders, and no, I haven't given an African orphanage the big hug I'd love to give. All in due time. I'm ready to move on to Lesson Fourteen.

Au revoir.

LESSON 14

Be One with Nature

This lesson is as trouble-free as it gets, dear sister. I am simply asking you to go outside and play! Our Universe, this planet, your Inner Goddess, they are one, deeply connected with one another (no matter how separate they may appear to the human eye). When discovering the union between body and soul, one must also make an effort to reconnect with the Divine Creation she is so intimately a part of. So, with that in mind, go outside and connect!

Find a spot under a tree for your yoga practice. Sit on a park bench, meditate, smile and be embraced by the sun's warmth. Stand still in the grass with bare feet and feel the earth's energy radiate up your legs and out through the top of your head. Or, something I personally favor, plant something and watch it grow. See what it's like to play a role in the majesty of creation, first hand!

Along with venturing outside physically, be there *mentally* as well. Bring more attention to the world around you as you perform daily tasks. You can transform the mundane into the extraordinary by noticing and relating to the amazement of all that surrounds you in the present moment. When you drive, when you walk, when you eat and breathe, pay attention to your environment; honor it with your awareness. There is no prerequisite in order for this to be worked into your everyday life, and learning to appreciate nature will never be hindered by weather conditions or scheduling conflicts. Its divinity is in constant expression and can be experienced anytime, anywhere; you have to make the decision to *be there* when it happens (ideally, this will become a daily practice in and of itself).

Over the course of this lesson, write about what you observe as you immerse yourself in the beauty of your environment. What can you learn from the behavior of animals? When you become still in the presence of a tree, do you begin to realize the magic of its essence? Do you notice splendor in things you might not have noticed before? Has this changed your awareness of everyday occurrences in your life? Take your time with this. See if your observations affect your perception of what you *thought* you knew about nature. The Source of Creation and all its manifestations, including YOU, are full of more power and wisdom than the human mind can fathom. Be still. Allow your Inner Goddess to connect with our Great Mother, my sister. Be open to what she has to teach you. *BLESSED BE!*

4/2/11

I don't think the timing of this lesson could've been better if I planned it myself! With the arrival of spring and the most ideal weather EVER, I know I'm going to have a lot of fun with this one.

Ever since that amazing sunset on the pier a few months ago, I've gradually been trying to reconnect to nature the way I did that evening. I haven't had much luck; mainly because I'll go and sit outside, trying to *will* myself into the mood.

"Okay, be touched by the beauty...and go...now...be touched." I've even tried recreating the scenario.

"Alright, let's see, nearing sunset? Check. Glass of wine? Check. Guitar? Check. Willingness to be moved? Double check."

Pathetic, I know.

After a few attempts, I conceded it was a onetime deal so I let it go. But I'm thinking maybe with the integration of yoga and meditation, I can get it back!

I already did yoga this morning, so that's done for the day. I *would* like to dive into this lesson though, so as soon as I get back from taking the kids to school, I'm going outside to meditate. I'll write later with feedback. This is going to be awesome!

. . .

So I worked in about fifteen minutes of meditation while Zoe took a nap. It was...nice?

I was anticipating some earth-moving experience, like being able to hear the grass grow, communicate with butterflies or some shit. It was nothing like that. The only difference between meditating in my room and outside was the birds were louder, distracting actually, and I was able to be acutely aware of every gnat that buzzed my face.

Each time one of them got close, I would have to exhale violently through my nose in an attempt to thwart nostril entry. In that instance, my ujai breath was indeed victorious. Other than that, it was business as usual. I had just as much difficulty keeping my mind still.

I wonder if those boots I saw in December are on sale now that it's spring. I could hop online as soon as I'm done doing this... Oh, right, focus... Of course my luck they won't be in style next fall...breathe, focus... I wonder how low-fat that muffin REALLY was...it was so good, they probably use a ton of butter...mmm, butter... I bet I could remake the recipe if—CRAP! FOCUS! ...Did I ever make an appointment for my Well-Woman exam?

That was today. Sometimes I think about a conversation that took place ten years ago; sometimes I think about what celebrity I'd like to look like or sleep with; other times I count calories because, YES, Skinnie Cooper is dying a slow, SLOW death. It's nonsense. Meaningless bullshit, that's the typical dialogue rolling around inside my noggin during meditation. I should come up with a technical term for it like "Dialoggin" or "Noggi-logue."

Am I discouraged from the less-than-stellar beginning to Lesson Fourteen? No. Every one of these chapters starts out with me being really excited or really irritated, and I usually end up having some huge, meaningful moment. It's par for the course at this point. Hell, I might even try to plant something so it can end in failure, invariably leading me to learn about the balance of life and death.

Tomorrow, I'm planning on yoga-sizing outside. We'll see how it goes. Most likely it will be amazing or disastrous.

4/3/11
DISASTROUS.

It wasn't the loud birds. It wasn't the annoying gnats. It wasn't the difficulty of doing yoga while wearing sunglasses. No, it was a force of nature I hadn't anticipated. My dogs. Loveable, yes, but these two canines are like a herd of bulls in a china shop, only more destructive. Excited to see me, jumping, nudging and sniffing my crotch the whole G-D time I was out there. I couldn't get away from them! And since they're the size of cattle and smell just as bad, I absolutely REFUSE to put them in the house. Finally, after I got knocked over during my eagle pose, I decided to say "Screw it!" and finish my practice inside. It's like they *knew* what they were doing!

"Okay, dude, when she moves into up-dog, that's when we lick the face; down-dog, muzzle up the butt; side plank, forehead to the sacrum. Remember, don't pounce on her until she does the pose where's she twisted up on one leg."

From now on, I think I'll go for a run instead and also work on becoming a cat person.

4/4/11
I'm going for a run this evening when Shawn gets home. I've got a busy day around the house and won't have the chance to do much for this lesson until later.

· · ·

Okay, note to self: If planning on going for a run, do so in the morning when motivation is high and before I have a glass of wine while cooking dinner. *duh*

I'm going to practice my guitar on the porch swing after the kids go to bed. Yesterday Seth faxed me the sheet music from that French playlist I gave him, and I'm eager to practice. Ooh-la-la.

4/5/11

Even though I stayed up until one-thirty this morning playing my guitar, I decided to jog home after taking my kids to school. Zoe's at Mother's Day Out and the play center is only about five miles away, so I thought it was a good plan for this lesson (the creek road between there and my house has some really pretty scenery). I figured I could always ride my bike back to the school, load it up in my car, and then drive home. *Easy-cheesy.*

I never run outside, much less the creek road, so hours of tread-mill work could never have prepared me for five *sandy* miles of hills, stray dogs and ninety-five-percent humidity—*on top* of being tired from getting hardly any sleep last night. If underestimation were to be made an Olympic sport, I would undoubtedly take home the gold every time.

One could say it was challenging. *I,* however, would say it was really effing hard. At the same time, surprisingly, I didn't *hate* it. I say "surprising." I should say "SHOCKING." Usually that amount of discomfort would have been HELL for me. F-bombs exploding everywhere, sulfuric regret burning my lungs, inner demons laughing at my pain. I'm glad to say, it wasn't that way at all. The most negative thing that crossed my mind was, "What the hell was I thinking!" But I pressed on anyway. A few times I was thankful I brought my phone in case I needed to call Blair to come pick me up, although I never did. I guess giving myself permission to do it somehow made it less tempting. Kind of like how allowing myself to have cake whenever I want dissolves the taboo.

At first I was frustrated with the level of difficulty in my run. After all, I've been running at a quick pace on the treadmill with ease. However, that's in a climate-controlled environment, with a flat, stable surface and a "Real Housewives" marathon distracting me the entire time. Circumstances are a *tad* different when running outside.

Ten minutes into my run, and after I realized the advanced level of the trail, I had accepted my lack of skill on such terrain, and un-characteristically forgave it.

I'm tired and I never do hill work or run in sand. I can't expect to breeze through something I'm not in shape for. I'll do my best, that's all I've got.

This is another example of how the "I SUCK" mentality has waned significantly. I welcome it!

And, since my mind was free of negative shit-talking, the scen-ery around me was actually noticeable. You know, I never quite re-alized it before, but I live in a really pretty area! The new grass is beginning to sprout. I could smell it, sweet and clean. The tallow trees are greening back up. Oh, and the oaks! Richmond has these gigantic oak trees, some of them over a hundred years old, creating these beautiful canopies all over the place. They're so stately. I never noticed that before. And then there were the butterflies, fluttering from one yellow flower to the next. I love butterflies. The cows, well, they looked the same as they always do, bored and unassuming. They simply stared at me as I jogged by. It was kind of awkward, really, like they didn't know what I was doing, nor did they trust it.

"Keep your eyes on this one, fellas… She looks like she's up to no good."

Anyway, from what I could see of the creek, it was full, winding and sparkled in the sunlight, precisely how you might expect a creek to look. It was prettier than I remember it being, though.

By the time I got home, my legs were less stable than a two-story Jell-O mold. My chest was pounding, my feet were throbbing and my face felt like it was on fire. Head to toe, I quivered from fatigue. My sense of accomplishment, on the other hand, turned all of this hammering discomfort into a glowing badge of honor. *Good job, kid!*

Now I need to figure out how the hell I'm going to get my car back because there's no freaking way I'm going to try that trail on my pink, banana-seated ten-speed.

4/7/11

Guitar practice on the porch swing. All I'm missing is a shotgun, a hound dog and a rusty truck on blocks in the yard. Where's my cowboy hat when I need it?

It's a beautiful day, eighty degrees, shady, the scent of blossoming orange trees is floating in the breeze. Springtime is the best and it makes me want to celebrate! The only downside to this celebratory mood is the old cravings and habits that accompany it.

There's something about beautiful weather and a patio that makes me want to drink cold beer. Just like winter has its own associations (snow, fire, hot chocolate), for me, spring is no different. Nice weather + patio = cold beer. Even with the personal growth I've experienced throughout this process, I could totally go for a cold one right now. By myself at ten-thirty in the morning on a Thursday, while Zoe's playing on the swing set.

Shouldn't I have risen above this by now? And does anyone else besides me and migratory birds have seasonal habits? It's weird. I never knew someone could have weather-specific triggers. I suppose this is what comes with being aware of my surroundings, although I have a feeling it isn't what the author of this workbook had in mind.

I *have* been focusing on nature more often. I try to pay more attention to the scenery when I drive, less on cell phones and loud music. In fact, I had to ban listening to certain songs when I drive, because the other day I almost ran off the road, singing my heart out with my eyes closed. I was relieved, upon speedy surveillance, that no one else was anywhere near me. I would've hated to run into another car, or more importantly, for anyone else to have witnessed a driving blunder only an amateur lip syncher would make.

Unfortunately, at this point, I'm unimpressed by what Lesson Fourteen has brought to the table. At the same time, I'm only five days into it, so I'm not going to judge too quickly. It's really taking me aback though. I expected to connect with this one immediately. I'll keep my eyes open and hope something shifts.

4/8/11

WHO-HOO! Shawn's parents are up in San Antonio for the week and want to have the kids this weekend! I'm going to take the boys out of school early and meet my mother-in-law halfway. SO PUMPED! Shawn gets home from the Vegas sales conference this evening and I'm totally going to surprise him with our first date night since *February*! U-S-A! U-S-A!

4/9/11

Shawn and I had THE BEST time last night! He got home from the airport and was pleasantly surprised to hear music playing instead of the chatter of Nickelodeon. The kitchen was lit up with candles, I had champagne chilling and Madeline Peyroux set the mood with her sultry, Billy Holiday style. I even got dressed up, heels and everything.

We toasted to sunset and hung out on the porch swing while we snacked on a yummy cheese plate I threw together. Brie and champagne, so lovely.

"We are SO French right now, dude."

"Oui," he said, then gave me a quick kiss.

"What would it take to see if you could have your sales territory changed from Texas, Oklahoma and Louisiana over to France, Italy and Spain? I could travel with you and your company could pay for the trip. Win, win!"

"Why didn't you say something sooner? They originally offered me Europe, but I figured I should stay closer to Arkansas."

This morning was fun, too. We ate breakfast in bed and gossiped about the Vegas trip.

"Pete got so laid, babe."

"No way!"

"Yes, dude. Like, *Champagne Room* laid."

"GROSS!"

"And Scott Brown, remember him?"

"The guy with the dart?"

"Yeah, he got so drunk the first night, he THREW UP in the sales meeting the next morning!"

"IN the meeting?"

"All over the table. It smelled so bad, poor guy."

We've really been missing each other. With work, kids, extracurricular stuff, we're a great team but there's very little intimacy anymore. In order to keep everything running like a well-oiled machine, it takes work, like a business. There aren't a lot of warm and fuzzies in *business*. We talked about that, too, vowing to start making time for "us" again. It's a vow we've made before, but life happens and certain things fall through the cracks. It's okay, it's the way it is. I guess the important thing is that we keep coming back to that vow.

While we were talking, he asked me how my guitar lessons were going.

"They're awesome. I'd play you something but my guitar is in the other room and I'm lazy, so."

He sat up and held out his arms. At first I thought he was going to sing "I'm a little teapot," but then he said, "Play *me*." So cute.

I smiled and said in my best Texas accent, "I'll play you like my six-string, boy," as I crawled to his side of the bed and sat in his lap. He wrapped his left arm around my waist, pulled me close, then lightly ran his lips back and forth over my heart.

"You can play me all you want, as long as it keeps me close to this," he said.

Damn, that man is smooth.

With my right hand on his back, and my left holding his outstretched arm, I hummed the chords, picking and strumming my way through the first few notes of "Quelqu'un ma'a dit." I didn't make it very far into it because the kissing around on my neck and chest got distracting...

I still have butterflies.

4/13/11

You know what I *don't* like about spring and the weather warming up? Mosquitoes! Those disease-spreading vampires of the insect world annoy me to NO end! They're back, and they're HUGE.

Due to the mild and wet winter, our mosquitoes are so freaking big that I felt one land on my arm this morning when I popped outside to get my flip-flops off the porch. Do you know how *big* a mosquito has to be in order for you to *feel* it land on you? It was like a G-D pterodactyl! I felt this "thud" on my shoulder as if someone had tapped me to get my attention. I turned my head to discover this bat-sized bloodsucker draining the life from me. I squealed like a little girl and, with the grace of a lioness, began feverishly running in place. With all my might, I swatted at it as hard as I could, slapping the shit out of my arm and missing the mosquito entirely. It dove in several times, taunting me as I spun in circles, thrashing my arms and slapping at the air. It was a ridiculous attempt to kill it before it had the chance to bite me again, but why it didn't dawn on me to simply go inside I'll never know. For a moment it was gone, and I thought victory was mine. Then suddenly it was there hovering in front of my face. Before it flew away, it looked me dead in the eye and pointed at me as if to say, "First you, then the children."

The battle line's been drawn. I know violence is never the answer, but I will do what I must to protect my family and myself from future months of itchy hell. This warrior princess has a Mosquito Magnet, Skin-So-Soft and more citronella than a Florida Wal-Mart in July. If I can't kill them all, I'll at least do my damndest to repel them.

On a side note, is it wrong to abhor one of God's creatures while doing a lesson geared toward nurturing my connection with all living things? I think that has to be the best example of irony I've ever come across.

4/15/11

Well, I've been keeping up with my Spanish soap opera and guess who's pregnant? Yep, *Consuela*. But here's the kicker: Is it Alessandro's baby or Mateo's? *Quien sabe?* Not me. But I'm sure we'll find out soon enough. Knowing her, it'll end up being the love child of Joaquin, the stable boy. Can I get an amen? That crazy Consuela.

4/18/11

So, I've made it pretty apparent this hasn't been my favorite lesson so far. The mosquitoes have made going outside less than desirable, and my inability to connect with nature has been discouraging. I guess my excitement turned into irritation after a few failed attempts to be one with the Universe.

That was until today. I had, what I would consider, a pretty significant A-Ha.

I went to the store last Tuesday. I bought the usual groceries: veggies, fruits, lean meats, and cereal, along with some extras like toothpaste, Q-tips, bubble bath and body lotion. I was running late and only had time to put the things in need of refrigeration away before I went to pick up the kids from school. I had pantry items and toiletries to organize and shelve, so there were bags still sitting in the kitchen when the kids and I got home. I told them I wanted to get the stuff put away before I made them an after-school snack.

Ryan, being in "superhero mode," offered to assist me with the task. "Ma'am, can I help you?" he asked with his fists planted on each hip.

"Oh yes, sir, you're so strong," I said. "Can you take this bag to my bathroom, please?"

He nodded, grabbed the bag and charged out of the kitchen. After about ten or fifteen minutes, he came back from my bathroom and proudly told me he had taken the liberty of putting all of the stuff away for me. With apprehension, I thanked him, and then worried I would never again see the contents of that bag.

To my surprise, however, I was able to locate most of the toiletries: Q-tips under the sink, bubble bath IN the bath tub and toothpaste IN the sink. My son had done a pretty good job of figuring out the appropriate place for bathroom items. The only thing missing was my lotion. I looked everywhere, in the hamper, in my bedside table, by the toilet. No luck. I told Shawn yesterday I was going to have to buy a new bottle because I didn't know where Ryan put it, "bless his heart."

This evening, after I got out of the shower, I found the lotion sitting next to my sink.

"OH! Here it is! Where did you find it?" I asked while Shawn was brushing his teeth. He laughed, and with a mouth full of minty foam, he said, "Oh, it was in the shower right next to the body wash. I guess he put it in the place that made the most sense to him."

At first I felt silly. I've been looking for that bottle since *last* Tuesday. It's now Monday night. I've taken no less than five showers in the meantime, reached for the body wash on each occasion and never *once* noticed that bottle of lotion there.

I chuckled and said, "I guess I was so busy searching everywhere else, I didn't bother looking right in front of me."

A-HA. From the depths, there was an "A-HA."

I immediately started thinking about this lesson and how I've spent this whole time searching for the magic outside, like I was on some sort of scavenger hunt. I traced my steps back to the sunset on the pier and remembered something that had gotten lost in the shuffle along the way.

When I went to the pier that evening, I wasn't *searching* for anything. My intention that night was to change up my goddess ritual and go practice my guitar outside. That was it. I wasn't there to meditate or fulfill an assignment. There were no judgments placed because there were no guidelines or expectations. I was there because I *wanted* to be. The enthusiasm of *being there* was enough for me to be open to bigger things, even with my mind running in the background the whole time.

I think I understand more clearly now. It's the awareness beneath the thoughts, the stillness *inside* that creates space to connect with the magic on the *outside*. I totally get the whole sky/clouds metaphor the author was talking about in Lesson Nine. I know she explained it, that I am the sky, still and unchanging, and my thoughts are the clouds, they come and go, but it didn't click until now. That's what I've been missing during all my previous attempts to do this lesson "correctly."

I started this plan thinking the connection needed to be *discovered* by going outside and meditating or doing yoga in a garden or going back to the pier with my guitar. But I got so busy *not* finding what I was looking for, I allowed a very simple process to be overcomplicated by ridiculous standards. I diligently focused on the *clouds* and completely forgot that the *sky* is the key.

This can easily be paralleled to the person who is so busy searching for their glasses that they don't realize they're wearing them on their head. Or the woman searching for the bottle of lotion in the laundry hamper. *smile*

With fresh perspective, I think I'll go back and begin this lesson again tomorrow.

4/19/11

Well, the battle ensues. I made the mistake of heading out for my "nature hike" without bathing in bug spray this morning. I don't know what I was thinking. Evidently I wasn't. The mosquitoes have been lurking in the shadows, studying my habits and waiting for an opportunity like this. They've done their homework.

The good news is my walk turned into a sprint, so it was great exercise. Along with that, it was the fastest three miles I've ever run. The bad news is it was a five-mile hike, and I was still two miles away from my house when I started losing steam from galloping at full force.

It was such a magnificent combination of stooge-like comedy and athleticism. I'm truly jealous of the lucky bastards in passing cars who were blessed enough to witness it.

"Dear God, why is that poor girl running for her life? And why does she keep punching herself in the throat?"

Despite my efforts, flailing and cussing proved useless in keeping the pesky parasites away. I ended up looking like I was in desperate need of an exorcism. It would've been so much funnier if it were happening to someone else.

I've counted fourteen bites around my ankles, calves and neck. I haven't checked, but I'd be willing to bet there are at least three on my ass. I feel violated.

On a much lighter note, I *did* learn that a swarm of gnats will adhere nicely to a sweaty face and freshly applied ChapStick. Ah, nature.

Do I hate mosquitoes even after my big A-Ha? Passionately, yes. But I can at least appreciate the gift of a good story. And so can Shawn, who is still laughing.

4/24/11

Today I thought I would be smart and open the windows while doing yoga. I figured this way I could have a dog-free practice while reaping the benefits of the outdoor experience. I inhaled a bug, gagged and then decided to close the windows. Even *I'm* still laughing at that one.

I swear if insects were forest animals, I'd be Snow-fucking-White.

4/26/11

Zoe and I stayed outside most of the day today. With the weather being a gorgeous seventy-five, I couldn't bring myself to come in. We drew on the driveway with sidewalk chalk, went down to the pond and fed the ducks, had a picnic on the pier—a great mother-daughter day!

I'm about to go get the boys and I'm planning a picnic at the pier for dinner, too. Who's the shit? I'm sorry, *who?* I think we all know the answer to that question.

• • •

How have we not done that before? Dinner at the pier? Awesome! Yes, the flies were annoying, but actually worth it! Everyone had their own job—Ryan spread the blanket out at the end of the pier; Tyler brought the basket of food from the back of the Suburban and Zoe got to set the plates out, exactly the way she does when we play tea party. We ate our turkey and Swiss sandwiches as the sky turned colors. Then over chocolate chip cookies, Tyler told me about a girl he's interested in asking out. After I stifled tears and refrained from screaming, "She'll do nothing but hurt you!" I asked him to tell me about her. He said her name is Hanna and that she's a cheerleader. God help me.

"You'd like her, Mom," he tells me. "She really likes clothes and stuff." *cringe*

We packed up once the sun set, and as we were driving down the block towards the house, Tyler looked at me and said, "We need to do this more often." I was really touched by that.

I'm off to bed.

A cheerleader? Really?

4/27/11

Well, I'm having lunch with Blair and Jaysin today. Shawn said he's jealous because he won't be able to go, but since I know his reason for being jealous isn't a nice one, it's best he can't make it. I'll write later. It should be interesting.

· · ·

OKAY...the dude is EFFING HOT. 6'1", 220, brown floppy hair and skin like a Greek god. He's just straight-up delicious. When they walked into the restaurant I looked at him and it was clear to Blair that I was impressed. She had her eyebrows raised like, "Right? What'd I tell ya?" Put about twelve more years on that kid and he is going to be *dangerous*.

Something I found to be hilarious is that he knows Seth, my guitar instructor. Seth has mentioned me to him. God help me, deep down I was so flattered (and shamefully wishing Seth was as hot as this guy).

We had a great lunch and Jaysin is charming and GA-GA for Blair. He couldn't take his eyes off of her and when she excused herself to the ladies' room, he gushed about how "beast" she is. After a few seconds he clarified by saying, "she's awesome."

Ah, my bad poker face strikes again.

"I'm only thirty-five, but you're making me feel a lot older, dude. Knock it off with the obscure lingo."

He obliged with a, "Yes ma'am."

I then had to tell him NOT to call me ma'am. Vanity's a bitch. *eye roll*

We hung out at the restaurant for two hours and I pretty much got the full scoop on the boy toy. He grew up in Oklahoma, but relocated to South Texas for college to major in wildlife management. He's graduating in May and has already been accepted to the game warden academy.

When lunch was over, I said my goodbyes to Demi and Ashton and headed to my car. Before I was out of the parking lot, I received a text from Blair.

Isn't he so beast? she wrote.

I simply replied, *Grrrr!*

I'm really happy for her, but if she starts shopping at Abercrombie, I'm staging an intervention.

4/29/11

No official date night tonight, but Shawn and I hung out on the porch swing and celebrated the sunset with a beer while the kids ate pizza and watched a movie. We didn't do much talking; we sat, watching the birds and listening to the crickets. I started noticing lightning bugs flicker around the pond and I couldn't help but smile. Lightning bugs will always take me back to the age of four in my Granny's backyard.

When we made it back to the house, I had a text from Libby.

Lightning bugs are back. I guess she's being one with nature, too.

4/30/11

On a typical Saturday, the house sleeps in until about eight or so. Sometimes I set out to wake up early and surprise everyone with breakfast, but more times than not, I get woken up by my daughter tugging at my pillow case asking for chocolate milk (*organic*, thank you very much).

It was ten after six when I awoke to the sound of my porch chimes clanging in the wind. April rain is my favorite part of spring and it was the first shower since I started this lesson. I didn't know why, but I was excited to wake up and go watch it, like a kid going to see the first snow of winter.

I knew I had at least an hour and a half before the rest of the family woke up. I listened to the rain drumming against my kitchen windows as I flipped on the coffee pot for Shawn and heated the kettle for my tea. I prepped some pancake batter for the kids, and as soon as that teapot started whistling, I poured myself a cup and made a beeline for the porch. It's what the Universe guided me to do, so I followed like a willing puppy dog.

I could feel the mist from the rain, cool on my face as I sat on the porch swing, going in and out of meditation. With my eyes closed, I listened for a few minutes, and then I would open them to watch how the trees responded to the downpour. Each time was a new experience, just as beautiful as the first.

It brought to light the harmonious ebb and flow of the world, the exchange of energy. Everything in nature is given or taken and then eventually returned. I know this is pretty basic science any third grader could fill me in on, but there's obviously a significant difference between reading about it in a textbook and actually observing it.

After a while, I found myself thinking about where we, as a species, fit in to all this. The trees, the grass, the animals, they're all provided for. They do what comes naturally to them, and that's all there is. There's no stress, no bustling, no worrying about when it will rain next or what they need to do about the mischievous ant colony moving in next door. They get what they need without asking, "Is that it? What if this isn't enough?" I guess they instinctively rely on the natural cycle they're a part of; it doesn't occur to them to do anything else because they aren't plagued by *thought*.

And then there's us: taking with very little giving, fearful of losing what we have or denying that what we take has repercussions. I felt sad and happy at the same time. Sad to consider the state of humanity and the toll it's taking on its own race *and* the planet, and happy to be one with the cycle of creation, in spite of those who choose to reject it.

Shawn interrupted my trance-like state, handing me a pancake and a refill for my tea.

"Move over, bacon," he said while making himself comfortable on the swing next to me. When I saw he had cooked the pancakes, I thanked him and asked what time it was, learning I had been out on the porch for over an hour.

"Wow, an hour? You're either having some really deep thoughts or none at all," he said, leaning over and taking a bite of my pancake.

Nudging him and turning my shoulders to guard my breakfast, I told him it was a bit of both.

"Do you need more time with the trees?"

"No, I think I'm good."

"Sweet," he hopped up. "There's a 'Buffy' marathon starting in ten minutes."

That was his parting shot before he went inside. I shared his excitement; this was the perfect weather for a marathon of vampire slaying, and we were long overdue for a lazy day with quality time.

Before I got up, I felt the need to ask myself what I could learn from the trees, as the author had mentioned in the lesson plan. Did I need to spend months studying the outside world, or could I simply sit and be taught by the nature of nature? Noticing again the trees in the wind and rain, I gained a better understanding of how to *be*.

In the midst of a storm, the branches may thrash, the leaves may tremble, and the trunk may bend, but the *roots* remain still.

I'm grateful for this moment, and can only hope the trees will forever serve as my reminder to bend with the wind, to stay grounded at all times and to give selflessly, without expectations.

I can't think of a better lesson to learn than that. Thank you Lesson Fourteen.

LESSON 15

Giving Back

Part I

What's your point of view on the world today? Is the glass half empty or half full? Look around you. What do you see? Many turn to the
news for a worldly perspective. Flip on the TV, you'll get a full report
on war, strife, hunger, disease, pollution killing the earth and its in-
habitants. And the news is right; what they say cannot be debated.
We're not only terrorizing and killing each other, we're wreaking
havoc across the globe, beneath its surface and above. Our Great
Mother is being abused by Her children; anyone who disagrees is
either living in denial or selling something.

But what about the other end of the spectrum? There are those
who are of the belief that humanity is not on the edge of annihila-
tion, but on the rise of an *awakening*. We don't hear about them,
because "happy" doesn't sell. But there are many who choose to live

in the light instead of battling their way through the dark. Instead of fighting with war, they're advocates for peace. Instead of worrying about poverty and disease, they live a life of service to those in need. Instead of complaining about intolerance, they embrace their fellow man with compassion and love. Instead of being *anti*-negativity, they are *pro*-positivity. There's a lot of power in that.

Now I ask you, sister, what role do *you* play in all this? Or more importantly, from this point on, what role do you *want* to play? No one knows how far you've come but you, my dear one, and over the last the fourteen lessons you've gone through a great amount of spiritual excavation and construction. You've learned, you've laughed, you've cried, but more crucial than anything else, you've become *aware*. It's time to take that awareness to the next level. My sister, it's time to *join* the awakening. By now, you know who your Inner Goddess is, and your next step is to bring her into expression.

I want you to think about your global responsibility. What, if anything, do you contribute to the collective, the greater good? Is there something you would like to change about that? What is it, and why? Write it out. This is your assignment for the first part of this lesson.

You may know exactly what you contribute, or what you *want* to contribute. Then again, you may not have a clue, and that's okay. With a still mind and a *light heart*, ask yourself, "How does the Source of Creation want to express itself through me?" Eventually, you will have an answer. As in all the lessons, there is no time frame; if you need a day, a week, a month, take it. You can come back when you have the clarity you need.

Proceed to Part Two when this has been completed and you are ready. *BLESSED BE!*

5/01/11

So, what? Discovering my Inner Goddess isn't just about being Zen and fabulous all the time? I want to say, my entire intention for doing this workbook was to learn something deeper about *myself*, something that would help me to better handle my *personal* responsibilities. Now I need to worry about my GLOBAL responsibility? Jesus, no pressure there!

I feel completely unprepared for this. It's my freshman year of college all over again; just thinking about it now makes me cringe. Back story: I was accidentally placed in Mathematical Foundations of Continuum Mechanics instead of Algebra. Contrary to popular belief, there's only a *slight* discrepancy between the two, really. *eye roll*

The classroom *alone* was intimidating. It was an auditorium of 300 seats, each of them filled with fourth year students who were all smart enough NOT to sit in the front row, the *only* row with vacant seating, lucky me. The professor began the class in perfect English, but to me it sounded like some dead language because I had NO idea what he was saying. Mystified, I looked around the room as the rest of the students listened and took notes with obvious understanding. My chest filled with panicky confusion. The sound of my heart pounding in my ears drowned out the alien lecture, and as I attempted to crawl inside myself, my breathing became quiet and shallow. If I had been naked, it would've been my worst nightmare realized. It's a good thing college professors at major universities are completely unfazed by students leaving their classroom in tears. He didn't even break stride, he kept on lecturing in his own mathematical idiom (today's word of the day).

That particular scenario was much more stressful than this, of course, but I *am* experiencing the same, "Am I supposed to know this?" sense of dread.

"By now you know who your Inner Goddess is"? Awesome. What if I *don't*?

I know I've had some pretty magical and moving moments, but I'm the same neurotic person I was when I started this a year ago! Does this mean I've been doing something wrong? Should I start over from Lesson One and go back through each chapter more thoroughly? Is this because I cut my four-week cleanse to three? I'm not hurling myself into a full-fledged panic, but I'm puzzled, to say the least. If my Inner Goddess was supposed to have been discovered by now, I must've lost track somewhere along the way. It's making me feel ill-equipped to continue with this lesson. I mean, how can I possibly be a useful addition to the collective "awakening" when I'm *clearly* drowsy from decades of spiritual Ambien?

There's a part of me saying this was all a monumental waste of time.

Cut your losses and move on. It's just a stupid workbook, it doesn't mean anything. And you did well, sticking with it this long; you usually quit everything much more quickly than this. Go have a drink and reward yourself for at least giving it a try.

At the same time, there's another part of me saying, "*Oohh*. Hello, anti-goddesses, unleashing the titans again, I see." *deep breath*

Knowing what I've learned, once again, this is when I go within and observe the voice in my head instead of getting caught up in its story. Doing this has worked pretty well in the past. But it feels different this time. I need to walk away for a bit.

. . .

You know what I've learned today? Fighting with my own ego is a lot like professional wrestling. There's a lot of smack talking, mixed with flashy distractions, followed up with violence that only *appears* to be real, concluding with the illusion of victory for one of the contenders. Another way to explain it is, "It's fucking stupid."

I was prepared to tap out when I first read the lesson plan, I really was. Which is on point for me, characteristically speaking. That's been established a thousand times over.

There I was, about to be struck down by my imaginary opponent. As my ego leaped toward me with a final "I told you so," I turned around and left the ring. It really was that simple. No countermove on my part. No attempt to strike it down. I realized if I try and fight my ego, it wins no matter what. So I left it standing alone in the ring, screaming at me to come back and fight.

You need me, you can't do this by yourself!

Before I began this journey, I would've believed that to be true, but now there's something stronger in me that knows this is a lie.

I thought about where I was last year at this time and considered how far I've come since then. Even though I don't know my Inner Goddess yet, I at least know she's there, and I have gone through a great deal of personal growth and felt things I didn't know were possible for me to experience.

Because of this book, I discovered yoga and it's become a true practice, a way of life. I started learning the guitar, something I've wanted to do since junior high and have been too timid to pursue. I don't allow my laziness to bully me anymore, and our family as a whole is closer because of it. No, I'm not at complete peace with my body yet, but I have accepted that health and happiness are not rooted in skin and bone. I've learned pleasure seeking in food and alcohol is a sign that something is wrong on a deeper lever. I discovered America is not the only country to produce great movies or tasty cuisine, and stepping outside the box is like my very own mini-adventure. I was happy to learn meditation can take on many forms, and I don't have to be a Zen master to do it. I found out that my comfort zone is not my friend, my vagina is not my enemy and my past is not my albatross.

This isn't a stupid workbook. This is a watershed in my life. And being asked what part I play in the grand scheme of things isn't an offensive question, and it isn't something I should feel diminished by. I don't know what my global responsibility is because, up until now, I've been too self-absorbed to consider it. That doesn't make me a bad person, and it doesn't mean I can't start thinking it about *now*.

I'm grateful for this moment and for what I'm uncovering. I'm grateful for this book and whatever urged me to purchase it a year ago. I'm grateful for time. I'm grateful for love. And most of all, I'm grateful to my ego. Had it not attacked, I might never have learned to simply surrender.

I'm going to take some time to think. I'll be back tomorrow.

5/02/11

I almost started this with a list. I've been thinking about this lesson since I wrote yesterday morning and I had planned to write up different ways in which I can contribute to the collective.

Okay, I actually *did* begin with a list and then realized halfway through it I was writing a bunch of ridiculous goals my lifestyle doesn't even allow right now. Volunteering at local soup kitchens, working with troubled teens. I even thought briefly about opening our home for fostering. These are great and noble causes, but each of them is completely unavailable to me, because there are no such programs where we live. We don't even *have* a local soup kitchen! These were things that sounded really heartfelt and looked good on paper. Another distraction. Twisted Lister is a crafty one.

I took a deep breath and started over. I realized if I begin this lesson the same way I began so many other fruitless searches, what would be so different about this one?

"We can't solve problems by using the same kind of thinking we used when we created them." Albert Einstein (smart guy, that one).

After a minute or so of wondering where I should begin, it came to me when in reflection. The best place to start is by asking the right questions and answering them honestly.

What is my global responsibility? *I don't know.*

Anticlimactic, yes, but it's the truth. I could pretend to know and say things like, "help bring about world peace, feed the hungry and plant trees wherever approved to do so." Well, yeah, that's EVERYONE'S responsibility! We should ALL be doing that. But I'm not running for President or Miss America.

What do I contribute to the greater good? *Um, not much.*

Why lie to my journal? Other than taxes, I contribute very little to society, and even those tax dollars come from Shawn's salary, so I don't even contribute *that*! I stay inside my bubble most of the time. Every now and then I send cupcakes to the school when there's a party for the kids, but that's usually holiday specific. Shawn's involved in several charity organizations through his work, so I guess I could live vicariously through *his* contributions, but probably not.

I *do* recycle; that's a big deal to me. I'm the only one in my circle of friends who does. Some of them find it annoying because of my inability to throw things away.

"One of these days we're going to see her on "Hoarders," just wait."

Typically, I'll come back with something equally as passive-aggressive, like, "Oh, I'm sorry I don't hate the earth like you do." We laugh, flip each other off, true communion.

What else? Before Shawn started traveling so much, I really liked throwing parties. I still do. I don't do it as often anymore. I could say I'm good at bringing people together.

I make people laugh. Although, that's not really a "greater good" kind of thing, is it? And it's usually at *my* expense from doing something stupid, so I guess that doesn't count.

I can't really think of anything else. I recycle and bring people together.

What do I *want* to contribute to the greater good? *Hmm.*

This took some time to answer. I sat repeating this question in my head, over and over until it hardly made sense anymore. Strangely, once the question became ambiguous, it became less scary, I guess. I no longer felt pressured to answer, and the release of that pressure opened space for the answer to float to the surface. *Inspiration.*

To lead by example. It's the only thing I know I *can* do. I had to put it in terms of parenting. As much as I hate to think about it, I don't have control over what my kids are going to do once they're grown and on their own. But I can guide. I can choose to live in a way I want *them* to live and have faith that they'll be healthy, happy people because of the example they were led by.

The only thing I can do is take Gandhi's advice and *be* the change I want to see in the world.

I can be a part of *the* awakening through *my* awakening. I can embrace mankind as my brothers and sisters and have compassion for the all the assholes out there.

"Forgive them, for they know not what they do." Well said, Jesus!

I *can* be nice to the cashier who gives me a dirty look and doesn't speak to me the whole time I'm standing right in front of her. She hates her job. I get it! Being a bitch to her isn't going to help her out! Maybe my being nice to her will change her day, and she'll go and be nice to someone else, changing *their* day, ending up in more positive energy to radiate. Being nice to an asshole doesn't make me a pushover. It means I'm tolerant.

If all I have to offer is peace and love to all those I come across, surely that peace and love is bound to spread? Maybe I'll make people laugh and give them space to feel okay and not judged. Maybe if I can lead by example, my example will *inspire* others to do the same.

Inspiration, this is what I want to contribute to the greater good. *This* is what feels genuine. *This* is how my light can shine.

Someone needs to stitch this shit on a pillow. I'm on a *roll*.

Lesson 15

Giving Back

Part II

Alright sister, you've talked the talk. Now it's time to walk the walk. Your Inner Goddess is flowing through you, you know what you want to do, now go do it! Before you move on to your final lesson, I ask you to write a summary (in whatever detail you see fit) describing how you intend to go about living your life of service. What's the first step you need to take in your initiative? In a world full of distractions, how do you intend to stay committed to this lifestyle? I don't want you to launch a new journey without a map, so take all of this into consideration. Be thoughtful, get excited and write it out. Oh yes, and don't forget to declare it once you've developed it. It's a well-known fact that we are more likely to stick to our commitments when we tell other people about them, so share this with your loved ones and utilize your support network! Welcome to the second part of Lesson Fifteen, my sister. Welcome to the first day of the rest of your life! *BLESSED BE!*

5/03/11

Say what?

Dude, refer to what I wrote yesterday. I pretty much spelled it out. I'm going to be awesome, and that awesomeness is going to be so awesome, it will inspire all who cross my path to be awesome in the ways in which *I* am awesome. Voila! Consider my plan declared. Done.

5/05/11

sigh

I know, I know, these lessons are *never* that cut and dry. I won't delude myself. Even after my "hallelujah moment" the other day, I guess I'm still feeling scared I might ruin this new journey with old habits. Declaring that I'm a changed woman makes me feel vulnerable, like all those I declare it to will be waiting for me to screw up.

And there's *another* fear…What if I *do* screw up?

5/07/10

I got a call from Casey today. She wanted to talk to me about the workbook.

"Okay, I wanna know about the Kool-Aid you've been drinking. What's the book called again?" she asked.

Out of all my friends, I'm shocked *she's* the one who's going to buy it. Blair talked about it but never did. I'm interested to hear Casey's take on it.

Speaking of Blair, she and Jaysin broke up. He was getting too clingy for her.

"He totally choked the puppy," she said over lunch yesterday.

"Is that some sort of new sex thing, or are you saying he's too overbearing?" I asked. I couldn't help but be jealous of her creative metaphor. Choke the puppy? I'm totally going to start using that one.

We were all curious as to what changed. Two weeks ago she was seeing the world through Jaysin-colored glasses. Now she rolls her eyes, "He's SO immature."

No shit, Blair. He's twenty-two. *eye roll*

I nearly spit my wine out when Marissa asked, "Did he start calling you 'Mom'?" Blair tried to act irritated, but she started laughing after she told Marissa to kiss her ass. All joking aside, she said she feels bad.

"Y'all, he cried when I told him it was over."

So did Pete, but I chose not to bring that up.

She said she's going to enjoy her singlehood for a while. I told her to keep a journal of it all so we can all enjoy her singlehood, too.

05/9/11

Big A-Ha today, but it's late and I'm going to bed. A sick kid is a bit of an energy drain. I'll write tomorrow, it's good stuff...

5/10/11

So I realized what's been intimidating me about this lesson is the challenge to stop talking shit and take action.

What if I fail? What if I can't change?

Just because I came face to face with my anti-goddesses doesn't mean they don't still creep up. Epiphanies or none, the "evil sisterhood" has been with me longer than my growing goddess, so an appearance by Cruellica or Babette is understandable in a moment of weakness. Having compassion for this truth has given me the ability to view my fears in a different, more positive light. Each anti-goddess is a red flag, a reminder to do what needs to be done, *especially* when I'm scared shitless.

"You're scared? Good. That means you need to act on it."

Normally I wouldn't be thankful when one of my kids gets sick, since thinking about it makes me feel like a Munchausen mom. Nevertheless, I've got a pretty good idea of how this lesson needs to come full circle.

Yesterday morning Zoe woke up feeling yucky. The twenty-four-hour stomach bug has been running rampant and unfortunately tagged her smack dab in the middle of her super cute belly. After she threw up her juice, I was worried she was going to have trouble keeping fluids down. Obviously, I wanted to keep her from getting dehydrated, so while she rested on the couch, I asked a neighbor to come over while I ran to the nearest convenience store. No matter the flavor, none of the "Pedia" drinks have ever appealed to my kids, so I figured Gatorade was my next best choice.

After three and a half minutes inside the Speedy Shop, I had an arm full of crackers and brightly colored sports drinks. At that point, I chose to ignore the high fructose corn syrup and Red #40. I wanted to get my daughter comfortable and feeling better.

I stood in line at the checkout and couldn't help but notice the ornery "vibes" radiating from the cashier. With a near scowl on her face, she spoke to no one. She scanned items, practically throwing them one by one into a plastic bag and then moved on to the next customer without a word.

I looked around and noticed other people in line watching her, giving dirty looks and making comments amongst themselves.

"Looks like *someone's* having a bad day."

She was being extremely rude and everyone else started to become as put out as she seemed to be. As I began to detect my *own* energy turning toward the negative, I suddenly remembered this is *exactly* what I was talking about in my previous entry. This is where I'm supposed to be compassionate instead of irritated. I quote, "Being a bitch to her isn't going to help her out!" I was shocked to be faced with such a similar scenario only days after writing about it; then again, we have a lot of rude cashiers around here, so that's probably why that example came to me so organically. Anyway, it was this moment when I realized that because someone else is bitter or unhappy, doesn't mean it has to affect *my* path or the kind of person *I* want to be. So I made a decision.

When it was my turn to check out, I walked up to the counter and said, "Hey, how's it going?"

I unloaded my loot in front of her, and without looking at me, she grunted, "Hi." I asked how her day was coming along and her response was as sharp as before. "Fine."

I stood there, watching her scan the last of my drinks, trying to think of a way to make her smile. I got an idea, and before I could question whether or not it was a *good* one, I heard myself blurting it out, "Well, if it makes you feel any better, you're having an *amazing* hair day!"

She looked up at me as if I had asked permission to smell her feet. I stood there perfectly still. Having nothing articulate to add, I shrugged and settled for the universal topper, "I'm just saying."

She gave me a cautious smile. "Um, thanks," she said after an awkward pause.

At first I felt like an idiot, but after she gave me my change, she said, "Have a nice day." I returned the sentiment, and as I walked away, I heard her greet the customer behind me. Sure, it was unenthusiastic, but it was better than the "Go to hell" look she was giving everyone before.

Holy shit, that actually worked!

Disclaimer:

There will be times when the bitchy cashier may get the best of me. There might be situations when I'm absorbed in thought and forget to greet each passerby with love. There will *undoubtedly* be times when I bypass the "happy place" and jump right into flipping my shit because my kids are doing something that drives me *crazy*.

I think my best plan of action is simple. Like I mentioned in Lesson Fourteen, I need to live like the trees in my front yard: accepting, selfless, bending and grounded. If I can practice this every day, eventually it will be the norm. I will become the change I want to see in the world. Practice, practice, practice. And on days when I forget to practice, I will practice practicing.

It's funny, I thought I was so geared up to get to Lesson Sixteen and finish this workbook. Here I am, standing at the threshold of the end, and yet I'm hesitating to turn the page.

This is exactly how I felt when I approached the final chapter of the Harry Potter series.

LESSON 16

Reflection

Well, here we are, my Sister Goddess, at the end of a road we've traveled together. I thank you for spending your time with me and for your commitment to finding your True Self. I can only hope these pages have helped to provide you with what you were looking for. As this journey comes to an end, with pride and honor, I send you off to begin anew. But before I do, I have one final task for you.

In the introduction of this book, I asked you to think about your idea of a goddess. What does the word "goddess" mean to you? Who is she? Who do you want *yours* to be? For the closing lesson, I want you to go back and reread your initial response to these questions in the introduction. If nothing gives you an idea of how far you've come, this will! Throughout the preceding assignments, you have broken down barriers, allowing you to embrace your Inner Goddess, inviting her to shine through. You went from thinking about the *concept* of a goddess, to *becoming* one. After you've read your response to the introduction again, smile, and take in what you know now. Do this, and then answer the question once more. Who is your Goddess now?

In light and love, my sister –
BLESSED BE!

5/13/11

Oh, sweet reflection. I began this final lesson emotional and excited. I was thinking I would write something beautiful and poetic, something I could be moved by, something I could come back to in the future for an enlightening reminder or inspiration.

Spoiler Alert: It didn't go as expected. Shocking!

So, with butterflies in my tummy and great anticipation, I went back and read my first entry. To my surprise, after a few lines I found myself becoming irritated by who had written this. I felt the urge to read on to my second entry and then my third. By the second paragraph of Lesson Three, I was straight up disgusted.

I can't stand this woman!

I love my children dearly, but you wouldn't have known it reading through those entries. Whiney, lazy, self-serving—I was unnerved, to say the least. It's a lot like when you hear your own voice on a recording and you think, "My GOD, is *THAT* what I sound like?" It was like that, only worse because, well, it's my *personality* I was so horrified by.

I wanted to stop reading, but it was like a train wreck, or "The Jerry Springer Show." I couldn't turn away. I had to continue.

Then I read further into fear, my anti-goddesses, negative habits; I remembered writing about those things. Between the sarcastic remarks, I remember the amount of control those things had in my life at that time, and I remember how much shame I felt. I disliked myself so much. I noticed my annoyance turning into compassion as I read on.

Things lightened up when I got to Lesson Six. I couldn't help but laugh and roll my eyes when I read about instilling positive habits and the *ridiculous* amounts of change I planned to undertake in a twenty-four-hour period. I don't have a milking cow or laying hens, if that tells you anything; and if you check back a year from now, I'm willing to bet I still won't. But at the same time, I was pleasantly surprised to find how many of those habits are very much a part of my everyday life now. It makes me smile.

I can't say I've come remotely *close* to forgetting my adventure with the colon cleanse, but it was really funny to go back and read about it through my perspective that day when it all hit the fan. The whole "crapping myself" debacle overshadowed the great things that happened during that lesson. I was introduced to a lot of vegan and vegetarian dishes, which I now incorporate into my menu on a frequent basis. Because of this, my kids eat more vegetables and Ryan actually requests hummus in his lunch (even though his friends tell him it looks like throw up). I was able to step out of my own way and look at my relationship with food objectively. Very helpful.

Ah, and then there was yoga. If I got nothing else from this workbook, I will have considered it a success because I'm so grateful to have found this practice and the group of beautiful women who are now my friends at the studio. And, even though I wasn't interested in the beginning, I'm thinking about getting certified to teach so I can share this gift with others.

Meditation is a work in progress, but what isn't? Because of Lessons Eight and Nine, my body is stronger, my mind is more easily calmed, and I feel more connected to my spirit than ever before. I'm grateful for all this. It's a sad truth that many people don't *ever* learn to love themselves, much less by the young age of thirty-five. To all those who find it earlier in life, I commend you.

Lesson Ten changed my life. I came to terms with a great deal of buried pain this past holiday season, and I became liberated because of it. I feel like a part of me died that day after my yoga class. I have made Suffering my guru, and I learn from it all the time.

My goddess ritual is something I continue to make time for. Life happens, so I don't always have a full day to pamper myself. But whether it's a luxurious bath, yoga on the deck or twenty minutes to sit in silence with a cup of tea, I always make time to honor that which needs to be honored.

I loved Lesson Twelve. I smiled the whole time I read it. Although I haven't been practicing my guitar much over the last month or so, I refuse to allow Cruellica's smack talking to bother me.

"See?" she says. "It's like the new puppy. It lost its cuteness, and now you don't want to play with it anymore. Shocker."

Yeah, yeah, yeah, you're so silly, Cruellica.

Lesson Twelve also gave me that incredible night on the pier, which opened up a whole new realm for me. Sometimes I'm too busy to remember to live like the trees, but I'll never again go through a day where I don't acknowledge our Mother Earth and offer gratitude for her grace.

Getting in touch with the world was so fun. I watch "Sophia" every chance I get and, believe it or not, I'm to the point where sometimes I know what they're saying! (P.S. Consuela was FAKING the pregnancy, that vixen!)

Every time I enter the Taj Mahal Restaurant, I'm greeted by my enthusiastic friend, Amar, who knows to NEVER bring me chicken curry. I enjoy our foreign movie night, even though it's gone from weekly to monthly, and I loved reading about my surprise date night with Shawn. I'd like to repeat that one. I bought pictures of the Sacred Mountains in China and set them up where I do yoga and meditate. My plan is to manifest an excursion to there. I'd actually love to travel the world and journal through the whole adventure: the people, the emotion, the *food*. Imagine all the different countries I could get diarrhea in. Seriously.

Lesson Fourteen was great because it taught me to look for the lessons in life. When searching for something, begin with what's right in front of you or what's *inside* of you. And trust. That's what this lesson is all about. Trust that life is divine, and it's playing out exactly the way it's designed to. Trust that there is no lacking. Trust the perfection in the imperfect. Trust the lessons hidden in my six-year-old son's logic.

And finally, Giving Back, Lesson Fifteen was validating because I sat there with my self-doubt and hung out with it. No longer my nemesis, it became yet another lesson. Again, Suffering will keep knocking until you finally get it over with and answer the damn door.

The other thing I loved about this lesson was how it made me aware of the power I have with every choice I make.

"I should be compassionate towards this person, but it's so hard!" *What is Suffering trying to teach me here?*

There's so much power in that.

"I'm in a bad mood. I don't want to be anymore. I think I'll decide to be happy now."

That's power, my friends. Lesson Twelve gave me that.

Of course some days are harder than others. At the same time, I like the idea that life's journey is thousands of baby steps instead of one giant step from A to B. The beginning and the end are not *life*. Life is the passage between the two. The truth in that really resonates with me. If I can remember it, this truth can always serve as an entry point for forgiveness and compassion…for myself as well as others.

So here I am. I'm reflecting on the past year, where I stood and where I stand. I made the comment the other day that I'm still the neurotic person I was when I began this journey. To a certain extent, that's very true. I have my human moments.

I beat myself up for losing control or being less than perfect. I still and always will salivate over haute couture and salon shoes because I appreciate their beauty. There's as much creative genius that goes into Valentino as that which goes into a flower; I choose to honor that. Is veganism in my future? Well, I don't know where my path will take me ten years from now, but today it leads me to BBQ and a milk mustache. I scream the F-word when I stub my toe. I fail to find beauty in the cellulite on my thighs. I still get irritated by my kids bombarding me with questions, even when they can clearly see that *I'm on the damn phone*. I deal with the wonky libido that comes with a hectic family life and fluctuating hormones. And I, for the love of God, am constantly asking, "Am I doing this right?"

All of these things are still here. The only difference now is…I love me *anyway*.

I live on this planet, in this body, to experience what this incarnation has given me to experience. To live life fully is not limited to being adventurous, dancing naked in the rain and learning to surf when you're 80. Living life fully is being there for every baby-step, in every moment, even when some of them hurt like hell.

So what does Goddess mean to me now?

I don't know if I have an answer for this anymore. It changed as I changed. It evolved as I evolved. It has grown as I have grown.

So I guess if my personal definition of "Goddess" is *one* with me, the only possible conclusion is the Goddess *is* me.

Whatever *that* means.

Dear Reader,

Always remember that YOU are the Goddess. May you be inspired to laugh, grow and live mighty.

Do this, and you *will* change the world.

~Namaste

Michelle

14151040R00173

Made in the USA
Charleston, SC
23 August 2012